PANIC!

John Creasey

Master crime fiction writer John Creasey's 562 titles have sold more than 80 million copies in over 25 languages. After enduring 743 rejection slips, the young Creasey's career was kickstarted by winning a newspaper writing competition. He went on to collect multiple honours from The Mystery Writers of America including the Edgar Award for best novel in 1962 and the coveted title of Grand Master in 1969. Creasey's prolific output included 11 different series including Roger West, the Toff, the Baron, Patrick Dawlish, Gideon, Dr Palfrey, and Department Z, published both under his own name and 10 other pseudonyms.

Creasey was born in Surrey in 1908 and, when not travelling extensively, lived between Bournemouth and Salisbury for most of his life. He died in England in 1973.

THE DEPARTMENT Z SERIES

PANIC!

Department Z

JOHN CREASEY

ipso books

This edition published in 2017 by Ipso Books

First published by John Long Limited 1939, revised by Arrow in 1969

Ipso Books is a division of Peters Fraser + Dunlop Ltd

Drury House, 34-43 Russell Street, London WC2B 5HA

CHAPTER 1
SAYS MARK

A ny man or woman with a sporting turn of mind would have offered long odds, on first seeing Mark and Michael Errol, that they were not only brothers but twins. The bet-taker would have won, for in fact they were cousins—a relationship from which they appeared to derive singularly little pleasure. Indeed, the same casual and careless punter would have considered them bad friends, despite the fact that they shared a Brook Street flat as well as that unmistakable Errol chin.

The chin, on a day in August which each spent blaming the other for the decision to stay in a now sweltering London instead of escaping into the countryside, was a subject of some bitterness between them.

'If you,' Mark announced, with a scowl, 'would learn to use a decent razor, you'd get a shave that wouldn't make me ashamed to take you out.'

Their voices, let it be said at once, were not alike. Mark's was deeper, almost rough at times, and he clipped his words. Michael's was fuller, more mellow; and he was inclined to drag his words. But being what they were—two young, popular but unattached bachelors, wealthy enough to spend twelve months in the year in sheer idleness—and as yet untempted to do otherwise—they had perfected the art of imitating each other's voices for no better reason than to mystify acquaintances and amuse themselves.

'I,' Mike drawled calmly, 'do not propose to use a cut-throat for your or anyone else's benefit, little man. It is more than enough to be seen about with one.'

Mark rose to the bait in predictable fashion.

'One what?'

'One cut-throat.' Mike sprawled in his easy chair, a breeze from the open window behind him ruffling his dark hair. 'Did it ever occur to you, Marko, that your scowl, your squint and your bark combined are pretty forbidding? Dress you in a muffler and cap …'

'When you've stopped blethering,' Mark growled, 'perhaps even you will admit you need a shave if we're going to that perishing …'

'Don't say it!' grinned Michael. 'You know that polo is a sacred subject in the Errol family. Your respected father, my venerated uncle, would develop apoplexy if he knew how you feel about it. And after all—be reasonable! It's warm. All we have to do is sit there looking pretty …'

'With you there?' Mark said witheringly but he did not appear to enjoy the thrust. 'We've got to dress up, sit and bake in all that heat, be charming to old ladies and stay pleasant to pretty young things who don't give a damn about polo, and call ponies horses …'

'In fact, you are feeling somewhat rebellious,' Mike summed up.

'It was your confounded idea!' said Mark, bitterly. 'The old man had about given up expecting to see me at Hurlingham, and you have to go and offer …'

'By admitting that we were free this afternoon, little man,' Mike pointed out, with maddening logic, 'you started the ball rolling.'

'Oh, forget it!' Mark pushed his hand through hair which was rarely as well-groomed as his cousin's and so helped puzzled acquaintances to tell them apart.

They were almost exactly of an age—a few months short of thirty. They were both six feet tall to a fraction of an inch, both broadly—but muscularly—built, and both good to look at, if not entirely handsome. They had the same dark, almost black hair. Their eyes were grey, their lashes long, their noses regular—unlike the traditional Errol Roman—and both possessed that large, square chin with its unmistakable cleft. They were, as frequently happened, dressed alike in silver greys and Old Carthusian ties.

'What I was going to say,' Mark resumed, 'is that I propose we cut it. You can sprain your ankle or break a leg, and ...'

'Nice of you,' murmured Michael. 'Unhappily, I feel in the best of health, little one.'

'Don't call me little one!'

'Touchy,' mused Michael. 'That's a pity. You're a month early, y'know. It's September before you usually start agitating for something to do. But let me put on record here and now that I refuse to take part in any scheme for rehabilitating tramps ...'

'That was your crazy idea ...!'

'Or helping discharged prisoners—perhaps *that* was my idea? It cost me twenty-five quid and ...'

'It just didn't work out as it should have done,' snapped Mark. 'And I found Pitcher, didn't I?'

Pitcher was their man, and undoubtedly Mark had found him—through the humdrum medium of a Domestic

Agency. Pitcher was of a height with the cousins, but fat with it.

'And,' continued Mark, belligerently: 'Hurlingham is off. Dammit, it's nearly eighty in the shade already! And don't talk to me about filial duties. I've had ...' He stopped, and his scowl gave way to an expression of almost seraphic content.

'We will go,' he announced, with an air of finality, 'to Richmond, and take a boat out.'

Mike stared.

'Of all the crazy notions ...!'

'Let me remind you,' Mark imitated his cousin's drawl to excellent effect, 'that we have entered into an agreement whereby we have alternative choices of occupations and amusements, and solemnly we have declared that each shall respect the other's decision. You chose Brighton—*Brighton!*'—he shuddered— 'last week-end. I choose Richmond, this.'

Mike groaned. 'So be it. But you, in a punt ...! And I can't swim ...'

'Let's get off,' Mark urged, suddenly full of energy. 'Pitcher. *Pitcher*! Where the devil ...?'

'It's his day off,' murmured Mike.

'It would be! Well, you 'phone the pater that we can't ...'

'Whoever chooses an occupation,' intoned his cousin, with patent enjoyment, 'makes *all* the arrangements. Proceed, old son.'

Mark proceeded—and duly made excuses to a parent who was not noticeably surprised. The pair of them left 55c, Brook Street, collected their jointly-owned Talbot from its garage, and drove off—albeit unwittingly—into the service of that Department of British Intelligence known as Z.

There are those who have never heard of Department Z, and very many have no idea that it is the ultra-secret section of our entire Intelligence Service. Even fewer are aware that while its director, Gordon Craigie, is as little-known as a permanent Under-Secretary, virtually nothing can happen in the capitals of the world which does not reach his ears with astonishing speed.

Still less known is the large, ungainly-looking man named Loftus—William Loftus—who, at the time concerned, was leading active agent of the Department. Or of Ned Oundle, that spindly, spidery man with the improbably soulful-looking eyes, who acts as chief lieutenant to Bill Loftus.

But it happened that they were both near Richmond …

'Well, old son?' Mark demanded.

'Not bad,' drawled Mike, which was an admission.

They were lounging at either end of a punt moored to a shady bank, close to the Old Deer Park. The lapping of water was music in their ears as they watched two swans make their majestic way down-river. It was cool: they had lunched well at a riverside pub, and their pipes were drawing smoothly. For Mark, it was a triumph.

'No polo,' he murmured, dreamily. 'No noise. No baking in the Hurlingham heat. Above all, no …'

'Women,' Mike finished for him. They liked to be known as misogynists, although at times their behaviour hardly supported such a claim.

'Let us be fair.' Safe for the moment at least from feminine wiles, Mark could afford to be magnanimous. 'They *can* be all right. I mean, some of them are quite good to look at—and I've known some intelligent ...'

'But never a combination.'

'Agreed. Agreed!' Mark repeated, more firmly. 'Picture two here, right now. We'd have to make conversation, flatter them, feed them on chocolates, scrape out of a theatre tonight by the skin of our teeth. We'd—what the devil's that?'

'That' was a loud, sharp noise, quite close at hand. The cousins sat up abruptly, and stared towards a nearby thicket. They could see nothing through the mass of willow branches, bramble and shrubs—but about their ears, that sharp report still echoed.

'It sounded like a shot,' Mark murmured.

'Damn right it did.' Cautiously, Mike eased himself forward. 'It might have been a keeper ...'

'If it was a shot, it came from an automatic.'

Mike continued to peer around, saying:

'You could be right, but then, again, you could not. *Listen!*'

A new sound was coming towards them. Slow, almost stealthy, and certainly strange. It seemed all wrong that anything so untoward should be happening in that peaceful spot. Yet something about the shot, and the furtive movements following it, filled them with a sense of uncertainty, almost of foreboding.

And then a voice came: low-pitched, masculine.

'Through here ... steady with him ...'

'I can't see out the back of my neck—mind his head!'

'Don't shout!' snapped the first man. *'Anyhow—'* a low-pitched chuckle which was not of humour—*'he won't be needing his head again.'*

Mike looked at Mark, and the expression in his cousin's eyes mirrored his own. The stealthy approach was clearer; they could hear bushes being pushed aside, hear the snapping of twigs and dry branches. The implications were clear enough. A shot, the talk of carrying a body ...

'There's a gap ...!'

The Errols had contrived to reach the bank without making a noise. They could see, at the point where it met the river, the path along which the unseen men were coming. As they crept towards it, with the noise of approach growing closer, they heard the *chug-chug-chug* of a motor-launch further up the river. The chugging grew louder. The Errols cursed at the sound, which was muffling the movements of the men in the thicket.

And then things happened, it seemed simultaneously.

The launch came into sight, and made for the spot where the punt was moored. There was a man standing in it, a girl behind him, another man at the wheel. As it roared towards the bank the two men in the thicket, just visible now to the Errols, stopped in their tracks—and one swore.

'By God—that's Loftus!'

There was a pause, a heavy thud—and then suddenly a man's head appeared, face upwards. There was an ugly wound in his forehead, and he looked dead. At the same moment they heard a click—faint, almost insignificant—but to Mark and Michael Errol, ominous.

The safety catch of an automatic?

Mark chanced it. He moved—and Mike followed. As they burst through the undergrowth to the path, they saw a thick-set, grey-haired man with an automatic in his hand—which he was pointing towards the launch ...

Mark dived for his ankles in a perfect Rugby tackle, as Mike went for his taller companion.

The gunman swore savagely as his shot went harmlessly into the water. Almost in the same moment, the gun flew from his grasp as he and his friend were brought crashing down together. But in the moment of success, came failure. A boot struck Mike under the chin, and he loosed his hold, stars whirling in his head.

The tall man was up in a flash. With cold-blooded accuracy, he aimed a second, vicious kick at Mike's head—and this time, Mike slumped down unconscious.

Mark heard the launch cut out—and held on like grim death to his captive's ankles. But he sensed the threat from the tall man, in time.

As that vicious foot lashed out at him, he rolled sharply aside—then sprang up with the ease of a man in perfect trim, and cracked his fist towards the other's chin. He did not connect. The tall man moved his head a fraction of an inch—and sent a pile-driver to Mark's stomach. Mark covered, but only partly avoided the blow, and he gasped. Then the tall man flashed his hand to his pocket, and Mark saw the glint of grey steel—

He lunged for the man's legs, as the shot came.

The echo of it clattered about the thicket—but it hadn't hit Mark. His opponent, obviously an expert in rough-and-tumble, kicked again at his head. Mark, unable to dodge it completely, almost went the way of his cousin. He was expecting a bullet at any moment; he heard the crackle of shots close by, but felt no hurt.

Squinting through fractionally open lids, he caught a glimpse of a man—and darted out a hand as the fellow passed. There was a snuffled oath—and then a thud that seemed to shake the earth. Eyes gleaming, Mark scrambled up.

What looked like a young mountain was on the ground at his side. But before Mark could realise what was happening, the mountain erupted—the man on the ground came upwards like a volcano, and nothing short of a Camera could have withstood his weight.

Mark Wyndham Errol thudded into a tree.

The man-mountain came after him, his huge fists clenched. Winded, aching, alarmed—but thankful that there seemed to be no gun—Mark steeled himself for the unavoidable knock-out as one great fist was aimed his way.

Then:

'Bill—*that's not him!*' came a woman's voice.

In the split second between the start of that punch and the woman's cry, something quite unbelievable happened. The fist unclenched. Palm and fingers hit against Mark's face—but spread widely to cushion the impact: buffeting him only, like a blow from a broom. At the same time, a deep voice roared:

'Then where the devil ...?'

'That way ...!'

The big man swung round, and disappeared down the path. Gasping, bloody-faced and helpless, Mark stared at the woman who was hurrying towards him.

Two women!

Some minutes before Mark Errol had declared that some of the species could be quite good to look at—and assuredly, these were. One, slightly taller than the other, had the most glorious blue eyes, the loveliest corn-coloured hair imaginable. The other was as dark as the first was fair, very much smaller—almost *petite*—but of an equally dream-like loveliness.

Neither was smiling.

Mark gaped.

Mike, coming round, groaned as he tried to move—then opened his eyes and looked up. He saw the visions, and his eyes opened wider.

Suddenly from somewhere very close, there came the roar of a car engine. Even in their bemused state, the Errols heard the taller of the lovely women say·

'They've gone—we've lost them!'

And in her voice there was something akin to despair.

CHAPTER 2
SAYS MIKE

Mike Errol, still muzzy-headed but by no means blind, eased himself into a more comfortable position, and continued to stare at the two women. For this moment, at least, he had ceased to be a misogynist. Which was excusable enough—for the faces of both women showed character as exceptional as their beauty.

Mark was experiencing the same subconscious change of heart as his cousin, where the fair sex was concerned. Certainly, he could not fault the taller woman: the flawless perfection of her face and figure could not have been better served than by the tailored white skirt and blouse she wore, or that flaxen hair in its classically simple French pleat. But in her companion, he assured himself, there were flaws …

For instance, that minutest of moles, on her right cheek … the faintest of tilts, at the end of her nose …

Blemishes which were better than perfection …

But this was absurd, he chided himself, and made a conscious effort to concentrate on other matters.

The humming of the car engine was almost inaudible, now, and back along the path down which he had disappeared, came the large man. He was taller than Mark by several inches, and on his huge frame, loosely-cut grey flannels made him look considerably bigger even than he was. No one could have called him handsome, but that healthily-tanned face, under its thatch of mid-brown hair, held strength, character, and all those indefinable things which turn a naturally ugly man into an undeniably attractive one. Smoky grey eyes ignored the Errols and rested on the taller girl.

'They had a car by the road,' he said, shortly. 'I didn't have a chance. If these blasted nitwits hadn't butted in, we'd have had them.'

He transferred his gaze—bleak, now—towards the Errols.

Mike was still too befuddled to realise the implications of that comment, but to Mark it was the last straw. He was winded and bruised, he had set himself twice at the mercy of a gun, had done his level best to save utter strangers from injury or worse—and the reward was to be called a nitwit!

With some effort, he found his cigarette-case, selected a cigarette, lit it, and flicked a match towards the vast man, who stood regarding him with obvious annoyance.

'Thanks,' he said, acidly polite. 'And now, do you mind if we get back to our punt? Sorry to spoil the afternoon's enjoyment, and all that. Next time, we'll decide to sit and watch.'

There was a glimmer of a smile in the big man's eyes, transforming him. He took a cigarette-case from his own pocket and offered it to the girls—causing Mark to flush like a guilty schoolboy.

'I suppose,' the man said, resignedly, 'you thought you were playing heroes? These things will happen … Are you wounded, at all?'

'Only in spirit,' said Mark Errol.

The smile spread to the big man's lips.

'Well, you'll get over that. Try this on—' he glanced at Mike—'your brother.'

'This' was a whisky flask he produced from his hip-pocket.

'I haven't a brother,' Mark said automatically: 'He's my cousin.' But he accepted the flask, gratefully.

The big man and the taller girl made their way down to the launch—which, Mark now saw, had struck one end of the punt, splintering a floorboard. As a result, the punt was half-submerged, its cushions all but floating.

Mark handed the flask to his cousin, without comment. Mike took a sip or two, then stood up slowly. Between them, glances were exchanged, admitting a mutual course of action.

Watching the big man and his lovely companion board the launch, they were surprised to see that there was another man aboard. They were surprised, too, by the gentleness of the big man's voice, as he asked:

'Much damage, Ned?'

A new voice, taut with anger, answered.

'If I don't walk for a month, I'll not be surprised—the blighters! Who the devil stopped you getting them? Blast it, I don't mind being shot at if we get results, but ...'

'Shhh!' said the gentle-voiced giant. 'You'll hurt their feelings even more, and that wouldn't do. Now, let's have a look at you heroes. Di, get the first-aid box, will you?'

The Errols glanced in baffled wonder from the launch and its occupants to the delightful little creature at their side. She smiled—and Mark had time to note another engaging flaw: her front teeth were ever-so-slightly crossed. In a quiet, almost husky voice, she told them:

'It'll work itself out, I think. Don't take too much notice of them.'

Mark drew a deep breath.

'Heaven forbid! Tell me, are they friends of yours?'

He was taken aback by her reaction.

'They certainly *are!*' she said, fervently.

'Well,' Mike was recovering fast, 'we might have been shot and weren't; you might have been a hag, and you aren't ...'

A frown wrinkled the girl's forehead.

'You might have had the sense to keep quiet, but you hadn't!'

'No, that's a bit much!' Mike protested.

'Ingratitude is one word,' murmured Mark.

She started to speak, glanced towards Loftus, Di, and the wounded man on the launch, then at the men on either side of her. Something in their expression eased her tension.

'You might have a look at that fellow,' she remarked, casually, nodding towards the inert figure of the man the two others had dumped at the sight of Loftus. The man was lying off the path, partly hidden by overhanging branches. Both Michael and Mark had completely forgotten him, and were duly abashed as they realised it.

Mike reached the sprawling figure first—and straightened up in a moment, his face pale. Mark did not bend down.

'The rest of it might be a farce,' Mike's drawl was more pronounced than usual. 'But this fellow's dead, old son. It's past time we had a showdown, I think.'

'Odd,' Mark remarked, quietly, 'that the row's brought no one else out?'

'That can wait ...'

'Nothing can wait,' said the big man, behind them. The Errols had not heard him approach. They turned about, grave-faced.

'This man's dead,' Mark said, flatly.

'I'll say no prayers for him,' Loftus retorted. 'It's past time he died, my friends—and the pity of it is that it's only one and not all three of them.'

He pulled out his large, gold cigarette-case, and handed it round. 'We'll talk in a few minutes. Fay—if you'll go to the end of the path and turn right at the road, you'll find a telephone kiosk about three hundred yards on. Call Inspector Smythe of the Richmond Police, give him my name, and ask him to send three men and an ambulance along. You can say why—once you've mentioned me. He won't get so worked up, then.' With a quick smile, Loftus watched her turn and go. She walked easily, lithely, with a grace that seemed part of her.

Mike watched her, too—and sighed …

'Let's get to the launch,' said Loftus.

They had to pass the dead man to reach the launch, and the feelings of the Errols could be judged from the fact that they made no comment on that half-submerged punt. The wounded man sat propped against the tiny motor-house of the launch. The Errols eyed him uncertainly: both had the impression that they had met him before.

Lean, spidery, with saucer-like eyes as blue as cornflowers, he sat with both legs stretched in front of him. His right trouser-leg was turned up to the knee, and the girl called Di was binding a wound half-way between his knee and ankle. There was blood on the deck, and on his trousers.

'May you be forgiven,' he greeted the Errols, with a look of bitter reproach.

Mike snapped:

'Let's stop fooling! A joke's a joke, but this is long past it. If we got in the way, we're sorry—but it looks to me as if you fellows botched your own game. If game is the word.'

'We'd like to think it is,' said Loftus, easily. 'It saves us from taking life too seriously. Isn't your name Errol?'

'Yes. Yours Loftus?'

'Yes … How did you know?'

'One of the brace mentioned it.' Mike was still in bad humour: 'I've seen you before …'

'I've been trying to think where,' agreed Loftus. 'It could—dammit! Brook Street, of course! Yours is the Talbot with the cat and fiddle on the bonnet?'

'Right,' said Mark.

'H'mm. Well now, let me tell you a story—find yourselves a pew.' He waited till they were seated, then explained: 'We had reason to believe Benotti, Dodge and Merkle would be hereabouts, and we knew Benotti was for the long jump. We wanted to catch the three of them, and we were coasting up and down. We saw them coming, carrying Benotti—but before we could start shooting, you two horned in.' Again there was a glimmer of a smile on his lips, if none in his eyes. 'It was shooting you, or holding fire, and we used discretion. They didn't. Ned Oundle was hit, and the rest of us were lucky not to be. Got it?'

Mike nodded.

'So Benotti is the dead man. Which is Merkle?'

'The short, swarthy one.'

'And Dodge is the one who puts the boot in,' Mike said grimly. 'But that hardly explains why you wanted to shoot them—you're not the police, are you?'

'We are not!' Oundle snorted.

'Shut up, Ned,' said Loftus, easily. 'Errol, you saw that girl just now—Fay Loring?'

Mike nodded again.

'Well, the primary reason for our desire to put Dodge and company out of action was their keen desire to do likewise to her.'

'Oh!' For once, Mike was bereft of words.

'It's getting understandable,' Mark murmured, reflectively, and Loftus grinned.

'Fay does have that effect—I've noticed it before. Well, she's gone for the police, which ought to convince you that we're not scrapping off our own bat. For the rest, I can't tell you a damned thing—yet. But I can introduce you—the lady with the fair hair and the bandages is Diana Woodward—curtsey Di! The injured innocent is Ned Oundle—just nod your head, Ned. Your turn, Errol.'

'Michael, of that ilk.' Mike identified himself. 'And this is Mark. It's more or less every day we see you in Brook Street, of course. We're at 55c.'

'I'm 11g,' said Loftus. 'So we're neighbours. Now what brought you here this afternoon?'

The question was natural and seemed casual, but there was an expression in Loftus's smoky grey eyes which suggested a sting in its tail. Mike grinned.

'Are we suspect? It's Mark's fault—anything, to dodge Hurlingham!'

'I don't blame him.' Loftus grinned back. 'Well, the police can look after the body—although I'd better just see what Benotti had in his pockets. We'll take you down to the boat-house—just send the bill for the punt to me.'

'Right …' Mike Errol frowned—then brightened. 'The grey cells are beginning to work! Loftus of Department Z, isn't it?'

'A bane on all newspapers,' growled Loftus. 'But—yes.'

'H'mm.' Mike glanced at Mark, who nodded imperceptibly. 'Want any recruits, Loftus?'

The big man hesitated.

'It depends. How free are you?'

'As the air,' said Mike.

'This isn't a joke: it's …'

'If you're asking whether we work for our living, we
don't. We've all the time in the world to spare—and a little
arrangement whereby we take turns in choosing our occupation for the immediate future. And it's my turn.'

Loftus grinned.

'I take it that you're making formal application for
enlistment with the Department?'

'We are.'

'We'll make you sorry,' growled Ned Oundle. Diana had
finished bandaging his leg, and now he tried to stand. He
did so, with obvious difficulty, and she promptly fetched
cushions from the cabin and insisted on making him
comfortable.

If the Errols had doubted her perfection before, they
could not do so now. Everything about her suggested that
rare—to the Errols, non-existent—combination of flawless
beauty and intelligence. The slightest of American accents
gave her voice an added depth and warmth.

She smiled—and they were her slaves for life.

'If the parley's finished, Bill …?' she queried, joining them.

'All but—we're just waiting for the police,' Loftus told her.

'Are you sure it was safe for Miss Loring to go alone?'
Mark sounded anxious.

'Dodge and Merkle will be many, many miles away,' said
Loftus, with complete assurance. 'Don't start fretting about

Fay, old son—she's all right. Come with me, a minute, you two—I might need independent witnesses …'

There were the usual oddments, in the dead man's pockets. A penknife, some loose change, a watch, comb, matches, cigarettes—and a wallet.

Loftus laid them on the ground, one by one, before opening the wallet. It came only half-open, then somehow jammed. Frowning, Loftus held it to one side, and jerked hard …

There was a clang! and something flashed from it, too fast to see: they heard it strike the trunk of a tree behind them.

There was a moment's tense silence, then Loftus straightened up.

CHAPTER 3
INTERVIEW WITH CRAIGIE

There was, in Bill Loftus, an indefinable quality that lifted him at once from the ruck of ordinary men, something that in part at least explained his deliberate but complete control of any situation. From the moment he had returned from chasing the two gunmen, Loftus had been in control: the others—the girls and Oundle, as well as the Errols—had pivoted about him.

Now, the Errols began to see why.

Loftus looked round towards the tree, and his voice was easy and conversational.

'Nice playthings, our late and unlamented friend enjoyed—don't touch it, you fool!'

Mike, who was reaching for the small dart lodged in the tree-trunk, snatched his hand away.

Loftus went past him and, using a clean handkerchief, pulled the dart out. It was no more than two inches long and looked for all the world like a small diary pencil. But the long needle-point had gone half an inch into the tree. From his pocket he took a used envelope and dropped the dart into it, still wrapped in the handkerchief. Drily, he told Mike:

'Both ends might be poisoned, y'know.'

As the cousins gasped, Loftus turned again to the wallet.

It opened without the slightest trouble, this time. They watched him glance through the contents, none of which he appeared to think important. Then taking out a knife, he slit the pockets of the wallet and ran his finger inside. His expression hardened as he brought out a small sheet of tissue-paper, folded in four.

'That's what I'm after,' he said, with obvious satisfaction. 'Well, now—still hankering after joining us?'

Mike swallowed hard.

'Just what happened?'

'Dope!' snapped Mark. 'There was a spring in the wallet, and forcing it open released the dart. Any idiot could see that.'

Mike glared.

'Obviously one did!'

'Now listen, little man …'

'Peace on you, cousins!' Loftus grinned. 'But Mark's right—it was a neatly-arranged dart. Here—' he held out the wallet and they could see the small spring: 'The dart ran inside the wallet and to the casual eye would look like a pencil. Only someone knowing the gadget would know to press the catch to prevent the spring being loosed. Oh, it's a pretty idea—and worthy of Benotti. If a wallet refused to open, the normal reaction would be to bend over it—peer into it.' His jaw hardened. 'And so get the dart right in the face.'

'What made you turn aside?' asked Mark.

'Habit—caution—' Loftus shrugged. 'When a thing doesn't behave in a normal manner, it is open to suspicion.'

'Rule one, sub-section B, general regulations—Department Z!' Diana's eyes were twinkling as she reached his side.

'Quiet, America,' growled Loftus, and she laughed.

21

'Did Benotti invent it, Bill?' she asked, more seriously.

'I don't know—yet.' That little word was one of which Loftus was inordinately fond: it represented his belief that nothing was impossible. 'The reasonable inference is that any member of the Benotti association might have a duplicate, and it behoves us to be careful. One of the gentry invented it, certainly,' he added, grimly. 'So by now there could be a hundred and one like it.' He raised his head, suddenly. 'A car's coming, thank heavens! We ought to be on the move soon.'

Within the next three minutes, a car, an ambulance, four policemen and Fay Loring arrived. The middle-aged senior policeman, one Inspector Smythe, listened with some deference as Loftus made a sketchy but fairly comprehensive report. Fay called Diana on one side, and Mark tried not to stare as a powder compact was brought into operation.

Trust a woman! he thought, only hazily aware how much this utterly normal action reassured him, in the midst of so much that was so far from normal.

There was Loftus, who had hoped to kill or capture three men ... Fay Loring, whose life was in danger ... Merkle, Dodge, the dead Benotti ... the wounded Ned Oundle ... the obvious respect of the police ... his own and Mike's still hardly-credible involvement in the whole incredible business ... That powder-compact was reality, comfortingly mundane ...

Trust a woman! thought that erstwhile misogynist, Mark Errol ...

Loftus broke across his reverie.

'Come on, recruits—we'll get back to Richmond!'

Quickly, and in orderly fashion, they boarded the launch. Loftus had left everything but the wallet and its contents with the police, who had obviously had instructions to render him all possible assistance. He handled the launch as expertly as he did everything else, and soon the *chug-chug-chug* of its engine was echoing across the water.

The Old Deer Park on one side, and Isleworth on the other, looked serene and peaceful. Yet *someone* must have heard that shot, Mark thought.

'The Great British Public, much-maligned,' Loftus remarked, as if he had voiced his bafflement aloud, 'has to be known to be believed. I daresay a hundred people heard the shooting, and put it down to a car back-firing. Use a machine-gun in Piccadilly and no one will believe it, unless they're hit. What do you know about Department Z, Mark Errol?'

Mark had been envying Mike, who was sitting with Diana on one side of him and Fay on the other, obviously thoroughly at home. But even the lovely Fay could not compete with the fascination the mysterious Department Z had always held for both cousins.

'Oh, the usual bilge,' he said, awkwardly. 'As a matter of fact, I've always thought it had a pretty melodramatic ring to everything it does. You know—if anything unusual happens, blame it on Department Z—the public'll forget it in a week. That's about the lot.'

Loftus eyed him through drooping lids for a moment, then grunted. He seemed to condemn the Errols and the Great British Public with that grunt.

'As one might expect. All the same, you linked me up with it. Why?'

'Well, your name did get into the Press a few months back—over that Lakka business.* I was in Biarritz at the time and didn't see much about it, but the name stuck.'

'Good memory?'

'I can't complain.'

'Try not to be modest,' said Loftus. 'I want to find out if you'd be any use to us.'

'Well—yes, things do stick. Although I'm not a patch on Mike—he's a ruddy marvel, that way.'

Loftus grinned.

'Cousinly loyalty, eh? Can you use a gun?'

'Yes.'

'Married?'

'Heaven forbid!'

Loftus squinted over his shoulder at Mike.

'Susceptible?'

'I'll have you know,' Mark informed him, 'that we're neither of us even remotely likely to make fools of ourselves over women—if that's what you mean.'

'Good—too good to be true, in fact.' Loftus nodded ahead: they were almost level with Richmond Bridge. 'Which is your boat-house? You'd better arrange for them to salvage the punt.'

He turned inshore.

Mark did not try to bargain with a startled boat-house owner, who wished all clients doing damage proved as generous …

A little further down-river, they moored the launch and walked back to Richmond Bridge, near where the Errols had parked their Talbot—and Loftus his big green Bentley.

Oundle hobbled, supported by his massive friend. At the Bentley, Loftus stopped.

'I'll have to risk letting you drive her, Di—but scratch an inch of my paint and I'll sue you! Fay—in you get. Right? Ned, get in the back and make yourself as comfortable as you can. Take him to the flat, Di—and get Little over.'

'I don't need more doctoring,' protested Oundle.

'You're having it,' said Loftus. 'Errols—will you wait while I make a call?'

They assented, watching with mixed feelings as the Bentley drove off, with Fay smiling and waving till the big car turned the corner. As they disappeared, Mike shook his head suddenly, and gave Mark a wry grin.

'Is any of it true?'

'I started it,' Mark admitted, gloomily, 'but I'm damned if I know where it's going to end.'

'I suppose there *is* a Department Z?'

'We ought to find out, pretty soon,' commented Mark, drily.

Loftus rejoined them at last, apologetic but preoccupied. He stood eyeing them both for so long that it seemed certain he must have bad news to impart. He spoke at last:

'What time do they open round here?'

He grinned as they both gaped.

'Fact is, I've a couple of hours on my hands. At seven-thirty,' he added, drily, 'we go to see the Great Panjandrum.'

'That,' said Mike, 'is better.'

'More like,' agreed Mark.

'You haven't answered the question.'

'If we go to town, they'll be open by the time we get there,' Mike suggested.

'Idea. Let's go.'

If the Errols approved of his attitude, it continued to puzzle them. They had yet to realise that in order to keep their nerve at concert pitch—to avoid the risk of anything, no matter how catastrophic, destroying their mental balance—all Craigie's agents developed and took refuge in their own peculiar brand of humour. They faced too many

25

crises, saw death too near, met danger far too often, to allow it to affect them.

To Loftus, the afternoon's affair had been a mild one.

And, he knew, there was worse to come.

For he had not been jesting when he had spoken of a hundred and one possible possessors of a wallet fixed on the lines of Bruno Benotti's ...

Meanwhile, waiting until Gordon Craigie in Whitehall could see him, and the Errols—as well as make discreet inquiries about those ebullient young men—he took them to the Carilon Club, and drank beer heartily, and appeared to have no single trouble in the world.

Whereas in fact he had precisely a hundred and one.

The Errols followed Loftus along a narrow street leading from Whitehall, through a door which they had passed a hundred times yet never noticed, up a short flight of stone steps to a landing that led, apparently, to a blank wall. They did not see him press a button under the balustrade, but they stared as the wall slid open—to reveal the office of Gordon Craigie, Chief of Department Z.

Craigie was seated at a large desk bare of everything but telephones. Behind him were rows of steel cabinets and beside the desk, a dictaphone. There were no windows, but the room was pleasantly cool—despite the heat outside, indeed, a small fire glowed in the hearth.

At the fireplace end of the room were several easy chairs, a littered table, two small bookcases, and a cupboard which gaped open to reveal an astonishing miscellany of odd-ments, from eatables to linen, collar studs to cigarettes and a jar of pungent Navy mixture. On a rack by the fireplace were six meerschaum pipes, and a seventh was even then dangling from Craigie's lips.

He was a tallish, angular man, inclined to stoop a little, grey and lined before his time; but his hooded grey eyes were exceptionally alert. He had the somewhat bony features characteristic of so many Scots, and his chiselled lips drooped at the corners. In the past seven years Craigie had seemed to age at least fifteen, but he was still only a year over fifty.

As the little party entered—the Errols not unaffected by the precautions, for the door slid to as they passed it—Craigie took his pipe from his mouth and smiled.

'Hallo, Bill. So you've brought the pups?'

'They snarl a bit,' drawled Loftus. 'But when it comes to the crunch, they behave pretty well.'

The Errols did not see the slight lift of his eyebrow, or Craigie's imperceptible nod as he left his desk and crossed to the fire.

'Sit down,' he invited. 'You'll get used to Loftus, in time.' They sat down murmuring their thanks, and Loftus offered cigarettes.

'Comfortable?' Craigie asked. 'Good. I'll tell you without preamble that you've been screened thoroughly, that I've every reason to believe you're eligible for membership, and it just happens that you've come at a good time. I want two men—men useful with their fists—for a little job we have on hand. But before we go into detail and before you are told just what will be expected from you while you work with me, there's a question of some importance.'

As he paused, Mark gave a wry shrug.

'It's my turn to answer—let it come.'

Craigie smiled drily: over the telephone, Loftus had told him something of the cousins.

'Right. It's quite simple, and needs a direct "yes" or "no".' Gravely, he asked it: 'Are you, both of you, prepared to leave your flat to-night and disappear—if necessary, for as long as twelve months?'

* *Murder Must Wait* by John Creasey

CHAPTER 4
WORK FOR THE ERROLS

It was a question deliberately calculated to make applicants for service in Department Z think twice—and as many more times as they felt were necessary. It was asking no small thing. It meant, perhaps, leaving families and friends with hardly a by-your-leave—for before Craigie allowed them to answer, he pointed out that no one must know where or why they were going. It meant, he emphasised, not only offering to give a year of their lives to the Department, but *risking* their lives for it, not once but a hundred times.

'It probably sounds fantastic,' said Craigie. 'But it's not. You had a little—just a little—glimpse, today, of the things that do happen.' His expression grew sombre as he told them: 'I've had over four hundred agents, at one time or another. At least a hundred of them have just—disappeared.'

Mike stirred.

'It sounds grim.'

'It *is* grim.'

'Did you know Kerr?' asked Loftus, unexpectedly. 'Bob Kerr, the airman?'

'Yes ...' Mark hesitated. 'Didn't he have a crash—lose an arm?'

'It was called a crash,' said Loftus, heavily. 'Actually, he was lucky not to lose his life. He had seven bullets between the elbow and shoulder.'

Mike glanced at Mark.

'To me,' he offered, 'it looks as if they're trying to frighten us off, Marko. What about that answer?'

Mark blinked.

'Haven't I said "yes", yet? Sorry, Craigie!'

Craigie smiled: so did Loftus. There was an irrepressible spirit about the Errol cousins which made them remarkably fitted for service in Department Z.

'We're not trying to scare you,' said Craigie, 'we're just stating facts. Now ...'

He eased himself from his chair, crossed to his desk, and returned with a typewritten folio which he handed to the Errols. As they read it together, Craigie and Loftus smoked in silence.

It was a simple-looking document, containing just twelve paragraphs—a statement of the conditions on which any man worked for the Department. Among lesser and more predictable requirements, the Errols read:

'An agent will at all times hold himself ready for the service of the Department, will be prepared to leave his home or wherever he may be staying for an indefinite period, informing no one of his destination or purpose.

An agent carrying written information will be expected to destroy that information should his safety be imperilled: if possessing unwritten information, he will be expected to retain it at all costs, *even to death*.

An agent having direct orders to kill, will carry out those orders regardless of personal feelings. Without those direct instructions, an agent will not shoot or otherwise kill an opponent *unless* to save his own life or the lives of others, or to prevent an opponent escaping with information which might be of vital interest to a Foreign Power.

All instructions must be obeyed to the letter.

An agent ceases to be a member of the Department on (a) disobedience (b) proof that he does not put the Department's interest before all else (c) evidence of inefficiency (d) failure to observe the strictest secrecy and loyalty (e) marriage.

An agent will receive a yearly honorarium of £500 (five hundred pounds) and reasonable expenses to cover specific operative work.'

'Well?' said Craigie, as they finished reading.

The eyes of both Errols gave their answer before they spoke. In five minutes, the formalities were over; in fifteen, they had an outline of the activities of that remarkable organisation known, for want of a better name, as the League of the Hundred-and-One. Craigie gave them only such facts as were—to those who mattered—common knowledge. Before they were given information of more vital importance, they would have to prove themselves.

And the opportunity for that was close at hand.

While Craigie, Loftus and the Errols were talking in Whitehall, two men hurried furtively towards the Éclat Hotel in Piccadilly. There was excuse enough for their furtiveness. The blood of Benotti was on their hands, and although there had been no evidence of pursuit from the river, they knew enough of Loftus and his men to realise that evidence was not everything.

They hurried past the commissionaire, the reception desk, and the lift-boy. The commissionaire, used to less cavalier behaviour on the part of visitors, followed them discreetly, but on seeing them knock at the door of Suite 3, returned to his post. The present occupant of Suite 3 was the most generous man at the Éclat, and nothing must be allowed to upset him.

His name was Korrel.

He was a big, well-built man, running to fat, with the sleek, black hair and almond-shaped black eyes suggestive of Oriental ancestry. Immaculate as always in a superbly-tailored Savile Row suit, he stood now before the empty fireplace in the sitting-room of Suite 3, exuding an aura of benevolence.

His voice was low-pitched, mellow, suave, its cadence remarkable: and he spoke with a fluency rarely found in an Englishman.

'My dear Myra,' he was saying, in that melodious voice, 'the issue is perfectly clear: your instructions hardly need amplifying. Richard Anson is not, I will agree, your type. On the other hand, for the sake of the Association, Mr. Anson's interest is so essential that for once you must do something which is perhaps distasteful. Regrettable, but ...'
Mr. Abraham Korrel's shrug was eloquent.

The woman who faced him from the depths of a large armchair was wearing a flowered silk dress clearly calculated to emphasize the perfection of her figure. She was a magnificent creature, with her tawny hair braided about her head and her sultry, amber eyes—leonine eyes. The eyes glowed up at him.

'Yes, yes—I've heard all that before! But ...'
Her voice suited her: deep, husky, a shade imperious.
Korrel interrupted her.

'Let it be understood, Myra—there can be no arguments.'
Myra Clayton laughed, and it was not a pleasant sound.

'I haven't taken orders from you, yet, and I don't propose to start. Anson isn't my meat, and you know it—and so do the others.'

Korrel's eyes narrowed, hinting at an anger it would be dangerous to provoke.

'Myra, I have no wish to be unpleasant. I have already informed you that for the time being, I am the leading operative in England—and what I say *must* be obeyed.'

'Don't be a fool.' She spoke abruptly, but her expression was wary, now. 'Even if you do think you've the last word, over here, that doesn't mean your judgment's always sound. I tell you—I can't do a thing with Anson. You want a fluffy little bit, like Dora ...'

'Dora is already busy.'

'Well, Letty ...'

'Letty cannot be safely entrusted with an important commission. Let us have no more arguments, Myra. Anson is staying at this hotel, and I can arrange a meeting. It is comparatively simple for you. In all probability he will be of no use to us after a week or ten days, after which I may be able to find you something more attractive. But I want Anson at Moorton Road by to-morrow night, and you've got to get him there. I ... yes?' he called as a sharp tap came on the door. 'Who is it?'

Myra, her amber eyes smouldering resentfully, straightened up as a harsh voice answered.

'It's Merkle—an'...'

Korrel jerked his head and Myra moved swiftly towards the door to the other room. As it closed silently behind her, he called as if impatient:

'Come in—come in!'

Merkle entered first.

There was none of its earlier belligerence, now, in that brutal, swarthy face, and the small, beady eyes looked anxious: Dodge, following him in, looked equally uncomfortable.

Korrel, bigger than either man, stared at them in chilly silence, his lips twisted unpleasantly.

'Listen, Boss,' Merkle protested instinctively, 'we got Benotti, like you told us, and if it hadn't been for a couple've blokes ...'

'It is late for excuses,' said Korrel, coldly. 'Did you get his wallet?'

Merkle gulped.

'No, we ...'

Something happened to Korrel in that moment. His pale face flushed a deep red, his black eyes glittered, and his hand shot out to slap Merkle viciously across the face, with the palm and then the back of the hand. As Merkle staggered back and Dodge edged away, Korrel growled:

'Merkle was in charge, Dodge, but you're as much to blame. I won't have mistakes—understand? *Won't* have them! Make a hash of things like that again, and you're as dead as Benotti.'

'We did all we could, Boss!' Dodge whined. 'We nearly got Loftus ...'

Korrel seemed to freeze.

'*What* did you say?'

'Loftus an' two-three others were in a launch. They made for us, and if it hadn't been for these two geezers, we'd've got the lot.'

'*Loftus,*' breathed Korrel. 'How did he get there? *How—did—he—know?* And you ...' fury flared in him again—'you let *Loftus* get that wallet? The one man who ...' He made a visible effort to control himself. 'Get out!' he snarled. 'And stay under cover, you benighted fools. If the police get you, I won't lift a hand to help you—you deserve all you get. *Get out!*'

Dodge turned first, but Merkle beat him to the door. As it closed behind them, Korrel exuded a long breath.

Loftus, chief agent—and some said second-in-command—of Department Z, had located the spot where Benotti had been killed.

The plans had been made so carefully. Only a handful of people knew, and they were all trustworthy. But Loftus had managed to get foreknowledge …

Korrel shivered.

There was something uncanny about Loftus—indeed, about the way all Craigie's men operated. Korrel knew little enough of Department Z—had not heard of it before Loftus first began to work against the League of the Hundred-and-One. The police, of this country or a dozen others, Korrel would snap his fingers at. But Loftus and those other men …

Behind him, Myra Clayton sauntered out of the bathroom, hand on hip in a deliberately nonchalant pose, her amber gaze taunting, insolent.

'How well you're controlling the English side, Korrel …!'

There was murder in Korrel's eyes as he whipped round.

'*Get out of my way!*' he breathed. 'Get out and stay out, until you know how to behave yourself! If you haven't brought Anson to Moorton Road by to-morrow night, you're finished. Understand?' His voice reached hysterical pitch. 'Finished, finished, *finished,* you little …!'

Breaking away, suddenly cold with fear, she snatched up a linen coat and ran out. Korrel hardly noticed her go as he slumped into the nearest chair, breathing hard through dilated nostrils.

The reception clerk, the assistant manager and the commissionaire smiled and bowed as Myra passed, but for once she was not even conscious of their admiration.

Outside, she hailed a taxi and as it pulled up, said sharply '10, Moorton Road, Kensington.'

'O.K., Miss.'

Myra climbed in, the door banged, and the cab moved off.

Behind it, a small sports car also moved, a fair-haired, good-looking young man at the wheel. Carruthers, who was reputed to be one of the world's playboys, had been an amateur boxer of distinction. Although he would never reach Loftus's position in Department Z, he was one of a dozen of Craigie's most reliable men, possessing every qualification that perfectionist sought in his special aides save that one intangible but absolutely vital quality known as leadership.

Across the road, a tall, languid-looking individual with a long, irregular nose and soulful eyes surveyed the passing scene as though London on a hot August evening was the last place in the world he wished to be. The soulful eyes had noted the way Carruthers lighted a cigarette before starting in the wake of the taxi, then throw the packet to the pavement.

Mr Wallace Davidson mustered the energy to cross the road and retrieve the empty packet. He glanced inside it idly, as though hoping for a picture-card, and equally idly slipped it into his pocket.

Five minutes later, from a call-box, he 'phoned Craigie.

'Hallo, Gordon: N-O-S-D-I-V—'

'Carry on, Wally.' The Department practice of spelling their names backward to prove identity was, like so many things that Craigie organised, simplicity itself. And like everything that Craigie organised, successful.

'The Clayton woman,' Wally drawled wearily, 'has left the Éclat, looking fit to be tied—I shouldn't like to be her Little Boy Blue, tonight. Carrie's after her, and the address she gave was 10, Moorton Road, Kensington. Any orders?'

'No. I shan't want you for an hour or so, Wally—get some rest if you can. Number 10: you're sure of that?'

'Carrie said so.'

'Right, thanks.'

Craigie replaced the receiver, and Davidson made his lethargic way towards Brook Street, where he too had a flat. Half-way along it, he saw the vast figure of Doc Little, whom all the agents knew as the Department's consulting physician and surgeon.

Wally crossed the road.

'Hallo, Doc, where have you been?'

Little beamed.

'Just a little trouble with Oundle, nothing to worry about. No more than a scratch, in fact. Going to call on him?'

'Is Bill there?'

'No—Miss Woodward and Miss Loring—'

Davidson's sad eyes brightened.

'I'd better go and condole with Ned,' he said.

'Ned, my foot,' retorted Little. 'You lot expecting to be busy in the near future?'

Wally Davidson shrugged. 'You'd better ask Craigie. Why?'

'Oundle was more talkative than usual,' said Little cheerfully, 'and more absurd. That usually means—what's the matter, Davidson?'

Wally's lethargy had dropped away: in its place was an alert and catlike wariness which would have astonished any but his closest friends. He was staring towards the far end of Brook Street—towards Number 11g, in fact.

'Doc, 'phone Craigie—ask him to send three or four men to Loftus' place, fast! 'Bye.'

Little stared after him as he covered the ground at surprising speed, while still managing to create an impression of general fatigue.

Further along the street, two cars had drawn up. He saw two men climb from each—and all four head straight for 11g. And Wally recognised none of the four.

He had no way of knowing that a certain Mr Abraham Korrel had been on the telephone to a remarkable house in Moorton Road, Kensington, and that immediately afterwards, the four had left that house for the address of William Loftus. Nor did he know that all four men were armed, and had very definite instructions.

But as he instinctively quickened his pace, he was glad to feel the weight of the gun in his shoulder-holster.

CHAPTER 5
TROUBLE IN BROOK STREET

Ned Oundle, his leg properly dressed and the medical report satisfactory, reclined on a settee with his leg stretched in front of him, a cigarette dangling from his lips and a tankard of beer at his side.

Diana was pretending to read.

Fay was pretending to sew.

'My dear, sweet maids,' Oundle grumbled, 'what happened to the ministering angel bit? Why the devil don't you entertain me? Dammit, I'm injured!'

'The invalid must have quiet,' said Di.

'H'mm. Moping, eh? Just because Bill isn't here! How that poor mug allowed himself to get tied up with an undesirable alien ...'

Diana grinned at Fay.

'Isn't he a pet? He can go on and on like this, you know—hour after hour.'

'That's a relief,' said Fay. 'I thought he was getting delirious.'

'Pah!' Ned Oundle drank deeply, smoked, and regarded them moodily.

That they were at a high pitch of tension, he knew quite well. That Fay had even more reason to be worried than Diana, he also knew.

Diana, a few months before, had worked with the American Intelligence Bureau on a case which had also occupied Craigie's attentions—to put it mildly. War had, quite simply, been averted by a major miracle.

But for how long?

Wars and rumours of war abounded. Naked aggression stalked in Europe. Death, murder, pillage and worse ruled spasmodically, governed by loud-mouthed protestations of good-will by the perpetrators of outrages which, twenty years before, would have caused a European conflagration. To Oundle—as to millions of others—it seemed that the spirit of defiance, the spirit of freedom, had wilted. The map of Europe had altered vastly in the past year: altered with hardly a fight, altered under the aegis of a so-called axis—watched by democratic governments which had been bamboozled and confounded yet continued in office. Protests were lodged and ignored, elder statesmen looked grave. Cabinet Ministers made portentous speeches after each act of aggression and sounded grieved and hurt that the word of dictators was not as inviolable to the dictators as it was to the Cabinet Ministers.

And the dictators grew stronger, the voice of Russia rumbled but at first was barely heard above the platitudes of other powers, small states trembled, three monarchs had been exiled by foreign invaders and appealed in vain for help. A desperate last-minute effort to retrieve the errors of a generation was being made in the name of Collective Security, in which the bigger democracies only partly believed, and indeed viewed with considerable suspicion.

Most of the leaders, thought Oundle bitterly, appeared to expect a miracle—were hoping against hope that the German and Italian eagles would seek to devour no more tasty morsels. A blindness and paralysis was on the democracies, despite the warnings and predictions of men in the House of Commons with greater claims to knowledge than any in the Cabinet.

All of which made the work of Department Z more onerous.

It had not helped to have the press trumpeting stories of the ineffectual efforts of the Secret Service. Only Craigie, Loftus, Oundle and a dozen others knew how desperately they had presented responsible officials with facts which could not be denied—facts which were accepted, but of which it was said that there was no official confirmation, or that the position was still obscure—and which went with those officials on holiday, against the pleas of a negligible opposition ...

Just what part the League of the Hundred-and-One played in the activities of the dictator states, it was impossible to be sure. But it was considerable. The reason for the presence of so many League members in England was not yet known, but Craigie believed it was connected with the outbreaks of sabotage and senseless explosions which, for many months, had been rife up and down the land.

Oundle's chief grievance, now, was that they had had such a chance, that afternoon, and had muffed it. One dead League member and two escapees was hardly a brilliant score. It was no one's fault, but ...

He glanced across at Fay.

Odd, the way Fay had come to join the Department—which rarely used woman members. That her life was in danger, that she was wanted by the League, was an established fact. She had let that be known to Oundle—who had relayed it to Craigie. Craigie had judged Fay in that quick, rarely erroneous way of his—and asked her to play the League along, while being watched by his own men.

Fay had done so. The League, in time, had learned it.
Three weeks before, there had been a minor battle in Surrey,
with Oundle and Loftus and several other Department men
against a dozen of the League's lesser members. Fay, having
escaped with her life, had asked to continue working for
Craigie ...

He eyed her again—and found himself thinking, not for
the first time, that girls should not be enlisted. Diana was
different: she had been in the game before joining Craigie
as a co-opted member from the States. But Fay ...

There was a ring at the front door.

Diana put down her magazine, paused to leave her cigarette on an ash-tray, and went to answer it.

'Expecting anyone, Ned?' murmured Fay.

But before he could speak, there was an abrupt exclama-
tion from Diana—and then silence.

Oundle slipped his hand to his pocket and felt the cold
steel of a gun as he jerked his head towards Fay. Pale-faced,
she rose at once and crossed the room into the main bedroom. The door closed noiselessly behind her as Diana
demanded:

'What on earth does this mean? Who ...'

'Shut up!' snarled a rough voice. 'We don't want no talk
out of you. Get back in that room.'

'But ...!'

'Get back!'

A gun reinforced the order, and Diana turned back
towards the sitting-room. Her heart was beating fast: she
knew danger when she saw it, and these four were distinctly
ugly customers, and certainly all armed.

As they crowded in behind her, a suave, new, unmistak-
ably American voice came.

'Just one moment, honey!' The tallest of the quartet gripped her wrist. He had the dark, flashy good-looks of an Italo-American of the worst kind, and was dressed to suit. Holding an automatic against her side, he called:

'Loftus—if yuh're playin' with the idea of shooting, don't! The dame'll go first.'

Diana said evenly:

'Loftus isn't here.'

'No?' he jeered. 'We'll see. Go on, Luke.'

The shortest man—red-haired, pug-faced and with a peculiarly elastic manner of walking—went to the sitting-room door, his gun showing.

He saw Oundle.

'Loftus ain't around, Cy.'

'Hidin', mebbe.' The man named Cy tightened his grip on Diana's wrist, and shoved her into the room ahead of him. Oundle had taken his hand from his gun, for he could recognise a moment for action and this certainly was not one.

Cy was in the middle of the room, now, still holding Diana. His instructions had been to kill Loftus first, and any others with him afterwards. The strangely-named Cyrus Kalloni had served his apprenticeship in crime to a Chicago big shot who had recently gone to the electric chair, and the first lesson he had learned was obedience—to the letter.

Kill Loftus first.

'Check the joint, Luke.'

Red-hair went into the bedroom where Fay had gone, looked round, saw nothing, and withdrew. The second bed-room yielded the same results. So did the bathroom and the kitchen.

'He ain't here,' he announced, returning.

Kalloni twisted Diana's wrist, and she gasped with sudden pain. Oundle's lips tightened. Kalloni flung her roughly towards a chair. She staggered and half-fell, but recovered herself. On her wrist, the marks of Kalloni's fingers showed an angry red.

'Listen, sister. I ain't wastin' no time. Where's Loftus?'

'He's out ...'

Kalloni took a menacing step forward, and his eyes glittered.

'You're quite a looker, sister—but if you don't come across, pronto, you won't have no looks to speak of.'

He pulled a small, ebony cut-throat razor from his waistcoat pocket. He flicked open the blade, and the hollow-ground steel glinted in the light. There was a cold, deliberate callousness about his manner that was worse than any loud-voiced threats would have been.

'Get me, sister? Now—where's Loftus?'

Diana drew a deep breath.

'I'm expecting him any time.'

'That so?' He brought the razor up, suddenly; and petrified, she seemed to feel the sharp incision of the blade across her cheeks. But it flashed past, an inch from her face.

Kalloni was a third degree specialist of a high order.

'That's so,' Oundle spoke up, in a surprisingly steady voice. '*Any* time, wop. And I wouldn't like to see what's left of you, if that pen-knife touches Miss Woodward.'

As Kalloni turned—slowly, negligently—one of the others went to stand over Diana.

Still toying with the razor, Kalloni approached Oundle.

'Smart guy, huh? How'd *you* like a turn?'

'You damned fool,' said Oundle, dispassionately. 'Haven't you learned the first lesson, yet?'

Kalloni stopped waving the razor.

'Whaddya mean?'

'You'll find out—if you use that plaything.' Oundle turned to look at Diana. His heart was thumping: there was 'killer' written all over Kalloni's face, and a cruelty which might mean a lot of suffering before death came.

Oundle had no idea when Loftus would get back—or whether he would be alone, when he came. So it seemed to him that the most important thing was to give his friend a warning. Did Fay know Craigie's number? He couldn't be sure. He had to stall—and Kalloni would not be an easy man to bluff.

But Oundle's confident manner—and Diana's too, now—baffled Kalloni. Life, to him, was simply a matter of making himself feared. For a moment he had seen fear in the girl's eyes, but now he read something more akin to contempt. It puzzled him—and with the absence of Loftus, on top of it, nothing was going as he felt it ought to go.

'Mebbe I will,' he grunted. 'Listen, you—an' you, sister! One crack outa either of you, when Loftus comes—an' the dame gets the razor. An' you, smart guy, get lead where it hurts most.' He patted his stomach with his free hand. 'Barney, you stay by the front door. Marker, you watch the window. Luke, you keep your eye on the wise guy—I'll watch the dame.'

One-handed, he took a case from his pocket, extracted a cigarette, lit it with a lighter attached to the case and blew smoke into Oundle's face. He was watching the door out of the corner of his eye, and he saw the man named Barney stiffen.

Diana and Oundle watched, too, hardly daring to breathe, their only thought the need to warn whoever was coming. Diana was desperately certain that it would be Loftus, but she would have been little relieved had she known it was Wally Davidson, for whoever opened that door would get a bullet.

And if she or Oundle cried out, there was no guarantee that it would serve any useful purpose—but plenty of reason to believe that Kalloni would carry out his threats.

Then, sharp across the tension, came a *rat-tat-tat* at the door.

CHAPTER 6
WALLY WALKS IN

It is often said of Craigie's men that they have no regard for danger—which is absurd. They are more susceptible to moments pregnant with trouble than ninety-nine people out of any hundred.

Wally Davidson, for instance, had never been ashamed to admit—in the right company—that his knees still felt weak, every time he handled a gun. But danger was their life. They had learned to face it, coolly and equably, until it became a regular and natural part of their existence.

In the affair of the League of the Hundred-and-One, none of Craigie's leading agents doubted the ruthlessness of their opponents. There would be quick work, and fast killing—and withal, no quarter.

Which did not mean that any man should go bull-headed into trouble. So Davidson, to make it appear that he was unaware of the four men in the flat, knocked loudly on the door.

The move disconcerted Kalloni.

He hesitated a moment, then said in a low voice:

'Open up, Barney! Luke—keep the door covered.'

Barney slipped his gun into his pocket and reached for the door-knob as Luke moved swiftly to a better vantage-point, and Kalloni exchanged the razor for a Luger from his shoulder-holster.

Davidson, languid of manner and immaculate as always, started with apparent surprise at the thick-set uncouth-looking Barney.

'Is—er—Mr Loftus in?'

'Yeah, come in,' grunted Barney, and Davidson stepped into the large lobby. He saw Luke, and guessed why he was positioned opposite the door. He could not see Diana, but he caught a glimpse of Kalloni, of Oundle on the settee, and of the other two gunmen, and his expression remained the same: he did not bat an eyelid.

'Hallo, Ned! Entertaining?'

Kalloni glanced away from Oundle, which was a foolish thing to do. All four gunmen were eyeing Davidson, baffled at his attitude and wondering whether he represented danger. Oundle slipped his hand to his pocket and eased himself over so that he could fire through his coat; then as Davidson caught his eye, nodded imperceptibly.

Still out of Davidson's sight, Diana crowded against the wall, behind a book-case, as he drawled:

'Well, well—I didn't know such a collection lived in London!' and slipped his hand to his pocket.

'Keep your mitts in sight!' snapped Kalloni. 'And ...'

With the air of a conjurer, Wally produced a cigarette-case.

'Worried about something?' The complete disingenuousness of his manner had the four men gaping—introduced a note they would never be able to understand—which was one of the reasons Department Z was so often successful. Putting a cigarette to his lips, he beamed around. 'Four little Mafia boys, is it?'

Kalloni flushed. He pushed a hand into his pocket.

'Listen, wise guy, just cut the talk.' He jerked his head. 'Get over by the dame, and …'

'We don't seem to understand each other.' Davidson picked up a lighter from the hall-table and flicked it into flame, then streamed grey smoke towards Kalloni. 'I shouldn't move, handsome. The first mistake you make, you'll get hurt.'

'Why, you goddamn …!'

'The gun being here,' said Ned Oundle, gently.

Kalloni swung round, and the eyes of all four men were suddenly riveted on the gun in Oundle's hand.

'Awkward, isn't it?' He smiled, and his sorrowful eyes looked more innocent then ever. 'If I shoot first, one of you gets hurt. If you shoot first, you get hurt anyway—my friend here also being a crack shot. One way and another, it hasn't worked out quite as you expected—has it?'

'Why, you …' snarled Kalloni.

'Come, come!' Oundle taunted. 'Think of the lady!'

It had happened with the speed, silence and efficiency of the Department. The tables, if not completely turned, were at least half-way towards it. The four gunmen might win in a shooting match, but not now without loss.

Diana, as coolly as either of the men, picked up her bag from the table and extracted a small, pearl-handled automatic. She was smiling, although her heart was thumping. If the shooting started, there was no telling where it might end—certainly there would be little chance of them all escaping alive. Almost certainly the gunmen would make a fight for it. The swiftly-altered situation, the tactics of Oundle and Davidson, had taken them off-guard; but already Kalloni was recovering.

At least he could not use the razor, now, thought Diana, and shivered.

'Listen, wise guy,' he snarled at Davidson. 'You start anythin', an' we'll pump lead so fast you won't know what hit you!'

'Ah,' said Davidson. 'But we're not going to start anything. Unless you try to get away.' He beamed.

Luke's face twitched.

'Open up, Kalloni—we got no time!'

The tension was increasing, growing unbearable. One move of a trigger finger, and flame would stab from those guns: death would claim some of them, at least. Davidson had been hoping against hope that Doc Little had reached Craigie in time—that help was already on the way.

But less than ten minutes had passed since he had seen Little: if the showdown came now, it would be too late.

The paid killers stood motionless, guns poised in their hands, simply waiting for Kalloni's command. Only the ticking of the clock was audible, above their heavy breathing. Then:

'O.K., wise guy—you'll get in there.'

Kalloni had moved to the sitting-room doorway. He jerked his head, and the other three backed into the big lobby, their guns trained on Davidson. Kalloni, obviously, was aiming to get away without shooting—if he could.

Should they let him?

'Thanks,' drawled Davidson, and stepped forward. For a split-second, he was alongside Kalloni. His shoulder brushed against the man …

Three guns warned him, unwavering.

They passed each other in the doorway—and then Davidson back-heeled. His foot caught Kalloni under the knee and as the gangster staggered forward, he flung himself to one side and yanked out his gun …

Immobilised on the sofa, Ned was in more danger than Wally or Diana. But Kalloni, on the floor, was worse off than any. Wally fired—and took him in the right leg, below the thigh. Shooting almost wildly, his three henchmen made for the door, and Oundle fired twice to hasten them.

Kalloni's fall, followed by his gasp as he was hit, completely demoralised them: they got the door open and fled.

Davidson stopped only to kick Kalloni's gun out of reach, and was just starting after them when there was a tap at the window. He swung round—and saw Loftus!

The window went up with a bang.

'Leave them,' said Loftus calmly, climbing in. 'There are two or three of our lads downstairs, and police each end of the street—they can't get away. Any damage in here?'

'N-nothing serious,' said Diana, weakly.

'How the devil did you get here?' demanded Oundle.

Loftus grinned.

'Fay called us from next door. Craigie was 'phoning fast when I left and by the time I reached Brook Street, we were half-a-dozen strong. It looks,' he added, drily, 'as if things are really moving—and this time we haven't done so badly. Was this the spokesman?' He looked down at Kalloni.

Davidson nodded.

'I winged him.'

The gangster lay without speaking, but there was a murderous glint in his eyes. Diana, still pale but steady enough, moved towards him.

'Is he badly hurt? Perhaps I ...'

'Look out!' roared Oundle, and Loftus leapt forward.

In one fluid movement, he caught Diana about the waist and thrust her aside—just as Kalloni whipped out the razor, and flung it. Had Diana still been approaching him, it must have struck her straight in the face. Instead, it struck the wall behind Wally and splintered, a piece grazing his hand as it fell.

Loftus turned on the gangster, and the expression in his eyes made Kalloni scream. Effortlessly, the huge man bent and hauled him aloft. Heedless of his wounded leg, he threw him into a chair. Loftus, at that moment was at his ruthless and merciless worst—and looked it.

Kalloni was screeching, now.

'Shut that row!' snapped Loftus, savagely. And when he went on screeching, struck him sharply across the face. The action was effective. Trembling, Kalloni lapsed into silence.

Davidson watched, gun in hand, as Loftus went through the man's pockets. Diana, still shocked, watched with him. The last-minute attack had almost unnerved her: she was terrified that the man might yet manage to do some harm to Loftus.

She saw Kalloni's eyes glint when Loftus took out his wallet, and fancied she saw an expression of disappointment when Loftus put it aside and continued in his search; She suddenly realised that Kalloni's screeching was an act—had simply been staged to reduce the chances of getting badly hurt—and that Loftus and Davidson had known it.

Loftus finished at last and stood back, his grey eyes ice-cold as he surveyed Kalloni. Two envelopes found in his pockets gave his name in full—and also the information that he was a resident of the Naveling Hotel, Bloomsbury.

Quietly, he picked up the wallet.

The glint returned to Kalloni's eyes.

Loftus tossed the thing into the gangster's lap, and said with apparent casualness:

'Open it, Kalloni.'

The man went rigid, his eyes wide with the shock of that unexpected move. Loftus waited a few seconds, then laughed harshly. He took the wallet back, half-opened it, pressed the spring to prevent the dart's release and looked mockingly into the gangster's eyes.

'Nothing will go right for you, will it?' He took out his penknife and cut the lining of the wallet, felt inside, and pulled out a piece of thin paper like the one found inside Benotti's wallet. He opened it, and Diana, Wally and Ned saw the spidery writing, which was obviously in code, for the letters did not make sense. At the head of the sheet were the numerals: '51.'

Loftus said, still easily:

'So you were twelve higher up than Benotti, were you? He was thirty-nine.'

'You—you know *that?*' gasped Kalloni.

'That, and much more, about the League,' Loftus assured him. 'But a lot less than we're going to know when we've finished with you.'

And again there was fear in Kalloni's eyes—and a look in Loftus' own which augured ill for the man who would have slashed a razor across Diana's face.

Outside Number 11g, Luke, Barney and Marker scrambled into the first of their cars. Luke took the wheel and let in the clutch. The car lurched forward, bumping on punctured wheels. Luke swore, and his hand dived for his gun, but before he could get to it, half-a-dozen young men, all carrying guns, surrounded the car.

'If you know what's good for you,' a huge man named Martin Best said conversationally, 'you'll put your playthings away and come with us.'

One by one, they climbed from the car, to the audible disappointment of at least three of the half-dozen Z agents present. It was a coup as complete as any dictator's. And no one in quiet Brook Street knew a thing of that wholesale arrest. Nor would any have dreamed that a man who was Number 51 in a League so far suspected by only a few, was shortly to be interrogated in a manner he would not easily forget.

The League of the Hundred-and-One possessed, as its name implied, a hundred-and-one members. Number 98, although Craigie did not yet know it, was Abraham Korrel. Nor did Craigie know the three High Members—as they were beautifully and dutifully known among the lesser brethren—and for that matter no one, not even Korrel, knew their identity.

Korrel was not even sure that they were in London.

Nevertheless they were. And they met, towards midnight on the day of the Errols' acceptance in Department Z, in a houseboat moored on the Thames near Maidenhead.

As befitted the property of a multi-millionaire, the said houseboat was fitted with every imaginable aid to luxurious living and the personal comfort of its middle-aged, bearded English owner—and his many, many guests.

Inscribed in gold-leaf on its elegant stern was its name: the *Luxa.*

As well as the three High Members, there were on board a dozen lovely women, nearly as many presentable men and two or three who could hardly be called handsome, a crew of six and a service staff of fifteen—white-jacketed, in the thundery heat of that August evening.

In the silk-soft padded leather comfort of what was, in effect, a floating study, the three gentlemen sat facing each other, brandy at their elbows and cigars alight. All three were past middle age; all three were men of some note in social, political and commercial circles.

If physically they were at their ease, mentally they were not. The room was sound-proof, but instinctively they lowered their voices as they spoke.

Now, the shortest of the trio was saying quietly:

'So Numbers 39 and 51 are dead, and three of the less important members in the hands of the police. They know nothing worth disclosing, of course.'

The tallest of the three pursed his lips.

'*Is* 51 dead?'

'He has not been charged, and there are two bodies at the Cannon Street morgue, being treated with more caution than the police usually display. We can call him dead, I think—but of course we will get further proof. For the moment ...'

The speaker was interrupted by the third man: plump, florid and benevolent of face.

'The police are difficult enough, but this Department Z ...'

'Forget it! I assure you—it is an elaborate but completely ineffective organisation, initiated more for effect than anything else.'

'You're sure?'

'I am sure,' said the shortest man, confidently. 'Now, to get on: as far as I can gather, Korrel was responsible for both these misfortunes. He must be rebuked—severely rebuked. However, they are not of major importance. Nothing need upset our arrangements. The explosions have been timed ...'

'For God's sake, keep your voice down!' snapped the florid man.

'No one can hear us,' retorted the first speaker, coldly. 'Now, as I was saying: the explosions have been timed for midday tomorrow, and their effect—' he gave a mirthless smile—'should certainly be far-reaching. The whole operation will be controlled by the lesser members, of course, if there are any accidents ...' He shrugged, eloquently. 'The men can be replaced. The necessary arrangements have been made for arrests, too. Seven I.R.A. officers will be unpleasantly surprised, eight Palestinian Arabs, three Jamaican labour-leaders, and four supporters of the Indian Congress will also be unexpectedly arrested. There will,' he added drily, 'be many comments from the bench on the perspicacity of the police, many outbursts of indignation in the press—providing the international situation allows it enough space. And once we have observed the results, we can begin our next efforts.'

The florid man dabbed at his forehead.

'It's all very well for you to keep calm, but I'm not happy about that trouble today. I'm not so sure this Department Z can be dismissed so easily ...'

'If I am wrong, I shall be the first to admit it,' said the short man, blandly. 'But remember—you have prophesied errors in the past and they have never materialised. There is nothing, nothing whatever, to worry about. All being well, Anson will be at Moorton Road to-morrow, and we can then get a little further ahead. Well, shall we join the ladies?'

The florid man gulped.

'Look here, how many people will get hurt in these explosions? Damn it, the idea of innocent people ...'

'Innocent nothing!' snapped the short man, almost ferociously. 'They'll all be British won't they? You're getting too jittery—a great deal too jittery!'

The florid man forced a smile, murmured an apology and stepped out into the cool river air with relief. But the other's manner had helped, with other things, to make him afraid ...

None of the other people on board knew of the series of explosions in Britain's key towns planned for the following day, at noon precisely. None of them knew that perhaps a hundred innocent men, women and children would be murdered. None realised that the three men who joined them just after midnight were organising—slowly, deliberately and terribly effectively—a terrorism aimed at the heart of the country.

Certainly Mr Richard Anson had no idea of it, nor any thought that he was wanted to play an important part in the arrangements of the League ...

Anson, at that moment, was leaning against a rail close to the river, and smiling into the eyes of a lovely little creature whose red hair gleamed in the moonlight.

'Don't be an idiot, Dickie! I haven't known you a week.'

'A week, a month, a year—I don't make mistakes.'

'The perfect man!' Sheila Cullen teased. 'Please, Dickie—can't we just dance, or sing, or ...' She broke off, laughing up at him. 'Or if you really must get serious, there's always Myra. She's been eyeing me fit to kill, all evening.'

'Damn Myra! I ...'

'She'll be much more sympathetic!'

Anson's eyes narrowed.

'I've a damned good mind to take you at your word,' he said tartly. 'Damn it, not every girl has a chance of ...'

'Marrying perfection, I know! Dickie, if you weren't the least bit sozzled, and if you hadn't proposed to half the women on board, and if you could learn to forget the conviction that the one man who counts in this li'l old world is Richard C. Anson Esquire, I might take you seriously. As it is …'

Laughing, Sheila turned away and disappeared through a revolving door into the large dance-room. Lighting a cigarette, Anson scowled after her.

He was not by any means drunk—although the rest of the accusations, he was compelled to admit, were true.

The doors opened again, and Myra Clayton came through them. She knew she was right about Richard Anson's preference for the light and fluffy and *petite*—into which category Sheila Cullen certainly fitted—but if she guessed his present mood aright, he would not be averse to sympathy.

Had Anson ignored her, it would—for the time being at least—have kept him out of the orbit of the League. But the moon was shining on Myra's tawny hair and adding seductive, shadowy curves and hollows to her magnificent figure. Anson flung his cigarette into the water, and as it hissed and flowed away, Myra said gently:

'Feeling lonely, Dickie?'

'Too damn' right I am!' said Anson. 'Look, Myra, do you know any place where we can get some fun, instead of staying on this floating morgue?'

Myra's laugh did not reveal the exultation she felt.

'Do I not, darling! Tonight, or …?'

'Tonight, tomorrow—every damn' night, if it's fun!' said the third richest man ever to come to England from Australia. 'Just let's get out of here—I'm stifling!'

'I'll show you round,' said Myra, and laughed again.

The things which had first worried the Home Office, and eventually demanded the Department's attention, were the deaths—in some cases murder, in others suicide—of five leading armament manufacturers.

That an arms racket existed was a fact known even to the man in the street. What perturbed Craigie and certain other highly-placed individuals in Whitehall was that the dead men had between them controlled a substantial quantity of all the armaments produced in Britain. The deaths of the five—all known to the public as leading industrialists—earned some space in the national dailies, but Foreign Affairs soon crowded them out.

Craigie and Loftus believed the deaths were very closely concerned with Foreign Affairs.

It had been good fortune to find in the daughter of one of the victims—Fay Loring—a woman who was prepared to help in the fight against her father's killers. Fay had been their most valuable informant to date, and much that they had learned from her had been confirmed by reports reaching Craigie through diverse channels ever since …

Richard C. Anson was primarily interested in the manufacture of arms in Australia, but he also had extensive interests in other companies, in England and elsewhere.

Anson, in short, was in considerable danger if he were not well-disposed towards the League.

And Myra Clayton was going to show him round.

CHAPTER 7
AT MIDDAY

Mr Robert Carruthers, who had dropped the message for Davidson as he followed Myra's taxi to 10, Moorton Road, Kensington, was a young man of considerable determination. He did not think Myra had seen him at Moorton Road, and since his hair was not only fair but fine, he was singularly suited to the wearing of wigs. Disguised in a dark brown one, he had followed Myra from London to the small landing stage from which a launch carried guests bound for the *Luxa*.

There, most men would have been stuck.

But not Bob Carruthers.

He parked his Frazer Nash at the end of the road leading to the landing-stage, lifted the bonnet, removed his wig, and began to tinker and curse. In five minutes, four cars passed him, all chauffeur-driven. The alley was so narrow that the chauffeurs had to go at a slow speed to get past Carruthers, with the result that he was able to see all their passengers.

It was by no means sure that there would be anyone but Myra aboard the *Luxa* to interest him, but he had a photographic memory for faces, and he just might see something useful. His real hope, however, was that he might see someone he knew.

There were, in fact, three familiar faces in the first four cars, but no one on whom he could count for help. The fifth car-load arrived after a five minutes' interval and was an open tourer, not chauffeur-driven. As Carruthers straightened up, the man at the wheel glanced at him in annoyance.

Carruthers beamed.

'Neil, old son! Of all the luck!'

The brakes went on with a jerk, and the man at the wheel smiled. His companions—two girls and a second man—did not know Robert Carruthers, but were used to being jolted when Neil Clarke was driving.

'Carrie, you damned nuisance! If you've got to break down, why choose this spot?'

Carruthers spread oily hands in comic dismay.

'You ask me?' he said. 'In the first place, I was told this would lead me to the Reading road, and it obviously goes to the river. In the second, I was almost reversing when the damned—I beg your pardon.' Carruthers beamed upon the two girls, who looked young and innocent—and intrigued by Carruthers. 'What I mean is, something went wrong. Joking apart, Neil, I've been tinkering with the bally thing for an hour. I'm hungry, tired, weary—I've been glared at by every car that's passed. What's going on here, anyway? Do the cars go straight into the river, or ...'

'Or,' said Clarke. He was a youthful and decorative member of the Stock Exchange. Like Ned Oundle, Carruthers knew everyone who mattered. 'We're going to Neb's houseboat.'

'Oho!' Carruthers grimaced. 'Drink, I suppose? Food, wine, women—and I'm stuck here ...'

'You'd better come in with us,' Neil invited, with a laugh. 'They'll let you pass, in spite of the oil—it's a dress-or-not night, anyhow. Unless you'd like to borrow the bus to get you to a garage?'

'I will later, thanks,' said Carruthers. 'But if I don't get a glass of beer within ten minutes, I'll be homicidal!'

'Right—hop in.'

To the displeasure of the second man—a youthful and passionate gentleman who had been holding hands with a platinum blonde and enjoying it—Carruthers squeezed into the back with them and was driven to the special car-park provided for parties on the houseboat.

'Neb' was the nickname of no less a person than James Montague Nebton-Hart, first Baron Nebton. A shipping magnate of fabulous wealth, he persistently claimed he was in fact on the border-line of insolvency.

A house in Mayfair, another in Surrey, a third in Scotland, a fourth on the Riviera, managing-directorship of the Nebton-Pyxe Line—which consistently paid big dividends—and a marked ostentation in entertainment, did nothing to encourage that gloomy view.

Neb was a tall, striking-looking man, white-haired and bearded, but alert of eye. He was not a stickler for formality in his guests, but the touch of vanity in his make-up which made him sport a monocle, also inclined him to personal formality in dress. He was in the small reception room as Neil Clarke's party came in, and stared—pardonably—at Carruthers.

Clarke explained. Lord Nebton smiled and offered his hand.

'Of course, Mr Carruthers—join us, with pleasure!'

'Thanks awfully—it's jolly decent of you,' said Carruthers, who felt an inexplicable but instinctive dislike for Nebton-Hart. Consequently, he shook hands with extra vigour, and his host watched his disappearing back with some annoyance, for his own smooth white hand was now daubed with oil.

The incident—if incident it could be called—did nothing to disturb the success of the evening. The houseboat parties were justly popular. Nothing was missing for the comfort of the guests, and Clarke grinned at a Carruthers clad in only his vest and shorts, as he sprawled in an easy chair in the bedroom placed at his disposal by a major-domo who had taken his oil-smeared clothes away for attention.

'Neb does his guests well,' Carruthers conceded.

'Oh, he's not a bad sort.'

'Come here often?'

Neil Clarke shrugged. 'Perhaps once a month.'

'He's a goodly collection of lovelies, I've heard?'

'It's mostly hearsay,' said Clarke, more seriously. 'Don't run away with the wrong idea, old man—everything's run on right and proper lines. I don't hold any particular brief for Neb, but when all's said and done, he's a decent old stick.'

'H'm,' said Carruthers. 'Likely to be anyone here I know?'

'Well, let's see. There's Dora Lambert and Letty Kingham ...'

'Male, please.'

'Changed your habits?' grinned Clarke. 'I'm not sure who'll—oh, there's a brilliant specimen from Australia: chap called Anson. Met him?'

'No ... Fellow who's been making a splash at the Éclat, you mean?'

'The royal suite,' nodded Clarke. He grimaced: 'Surrounded by secretaries and whatnot—come to conquer London as he conquered Melbourne. As a matter of fact,' he added, honestly, 'he strikes me as being all right underneath, but he's got a crowd of sycophants around him, giving him the Great Panjandrum treatment, non-stop. He acts as if he's beginning to believe it.' Clarke shook his head. 'Handsome devil, too.'

'H'mm,' said Carruthers.

The door opened at that moment, and a steward appeared with his clothes, sponged and pressed, and two tankards of beer. Carruthers began to warm up ...

It was a good party, and Carruthers enjoyed it. And, just before decency demanded that he should go, he discovered that Myra Clayton had, after considerable effort, managed to hook the handsome Australian called Anson.

He wondered just how important that was likely to be ...

The following day dawned as brilliantly as its predecessor. It was the seventh day of a heat-wave which threatened to break all records, for at nine o'clock the temperature in London had risen to over eighty in the shade, and by ten it was eighty-five.

For once, even Craigie let his fire out.

He had learned little from Carruthers, although the connection between Myra Clayton and Anson might prove of service later. Loftus had tried without success to get information from Kalloni. Had the gangster been in normal health, Loftus would probably have succeeded, for he would have admitted no limits in the way of persuasion. There were things, however, which he would not do to a man with a bullet in his leg, and the fuller interrogation of Kalloni had been postponed.

The Errols had been given their orders, and were working.

The endeavour to create the impression that Kalloni was dead had been aided by a statement to that effect in the press. It was a try-on, for Craigie did not know how important the American was to the League. He did not realise that by arranging the statement of Kalloni's death he had eased the tension of a certain florid, benevolent-looking gentleman who had been aboard the *Luxa*.

Two sheets of flimsy had gone to the Cypher Department of the Foreign Office, and were being tested for a code—but the lack of quick results suggested there would be no results at all.

The one thing Craigie had been able to do was to take a list from a drawer in his desk, and cross off five numbers. These numbers were on a sheet of foolscap, and ran from 1 to 101. He crossed off, of course, numbers 51 and 39, as well as 11, 14 and 15—for the three prisoners had admitted their numbers in that peculiar organisation, although they appeared to know little else of any import.

It was sheer chance which took Loftus, Carruthers, Wally Davidson and Dodo Trale—a short, stalwart and remarkably handsome member of the Department—towards the House of Commons that morning. There was—as often happened, these days—an emergency meeting of the House, which had started at eleven o'clock. Holidays were things of the past, it seemed, for conscientious M.P.s. There was to be another Foreign Affairs debate, and the four men, for once with nothing direct on their hands, were sufficiently worried by the international outlook to wonder how the latest British commitment would be dressed up for general consumption.

Westminster Bridge was crowded.

Buses, private cars, cyclists and pedestrians went over it in an endless stream. A cool wind was blowing from the river, and the quartet strolled towards the Bridge, for the Prime Minister was not likely to be 'up' until half-past twelve.

A small car passed them, and pulled up close by the Houses of Parliament. Its driver got out and strolled nonchalantly towards the parapet, and then, after a moment or two, turned back towards Lambeth. Policemen on point-duty were too busy to notice the man who had offended all traffic laws by parking a car on Westminster Bridge at one of the busiest hours of the day. Even had they noticed it, they would not have followed the driver with quite the interest Loftus showed.

'Now why,' said the big man, 'did he do that?'

'What?' asked Dodo Trale.

'Leave that car ...' Loftus quickened his pace, making for the vehicle—an Austin 7 of ancient vintage. Through all the hubbub of the traffic, the first sonorous note of Big Ben, chiming midday, came clearly.

'My dear William!' Davidson protested. 'Are you batty? We're not flatfoots, yet.'

Over his shoulder, Loftus answered him: 'Why should a man leave his car there? Damn it, only a nitwit or ...'

He reached the car, and glanced along the bridge. At the far end the driver, conspicuous in a pale-grey suit, was watching—and suddenly, he took to his heels and ran.

Loftus snapped:

'That fellow in the grey—after him! Carrie, give a hand, here.'

He had yanked open the door of the car—and saw the large suitcase lying on the back seat. As he bent over it, he heard the loud ticking ...

And Big Ben was on the tenth stroke of twelve, Loftus realised suddenly, some sixth sense connecting the two facts in his mind.

'Get it over!' he snapped. 'Hurry, man!'

The case weighed heavily, but they carried it without trouble to the parapet—and together, they heaved it over the side. At the far end of the bridge, Trale and Davidson were cursing people who got in their way, but they were less than twenty yards, now, from the man in grey …

It happened, then.

The explosion was muffled, because of the water. But a spout shot up, hundreds of feet into the air, and sprayed down over the bridge like a cataract. A wave ten feet high swept towards both sides of the river, crashing against the Embankment, flooding the terrace of the House. There was another explosion and another. Men came running, women screamed, policemen abandoned the traffic and hurried to the scene.

Loftus and Carruthers stared at the widening circles of water, and although they were drenched to the skin, did not move.

Both men were thinking of what might have happened on the bridge.

And both were wondering if it was an isolated incident.

Craigie, telephone in hand, looked even greyer than usual.

'Sit down,' he said, as Loftus and Carruthers entered. 'No, come here—you can read this … Hallo? Yes. Yes, go on …'

A voice sounded in his ear.

'I'm speaking from Birmingham—New Street Station is pretty well wiped out, sir. A dozen men were killed …'

'Steady,' said Craigie, 'let me know just what happened. Don't get flustered.'

The man at the other end, a young agent, gulped.

'Sorry. I heard the explosion, from the Town Hall. It's shattered thousands of windows, and—sir? Oh, exactly twelve o'clock. It ...'

Craigie replaced the receiver, making a mental note that the young Birmingham agent wanted relieving, for he could not make a coherent report. He watched as Loftus and Carruthers finished reading the three reports already on his desk.

They were in Craigie's own shorthand, but the two agents knew it well enough to gather the drift. Briefly, it read:

12.10 *Glasgow.* Second Power Station blown up at midday. Nine dead: at least thirty injured.

12.12 *Coventry.* Grain store-house in the centre of the city blown up at midday. Casualties, believed high, not yet known.

12.15 *Liverpool.* Liverpool end of Mersey Tunnel destroyed by explosion. Water seepage reported. Casualties heavy, numbers not yet confirmed. Emergency operations in force.

'And now,' said Craigie, thinly, 'New Street Station, Birmingham, and Westminster Bridge—or as near as makes no difference.'

The telephone rang again. Craigie lifted the receiver.

'Southampton ... yes, I've got that ... *what?*'

'No doubt about it,' said the man on the line. 'The AZ Submarine dock was completely destroyed ...'

'Any—damage? Apart from that?'

'No ships touched, I understand, sir. But a number of casualties ...'

As Craigie finished with him, another telephone was already ringing. Loftus and Carruthers eyed each other grimly, as the list grew.

Edinburgh.

Cardiff.

Swansea.

Harwich.

Plymouth …

All three men realised the tremendous importance of it, knew that sabotage and terrorism was in train in England on a scale hitherto unimagined.

The League's work?

They could not be sure, but all three believed that it was. And all three knew there would not be a moment's respite for them until the League of the Hundred-and-One was wiped out.

Manchester sent news …

Woolwich …

There seemed no end to it. No end to the casualties, the mounting roll of innocent deaths. And against that dreadful toll, the saving of some hundreds of people at Westminster seemed to fade into insignificance.

Thousands had been injured: hundreds, at least, had died …

CHAPTER 8

ARRESTS BY THE DOZEN

The spasmodic attempts of various terrorist organisations to undermine the peculiar confidence of the British public had—as similar outbreaks had done in the past—failed completely. The ability of the police to swoop, sometimes before outrages and sometimes after, was a sufficient proof that the authorities were alert, and active. For nearly a year, bomb explosions had been taking place, arrests had been made quickly, and before going down for long terms of imprisonment the perpetrators had sought to defend their actions by wild statements about British persecution of this or that minority or state or political grouping.

The press, generally a reliable barometer of public opinion, gave bomb outrages importance only if there was no other news worth the headlines. The country, in short, was getting acclimatised to home-made bombs in waste-paper baskets or on railway lines.

But there were limits.

A stunned public learned the news from radio and press, and still found the series of disasters quite unbelievable. Twenty-four explosions had taken place; only one without its toll of dead and wounded. No official statements were available, but early estimated casualties of two hundred and thirty dead, and three thousand injured, was certainly no exaggeration. The pin-pricks of the I.R.A. and others had suddenly been swamped by a devastating jab with a bayonet. The topic was on every lip, fear and apprehension were in every mind.

Three trains had been affected, and these had been responsible for the worst casualty totals. Despite strong forces of police at the London termini and all stations *en route,* despite the special constables on duty at the suburban stations, vast numbers of people avoided the trains that night and the following morning.

Had the explosions been in one place—had half, or even a quarter of them, been prevented like that at Westminster, the growing public nervousness would not have gained such a hold. As it was, the obvious fact that the police had been caught unawares added to the general apprehension.

Rumours flew.

The explosions were variously attributed to Russia, Germany, Italy, and the I.R.A. Lack of an official statement allowed the rumours to gain ground ...

Loftus waited at Craigie's office for a call from Wally and Dodo. When it came, at last, Wally did the speaking.

'We missed him, Bill—the beggar got across the road in front of the traffic lights. What's next?'

'Better get back to the flat.' Loftus replaced the receiver and turned to Craigie. 'You'll wait for the lords and masters to utter, I suppose?'

'Yes ...' Craigie's lips drooped. 'There'll be a quick investigation, of course. It—*damn* that telephone!'

It was twenty minutes since the last explosion report, but all three men waited tensely, afraid they were to hear of yet another. But Loftus sat down heavily in relief, and Carruthers found a smile as they saw Craigie's manner noticeably ease.

'Yes ...' he said. 'Yes ... Right—in one hour.' He replaced the receiver and turned to the others. 'Kingham wants me to go round to the Yard. Fellowes and Miller will be there—you'd better come, Bill.'

Loftus nodded: 'Right. Carrie—wait for me at the flat, will you?'

At the A.C.'s office at Scotland Yard, Sir William Fellowes, the Assistant Commissioner, and Superintendent Miller, were waiting for Craigie and Loftus with the Rt. Hon. Eustace Kingham, the Home Secretary. That Kingham had gone to the Yard was obviously a move to prevent the press learning that a conference had been summoned by the Cabinet Minister. Kingham, a middle-aged, grey-haired and handsome man, was perpetually afraid that something he did or said would give rise to misunderstanding. Socially he was popular, politically he was a mystery—few people understood why he was Home Secretary, although he was admittedly inoffensive.

'Ah—Craigie. We're waiting.' He looked worried, with good reason. 'And this is ...?'

'Loftus, my leading agent,' said Craigie.

'Ah. Yes, yes. Well, you've heard ...'

'We're worrying about the explosions,' Fellowes said flatly. He was an austere man of fifty, a martinet, yet liked as well as respected at the Yard. As he paced the large office, it was noticeable that his right leg was some inches shorter than his left—a relic of his war service. 'Have you any specific information, Craigie?'

That was typical of Fellowes. Straight to the point, without deferring to the Home Secretary or any man on earth.

'Nothing specific, no.'

'Craigie, it is positively essential ...' Kingham began. Then stopped, as though not sure exactly what was essential, and Fellowes broke in:

'We've a list of two hundred suspects—I.R.A., Arab Association—but I needn't enumerate. I've suggested bringing them all in, but Mr Kingham feels it's too sweeping a move.'

Craigie did not smile. Loftus exchanged glances with a tall, broad-shouldered man whose sandy hair, moustache and skin suggested that they had been sprinkled with flour: rarely did a man so suit his nickname as completely as Superintendent Horace 'Dusty' Miller.

'I can't agree,' said Craigie. 'We can't be sure which organisation worked to-day's outrages, and we can't be sure that they weren't all working in concert. We *can* be sure that anyone connected with terrorist organisations will look on this as a golden opportunity, so they're better under control.'

'Yes, of course: I quite see that point.' Kingham brushed a hand over his hair. 'But when all is said and done, they may have had nothing whatever to do with the dastardly outrages of to-day. I feel that such a far-reaching decision should be approved by—er—by the Cabinet. We are meeting to-morrow morning, at eleven ...'

'By which time every suspect will have disappeared,' Craigie pointed out, drily.

'Precisely what I suggested,' said Fellowes.

The Home Secretary looked, as if baffled, towards Loftus and Miller, but the two subordinates held their peace. Kingham shrugged.

'Well—if you both feel that way, perhaps ...'

Fellowes put his hand on a telephone.

'Miller, you'd better get busy at once, I'll give Sloan and Martindale their orders.' He lifted the receiver, gave instructions to Flying Squad cars, and through Superintendent Martindale sent orders to the various Divisional headquarters for a swoop on all terrorist suspects. Kingham, looking bewildered by the speed of events, murmured that he hoped they got the right men, and went out in Miller's wake. As the door closed behind him Fellowes exuded a long breath.

'And *that* is the type controlling Foreign as well as Home affairs! My God, no wonder we're in a mess! Well, Gordon ...'—he pushed a tobacco jar towards Craigie, cigarettes to Loftus—'how's the League? Think this is part of its game?'

'I'm reasonably sure,' Craigie said, soberly. 'It's too big for any other organisation. Too sweeping. Another two or three like this, and we'll have real panic in London and most of the big centres.'

'H'mm. That's what the League's aiming at?'

'It wouldn't surprise me. But we can't be sure, yet. You've found nothing?'

'No. Those two fellows at Cannon Street ...'

Craigie smiled drily.

'Two?'

'Yes—one in the morgue and one in the cell,' said Fellowes. 'The stories have gone round, all right: Kalloni is supposed to be dead. But I mustn't hold him much longer—that damned fool Kingham will be reading the *habeas corpus* act to me if I do.'

'I'll take him in twenty-four hours,' said Craigie. 'How's his leg?'

'It's nothing serious.'

'Good—I'll send for him.' As Craigie stood up, Fellowes hesitated a moment, then asked bluntly:

'How big, Gordon?'

'So big,' said Gordon Craigie, 'that it might end either way. All I *know* is that the League of the Hundred-and-One has been after a number of our bigger industrialists. My greatest fear is that it's a kind of sabotage organisation, aiming to break the spirit of the people—and to-day's showing doesn't change my views.'

'No ... You've got nowhere?'

'We learned about the League from Miss Loring,' said Craigie. 'That was our first intimation. We've had several indications since. We've caught two or three of the lesser members—but as for the higher-ups, we're quite in the dark. By the way, have you discovered anything about Abraham Korrel?'

Fellowes pursed his lips.

'He's rich, he's been an Englishman for eight years—he was born a Russian ...'

'A White Russian?'

'Very white, he claimed,' said Fellowes. 'He has no apparent business. He has a small house in Hampstead and a larger one in Bedfordshire, runs a small staff of servants at both places, but travels a lot. That's all we have.'

'H'mm. Myra Clayton?'

'The usual stuff, I'm afraid. Poor parents, good looks, a year or two at the theatre, and then taken up by Korrel. They still seem friendly ...'

'They had a quarrel yesterday,' murmured Craigie, 'but that might have been just between themselves. Well, I'll keep you in touch ...'

'Thanks,' said Fellowes, and the Department Z men took their leave.

'Where have you sent the Errols?' Loftus asked, as they walked along.

'Not too far,' said Craigie. 'They've gone down to Bournemouth, in the hope of getting something on Rogerson.' Rogerson, Loftus knew, was a suspect of the League. 'They should be back tomorrow. Any ideas?'

'Could they work the *Luxal?*'

'It's an idea; I'll think round it. Tonight, we'll have a look at this place in Moorton Road, I think. It might be useful.'

Loftus grimaced.

'It's certainly a night-club; there's probably gaming, and there might be worse. But ...'

'We've got to work on it,' Craigie insisted. 'Tell Carruthers and three or four of the others, will you?'

'Right.'

'And 'phone me just after eight, before you go.'

'I will,' said Loftus, and Craigie went alone to the office.

It was a serious, sober, worried Loftus who returned to his Brook Street flat—and a glance at the evening papers proved the need for his concern.

By eight o'clock, however, heavy headlines were screaming the news of the ruthless work of the police. Fifty arrests, it was claimed, had already been made. At least a hundred others were expected before midnight. Once again, the peerless organisation of Scotland Yard ...

'They might,' grunted Loftus, 'have stopped the damned things. Heigh-ho ...'

'Tired?' asked Oundle.

They were alone in the flat. Fay was staying with Diana, who had the one next door—which could be reached via a secret door in the main bedroom wardrobe. Dodo Trale, Davidson, Carruthers and Martin Best, all in evening-dress and cursing the heat, were drinking cocktails with Diana, and pledging Fay's blue eyes.

Loftus grunted ill-humouredly and reached for the telephone. He called Craigie, and heard the latter say:

'Nothing fresh, Bill. Get along to Moorton Road—and be careful. Carruthers had better not go: he saw Myra last night. Keep a careful watch on Anson and the woman, of course, and let me know as soon as you can who else is there.'

'But if there are many there from the *Luxa,* won't Carrie be needed?'

'He can watch from outside.'

'He'll like that! How are the arrests going?'

'By the dozen,' said Craigie. 'But they can't hold them on charges about today's efforts. Most of them have arms or explosives, but not enough to account for the shambles we've had. It's the League, Bill. It's as big as we feared—and we haven't much time to lose.'

Loftus put a goodly supply of beer close to Oundle, charged his man—Butler—to tend to all the invalid's wants, and went through into the next flat.

'Carrie,' he announced, solemnly. 'I've sad news for you. You're not coming.'

Carruthers raised a quizzical eyebrow.

'On the other hand,' said Loftus, 'you're not staying away. Watchman's duty, outside, And any you recognise from the *Luxa* ...'

Carruthers glared.

'No, it's too bad! Here's your best man, positively your star agent, and you want to make him a door-keeper. It's ...'

'Peace, friends!' Martin Best protested. Cheery of face, fair of skin, Best contrived to look untidy, even in a dinner jacket. He was not appreciably smaller than Loftus, and his pet vice was toying with mechanical and electrical gadgets.

'Never mind, Carrie,' Dodo soothed. 'I'll lend you my flask, while you're waiting.'

'That's all very well ...'

'What I can't understand,' said Davidson, stifling a yawn, 'is why we ever let Carrie join us—and since he came in, why we haven't kicked him out. Damn it, old son, you've a cushy job! Out of the line of fire, and all that ...'

Loftus smiled at Diana. 'Ready? Dodo, look after Fay for the evening. The other two will play it solo—come in ten minutes after each other. Di, Fay, Dodo and I will get through first. Let's go.'

The small party left the flat, *via* Diana's front door, and in fifteen minutes were near the entrance of Number 10, Moorton Road, Kensington. The house was one of a long row of early Victorian residences and in the light of the August evening, the grey façades looked more dreary than average, even for a drab neighbourhood. Moorton Road had lost 'tone' in the last twenty years. Minor politicians and the less important peers no longer occupied it, and most of the houses were split into flats.

Loftus had studied the available facts about Number 10.

It was rented on a five years' lease by a man named Nathaniel Stebber, whose earlier efforts in financing night-clubs had led him to escape prosecution three times by the skin of his teeth. He was always assisted by his wife, a woman some years older than Stebber, and whose appearance sug-gested a righteousness far, far above what was to be expected in this wicked world.

It had been opened two months before and registered as the Ten Club—and although the police had it under observation, there had been no cause, yet, for action.

But Myra Clayton was interested in it ...

Myra, in fact, was already there when Loftus and his three companions arrived, went through the formali-ties of joining the Club, and were passed through into a shoddily-furnished dance-room. That the place was phoney was evident from the first.

Davidson and Best, gaining admittance without trouble on payment of a five pound 'entrance fee', felt exactly the same.

Carruthers, strolling at the far end of the street, and mildly confounding Craigie's orders, had kept an eye on the occasional couples and small parties of invariably young people who went to Number 10. He recognised none who had been on the *Luxa*, in the first quarter of an hour, and had begun to give up hope.

Then he had seen Myra and Richard C. Anson arrive.

On their heels came Neil Clarke, with the blonde who had been with him the previous evening.

Carruthers widened his eyes.

'Neil, if you're playing a funny game, God help you!' he murmured to himself.

He wondered whether Clarke would be recognised by Loftus or any of the others, deliberated on the advisability of telephoning Craigie from a convenient call-box, and decided to postpone action.

As he pondered, rheumy-eyed Nathaniel Stebber was eyeing Jabez Merkle with disfavour.

'He said you weren't to see him, Jab—I can't help you.'

'I've gotta see him!' snapped Merkle. 'I tell you I've *gotta* see Korrel!'

Stebber sniffed.

'Well, it's your own fault if you catch a packet.'

He led the way upstairs, tapped on a door at the top of the house and, after a pause, was told to enter.

Korrel had completely recovered his poise.

He looked magnificent in evening-dress, and his pale face was composed, his almond eyes apparently content. He listened, and frowned.

'Merkle may come in, Stebber.'

Merkle entered, breathing hard.

'Boss, I ...'

'Don't shout,' said Korrel, with distaste. 'If it is important, tell me quickly and get out.'

Merkle licked his lips;

'I—I was on the door, Boss. I see'd them come in, an' ducked outa the way. I been tryin' to see you ever since ...'

Korrel took a cigar from his pocket, sniffed it, rolled it by his ear, and placed it between his lips.

'Supposing, my friend, you tell me who you mean.'

'Why, Loftus, two skirts, and ...'

'*Loftus!*' All the poise disappeared from Abraham Korrel and the cigar dropped at his feet. 'Are you sure of this, Merkle? My God, if you're lying ...!'

'But it's true!' Merkle almost screamed.

Korrel began to smile—and his expression was a long way from pleasant.

'Well, well, well! Reward of virtue, my dear Merkle!' His voice was a purr as he went on: 'Summon eight of the men here at once. Warn them that they will have to be busy. Go along, hurry! I—no, just a moment. Before you go, point the other men out to Stebber.'

'O.K., Boss!' Merkle beamed. He had seen this as his chance to rehabilitate himself. 'I'm on me way.'

He sped downstairs and, through a cleverly-concealed door, pointed out Dodo, Wally, Best, the two girls and Loftus. As he went from Stebber to a telephone, Stebber's house-phone rang. Korrel's voice, high-pitched with excitement, came clearly:

'Get the men and women Merkle pointed out into the small room—yes, the baccarat room ... never mind about them being police: they'll want to try everything. Get them there, understand? And then clear the others out and close the door on them. Don't lose a minute!'

Stebber rang off smartly and proceeded to make arrangements, while eight men left the Naveling Hotel, Bloomsbury, not knowing that their job was the one which Kalloni had failed to do.

CHAPTER 9
MR KORREL'S MISTAKE

Like so many people who did not know it well, Abraham Korrel made the mistake of under-estimating Department Z. Twice in forty-eight hours he had tried, indirectly, to kill Loftus. It did not occur to him to think the third attempt, when the advantage was so clearly in his favour, could possibly fail. Nor did he know that if he failed this time, it would mark the final stage of the fight between the Department and the League of the Hundred-and-One.

Rheumy-eyed Stebber, ingratiating and suave-voiced, approached Loftus when Diana was dancing with Martin Best.

'Excuse me, sir …'

Loftus eyed him with disfavour. For that matter, he disliked the whole set-up. The band was poor, if not definitely bad. There were, so far, no more than two dozen people in the dance-room and only half of that number dancing, yet it seemed a crowd. It could not have been more obvious that dancing was not the chief attraction at the Ten Club.

Outwardly, Loftus looked large, benign, and brainless, the type of man with a lot of money to spare. So did his friends.

'Yes?' he said.

'It did occur to me, sir—it did occur to me that you might like a little flutter—strictly under *cover*, sir. No danger at all of difficulties ...'

Loftus's eyes showed interest.

'H'mm. What is it?'

'I could offer you a choice,' said Mr Stebber. 'The—er—rooms are on the floor above.'

It had all the hall-marks of a trick, thought Loftus, as he nodded agreement. Stebber, he knew, ought to be in jail, but had so far escaped because he always pushed his dirty work on to underlings. To approach a complete stranger with so direct an offer of law-breaking did not fit in well with the man's reputation. That made it interesting. Only in the certainty that he need fear no reprisal would Stebber have given that personal invitation.

'Of course,' murmured Stebber, still more ingratiatingly, 'there is no need for you to play, and I assure you that the tables are perfectly—er—straight.'

'I'm sure they would be.' Loftus rose, as expected, to the bait. 'Er—my friends?'

'They would be *very* welcome, sir.'

'Right—when they've finished dancing ...'

'I will be by the door, sir. If you will follow me, discreetly—in couples, say—I will take you upstairs.' Stebber went off to take up his position by the door—and the band stopped less than ten seconds afterwards. One by one, the dancers made for the small tables at the side of the room.

Loftus was studying those he did not know.

Three—two men and a girl—had the enlarged pupils and white, pinched nose of the cocaine-addict. Five—three men and two girls—were obviously of the suburban or country have-a-good-time type, hopefully believing that they were painting London red. The rest looked the type without enough money to make a splash in Mayfair, who needed something of this kind to make them feel they were established members of the beau-monde. The exceptions were Myra Clayton and Richard C. Anson, and a man with a blonde whom Carruthers could have identified as Neil Clarke.

Loftus had heard a great deal about Myra, and he was compelled to admit she really was a beauty. She wore a vivid green, daringly-cut creation, her magnificent hair was piled high on her head, and she had used make-up sparingly but to real effect. Her leonine grace was as out-of-place at the Ten Club as most of the girls there would have been in a jungle.

Anson made a striking companion.

Tall, tanned, with sun-bleached brown hair, not an ounce of spare flesh and obviously glowing with health, he was a magnificent-looking man. But his hazel eyes held a sullen dissatisfied expression, and his mouth drooped a little at the corners.

Spoiled, quite obviously—and yet possessing a 'something' which lifted him right out of the rut. Loftus recalled Craigie's description of him: disgustingly wealthy, and proud of it. None of his attendant sycophants appeared to be at the Ten Club.

So why had Anson been brought here?

And, more pertinently, why was Stebber anxious to get Loftus and the others to the gaming-tables?

Three small tables had been pushed together for Loftus, Trale, and the two girls. Diana was laughing as Best left her, for his own table—they had been soberly introduced, to create the impression that they had till then been strangers. Dodo Trale was eyeing Fay with obvious approval, and with a little encouragement would have grown discursive, but Fay clearly had a practised way of stalling would-be admirers ...

Loftus regarded her with considerable interest.

He recalled her introduction to the Department, her behaviour when she had been playing a two-sided game—when death might have come at any time. She had not turned a hair. The day before, she had slipped out of his flat and telephoned word to Craigie as coolly as she might have made an appointment with her hair-dresser. But she looked so delightfully fresh and youthful that it was hard to believe she was fully aware of the danger involved.

She caught his glance and smiled.

'Thoughtful, Bill?'

'Very.' Loftus glanced towards Stebber. 'We've been invited upstairs, to the gaming-tables—and there's a catch in it, somewhere. The band stopped short to get us there quickly. We'll go, but keep your powder dry!' He grinned encouragement, then as the band started again, rose and led the way towards Stebber. He noted with interest that Best and Davidson, not officially with his party, were being addressed by a dark waiter, and in a few seconds he saw that they also were coming towards the door.

Why?

That there was danger was obvious. That he would have been wiser to have kept out of the gaming-rooms seemed equally obvious. But dodging issues was not the way of Bill Loftus. He wanted to get at the truth behind the Ten Club, and he believed that this could prove a very good chance.

Had he not been suspicious before, he would certainly have become so when he found the baccarat room unoccupied. The room, some twenty-feet square, contained four tables, lined with chairs. Dreary plush draperies decorated the doors and the walls and in one corner there was a bar, without attendant.

Stebber smiled and rubbed his hands.

'We are just about to bring our other clients in, sir. Ah—here are two gentlemen, now …'

Martin Best and Wally Davidson came in together, Wally looking as weary as ever. Fay sensed the tension, but gave no sign of it, and Diana pouted prettily, as if disappointed.

'Bill, you promised me …!'

'Fun and games,' agreed Loftus, beaming. 'In a very little while, my sweet.'

'If you will pardon me for one moment?' Stebber gave his widest smile and backed towards the door—and as he went out, closed it behind him.

Fay's smile disappeared.

'Bill, are you sure …?'

'Sure of nothing,' grunted Loftus. Quietly, he added: 'Try the handle, Martin—but don't make a row doing it.'

Best moved to the door, silently turned the handle, and pulled. The door did not move.

'The spider and the flies,' muttered Dodo Trale.

Loftus frowned.

'Damn it,' he murmured, 'they can't do anything as simple as this—it's far too easy! Sure about the door, Martin?'

'Positive, William. It's one of those self-locking gadgets that…'

'Later,' Loftus stopped him, firmly. His smoky grey glance travelled swiftly around the room. 'I wonder if they can see us, in here? Di, you and Fay retreat gracefully to the bar—get behind it. Are there bottles?'

'Underneath, yes.' Diana nodded, investigating.

'Fine. Pour something out—anything will do. If they can see us, it'll look as if we're helping ourselves. Wally, wake yourself up for ten seconds, and wander round the room with your usual aimless gait. Looking,' he elaborated gently, as Davidson stared, 'for another door. Girls, if anything happens, get down behind that bar and stay there.'

'What are you expecting?' Fay whispered.

'Anything,' Loftus scowled. 'It was all so easy; so very easy—but the simple things are apt to get through. I've a feeling that it's just as well Carrie stayed outside. How long have we been here?'

Di, pouring beer, glanced at her watch.

'It's just turned nine.'

'Getting on for an hour, then,' murmured Loftus. 'No luck, Wally?'

'No door,' Wally reported, mouthing the words.

'No windows,' added Dodo Trale quietly, taking a glass. 'Here's how, folk! Bill—all joking apart, what do you expect?'

'Stebber's other clients,' said Loftus, softly. 'Not without guns. Martin, take the corner on the right of the door—Wally, the left. Dodo, get the girls. If there's ducking to be done, there's room for you three there.' He sauntered casually across to the remaining corner, picking up a chair as he went; then sat down, resting his arms on the back of it. The others took up their positions; equally casual, equally calm.

Yet each of them in fact was sharply on the alert, and prepared for anything. Loftus had an uncanny sense of danger, and they knew it …

Dodo started an inane patter which kept the girls laughing; Wally smoked, Martin Best smoothed his untidy hair and tucked in his recalcitrant shirt-front and wanted to know in a loud voice how long the Stebber beggar would be in coming. If they could be seen or heard, no one would dream that they were prepared for an attack.

Then, sharply, footsteps echoed outside the door.

Footsteps of half-a-dozen men, at least …

Loftus slipped his right hand negligently into his pocket. The others did the same, but Diana and Fay looked, deliberately, away from the door.

It opened suddenly.

Loftus caught a glimpse of Stebber, in the background—and more than a glimpse of the lanky Dodge, who stood there with a tommy-gun in his hand, and an evil grin on his face …

'Hallo, Loftus,' Dodge taunted, softly. 'You didn't expect us, did you? Take your hand out of that pocket, or we'll drill the ladies—that bar's made of matchboard, and these little fellas will slice right through it. *Move* damn you!'

It had happened with a bewildering suddenness, despite their readiness for danger. Even Loftus, had not expected a move on such a scale at quite such a speed.

He drew his hand from his pocket, and said easily:

'You do like trouble, Dodge—I should have thought one narrow escape would be enough for you. Mind if I smoke?'

'You just get over to your lady-friend,' Dodge snapped. 'You other two do the same.'

Loftus remained seated.

'And then?'

'Never mind about that!' snarled Dodge.

He was flanked by two other hoodlums, both carrying automatics. Loftus guessed at the rest of the party in the passage. More, he knew what was coming—knew Dodge aimed to get them all in one corner and open fire.

Could this really happen, in Kensington?

He felt a quick chilling fear, for in Dodge's eyes there was murder, cold and callous.

Loftus was used to the fantastic, but this was something beyond even his experience.

'*Move!*' snarled Dodge. 'If any one of you is thinking of shooting think again! Every corner is covered …'

Loftus, in his, the girls and Dodo in theirs, were faced by the tommy-gun. Best and Davidson were covered by automatics.

Loftus stood up slowly.

His face was set, and the tightness about his lips told the others that he knew how close they were to death. The girls were rigid. Loftus looked at the baccarat tables, wondering if they were of wood or iron …

His right eye, towards Best, moved imperceptibly.

And Best, his right hand still in his pocket, opened fire.

As simply as that.

It would be a shambles, either way, and they did not propose to die without fighting. Best's bullet, muffled by a silencer, struck Dodge's arm before anyone realised it had been fired, and as Dodge dropped the tommy-gun with an oath, Davidson fired from the right. One of the gunmen at the door staggered, and Loftus leapt for a table between the girls and the door. A bullet tore through his coat as he reached it and upturned it, shoving it towards the door with a force that sent it crashing against Dodge.

There was uproar!

Three of four men came running: the guards Loftus had rightly guessed to be on hand. Loftus was shooting fast now, with Trale following suit—they were the only men who could see into the passage itself.

'Wally's corner, Di!' Loftus yelled, and the girls obeyed.

Bullets sprayed round the room, riddling the bar as they raced for the one corner temporarily out of range.

Davidson sprang for another table, upturned it and thrust it, with less force than before, towards the door. Best was leaning on the wall, his arms limp, his mouth set tightly and perspiration bathing his forehead. He staggered towards a chair two yards away, and dropped on to it: had the others been looking, they would have seen the blood already seeping through the front of his shirt ...

So far, not a shot had been fired without a silencer: the noise of overturned tables and falling men had been louder than the reports of the guns. Loftus snatched the silencer off his Webley, suddenly: the more noise, the better. There was a fierce exultation within him. The first devastating attack had failed. Dodge was very still on the floor ...

But it was not over, by a long way.

The men in the passage seemed to be playing for safety. But there were more ways of causing death than by gunfire—a single stick of dynamite would blow that room to pieces. They were still alive, and might still have a fighting chance: but hemmed in as they were, the odds were weighted against them.

And then, clearly from the far end of the passage, came a man's voice:

'What the hell is going on?'

It was the voice of Richard C. Anson—and fast upon it, came Myra's imploring:

'Dickie, Dickie—get away, get away ...!'

CHAPTER 10
ANSON ACTS

Any moment, Loftus had known, an explosive could be flung into the room—gas could be used on them. To try to fight their way out—to enter a passage filled with armed men—was to invite suicide.

The sound of Anson's voice brought unimagined hope. For a moment, there was absolute silence. Then Loftus fired at a hand which appeared near the door—and the roar of the unsilenced Webley shattered the tension-filled calm.

A shot, from outside—and:

'Come on!' roared Loftus.

He leapt over the tables and Dodge, and Wally and Dodo were only feet behind him. From the doorway, they saw Anson and three others down on the floor, fighting—and the two remaining gunmen momentarily off-balance as they stumbled free of the sprawling, mauling heap at their feet.

Loftus sent three shots towards them.

As the first came, one fired back. The bullet took Trale in the shoulder and he spun round, but Davidson and Loftus escaped unscathed—and watched the two gunmen crumple up.

'Get the guns,' snapped Loftus. 'I'm …'

'Help him, Wally,' called Diana. 'We'll get the guns!'

She was close behind them, with Fay. Both girls held their automatics at the ready as they moved swiftly towards the fallen gunmen—and as one moved his hand towards his fallen gun, Diana fired a shot through his forearm. Fay covered the second wounded man, who made no attempt to move ...

Loftus and Davidson had already flung themselves at Anson's attackers.

At the head of the stairs, Myra Clayton stood watching, her eyes wide and fear in her heart. Loftus caught a glimpse of her—and of a big, pale-faced man who came rushing down from the top floor. And although he had no time to see more, he heard the man's deep, frantic voice:

'Get away, Myra—*get away!*'

Loftus and Davidson tackled one man apiece. Despite the odds, Anson had dragged himself to his feet and was slogging away doggedly as they came to his aid. One man felt himself spun round, saw Loftus's face ...

Loftus hit him, once.

The man thudded against the wall and slithered down, his eyes rolling. Davidson had jabbed his man in the back—and as he swung round, hooked him hard in the solar plexus. He lacked the devastating force of Loftus, who shouldered him aside now and cracked his giant fist to the unguarded chin.

The man crumpled up.

Anson had just ripped a right to the third man's stomach, and now followed it with an uppercut that sent him crashing back against Loftus—who calmly dropped him, senseless, with a clout on the head.

Diana was on hand again.

'We can handle these ...'

PANIC!

Loftus nodded, and Anson stared, bewildered, as the two men headed off down the stairs. He looked at the girls—then followed Loftus. On the main floor, screaming women and frightened men were rushing for the door: among them, but not screaming, were Myra Clayton and her big companion. Loftus glanced sharply around and recognised Korrel. But to shoot, in that crowd, was unthinkable. Loftus fought his way through to the door—but it was open, and Myra and her companion were already through it.

And then Loftus smiled broadly, as he saw Carruthers and three uniformed policemen …

He stopped short and Anson, cannoning into him, snapped:

'What's the matter? Why the devil …'

'Easy,' said Loftus. He waved an explanatory hand. 'There's efficiency for you!'

For Carruthers, with the policemen in tow, had made straight for Myra and Korrel. As Carruthers gripped the man's arm, a policeman touched Myra's shoulder …

She flung herself at him like a wild-cat.

Scarlet talons raked his face, and as he staggered back, Myra ran. Loftus, able to see but unable to get clear of the crowd, had never seen a woman run like it. She easily dodged a policeman hurrying from the far end of Moorton Road, reached Queen's Road, and disappeared.

But Carruthers had Korrel in an inescapable grip, and Korrel was quivering like a jelly. And Carrie kept him that way, as he searched unsuccessfully for Neil Clarke among the crowd being shepherded by the police.

Richard C. Anson, his jaw plastered in three places and the knuckles of his right hand bandaged, gazed at Loftus in bewilderment.

'Look here, man—what was it all about? I heard the shindig and shot up to have a dekko, but … '

Loftus grinned.

'It's as well you did—it helped a lot. You were just the diversion we needed.' He felt warmly towards Anson, who could just as easily have joined the general rush for the exits. Anson gave the impression of being a man who acted first and thought afterwards; he still managed to look as though he owned the world and all there was in it—but Neil Clarke's remarks that at bottom the man seemed a good type, appeared to be more than justified.

The fight was an hour old.

Summoned by Carruthers, via a sergeant on duty nearby, the police had arrived in force. Of the twenty-odd people who had been at the Ten Club, eighteen were under arrest, and the discovery of gaming-tables—roulette and chemin-de-fer, as well as baccarat—made a charge easy for the authorities.

But Clarke had not been seen. And Merkle, Myra, and three of the men with Dodge had managed to make a getaway.

On this, Loftus felt that he could look with equanimity.

Dodge was badly wounded; so were four other men—and although on their way now to hospital, they would all be well-guarded and, in the near future, well-questioned. Korrel, not physically hurt, had at Loftus' request been taken to Cannon Street. A general call had gone out for Myra, under the useful charges of 'doing bodily harm' to a policeman and of impeding the course of justice. The policeman's cheeks had been clawed from his eyes to chin, and he would be on sick-leave for a week or more.

Best and Trale were in a nursing-home.

Neither of them was likely to be more than a few weeks out of action, and Loftus had to admit things had worked out considerably better than he had had any reason to expect. At one time, a massacre had seemed inevitable; and hard-bitten though he was, the memory of that moment when Dodge had appeared with the tommy-gun persisted. The man's monstrously cold-blooded intentions had been all too plain.

He would come to answer for it, thought Loftus, grimly—and in good time be convicted for the murder of Benotti. Once the League was finished, eradicated …

It did not occur to him that the League would flourish much longer, for in Loftus there was a confidence little could undermine, and an absolute conviction that right would triumph …

He sat now in the small room at the top of the house in Moorton Road, where Korrel had been earlier in the evening. Diana and Fay had gone home, under police escort. Carruthers, Davidson, Loftus, Anson and Superintendent Miller, who had hurried to the scene from the Yard, were sitting about the room—relaxing, now, with their beloved tankards of beer.

'So O.K.—I helped!' Anson sounded impatient. 'Now what about telling me what it was I helped with?'

'All in good time,' smiled Loftus. 'For the moment, old son, you ought to be satisfied to know that you saved several people being convicted for murder. It was a holdup—with me and mine the victims.'

'But why the devil …' Anson, surrounded too long by toadies and yes-men, was used to prompt answers to his questions.

'All that comes later,' said Loftus, calmly. 'Give the man another drink, Wally—keep him quiet.'

'I'm damned if I'll keep quiet!' roared Anson. 'I demand to know …'

Wally approached him from one side, Carruthers from the other: Wally demanded, in sympathetic tones, just where it hurt? Anson, out of his depth with their nonsense and their utter irreverence for his worldly standing or his whims, stared in puzzlement from one to the other and saw something in their eyes which made his lips relax, at last.

'It's all very well,' he said, more quietly. 'But, hang it …'

Wally pressed his replenished glass to his lips.

Richard Anson spluttered, and then grinned.

'Oh, all right …!'

Loftus turned to Miller:

'We'd better have a good look through this room, Dusty—and the rest of the house, for that matter. I'd rather the Divisional men didn't try it, yet.'

Miller was the liaison officer between the Yard and Department Z. A stolid, almost completely humourless man, there had been a time when the antics of Craigie's men had annoyed him, for they were not always seemly. He had long ago come to understand, however, the reason for their apparent facetiousness, and even to appreciate their peculiar brand of humour. Moreover, he had developed a respect for them which nothing could shatter.

'All right, Bill, if you want it that way. Let's start.'

Loftus turned to Anson.

'Will you amuse yourself for half-an-hour with that beer, while we have a look round?'

'Why, surely.' Anson was finding himself strangely at ease with these unlikely characters. 'You carry on. Can I help?'

'Afterwards; a lot, I hope.'

Anson lit a cigar, and leaned back in the only easy chair. Loftus and Miller went painstakingly through the small room, while Davidson and Carruthers searched, unsuccessfully, every crevace on the floor. It was some time before Loftus—when all the papers they had found had been exhausted, when every cupboard, safe and drawer had been searched—kicked along the wainscoting, more for the sake of it than in the hope of getting results. He felt the wood give to the pressure.

'Half a mo', Miller!'

Anson watched, fascinated, as the big man went down on his knees and tugged at the panel.

Suddenly, there was a loud *click*! and in front of their eyes, a section of the wainscoting came slowly outwards. It was a yard long, and inside it was a shallow drawer.

'Well, I'll be damned!' said Richard C. Anson.

Neither Loftus nor Miller even heard him.

There was a file of papers in the drawer …

Five minutes' examination was enough to establish beyond all doubt the importance of their find. Loftus took an emptied brief-case from the desk—a case bearing the initials of the unfortunate Abraham Korrel—and pushed the papers inside.

'This is going to help,' he commented, drily.

'Yes.' Miller was equally phlegmatic. 'You've found something about the League, at last. You'll be wanting to see Korrel, of course?'

'I'll go into these, first. But look after him at Cannon Street, Dusty! All right, Anson—we'll get along to my flat and see what we can do about that curiosity of yours.'

It was in the best of faith that Miller had suggested Loftus would want to see Korrel. But one trouble with everything concerning the League was the devastating swiftness with which each incident occurred.

For as the open police car, with Korrel and two policemen as sole occupants, drove along Victoria Street towards the Yard, a closed Daimler overtook it. There was not much traffic about, for the theatres at that time were only in mid-performances, and in the sweltering evening heat, pedestrians preferred the Embankment or the parks.

The window of the Daimler opened.

The police-car driver turned his head—and saw the gaping mouth of the machine-gun. Desperately, he swung the wheel but he was seconds too late. The rat-tat-tat of machine-gun bullets sounded, sharp and clear. What few people were about, turned and stared in blank amazement. A man and woman walking arm-in-arm, on a level with the two cars, suddenly crumpled up. The police-car, out of control—for the driver was slumped over the wheel, his head spilling blood—crashed across the pavement and into the vast window of a furniture showroom. As the plate-glass smashed with a noise like an explosion, the car came to rest against the piled-up furniture it had carried before it. And as Abraham Korrel half-fell into the shop, a dozen bullets in his head, the Daimler sped noiselessly along to Parliament Street, up Whitehall, round Trafalgar Square, and safely away towards Bloomsbury.

Of this, Loftus knew nothing when he reached his flat.

Diana and Fay were there, and the ever-reliable Butler had prepared sandwiches and coffee. The girls were eating—dutifully, rather than with any real appetite—but Diana's eyes gleamed when she saw Bill, unhurt.

' 'Lo, folks!' he greeted them. 'Butler been doing his stuff, I see. Anson, have a sandwich—oh, sorry, old man: you haven't been properly introduced.'

Leaving Anson with the others, he went into his bedroom and telephoned the Department. Craigie, as he had expected, was in consultation with Kingham and others about the explosions. He had dropped the brief-case on the bed: now he hesitated a moment, then picked it up and went with it through the secret connecting doors to Diana's flat, where he tucked it at the bottom of a drawer full of lingerie.

When he returned to his own flat, Anson said wryly:

'Can't you stop these fellows playing the fool?'

Loftus smiled. 'Easy, Wally! Carrie, go and see if Butler can get some more coffee, will you? And now, old man ...'

He sat down, filled his pipe, and talked.

Actually he gave very little information away, but he said enough to make Anson's eyes and jaw-line harden, as he listened. He looked, in that moment, extremely capable.

'And so, if I'm right,' Loftus concluded, '—and it's reasonable to believe that I am—tonight's shindy was connected with today's explosions. Unpleasant, but true.'

Anson rubbed his chin.

'Yes, but where do I come in? I mean—you said this Myra woman is mixed up in it?'

'Afraid so—and I wish we hadn't lost her. But that'll come right in the end. As for where you come in, that's the big question. Myra's been making a play for you, hasn't she?'

Anson nodded.

The air of arrogance had disappeared; he was an ordinary decent, reasonable human being who had forgotten his wealth and his importance.

'Damn right she has, Loftus. She's been sort of around for the last three or four days—I met her at the Éclat first. I've only been here a week, y'know ...'

'You arrived eight days ago.' Loftus smiled. 'With three secretaries, two valets, and a dog you had to leave at Southampton, much to your annoyance. You travelled on the *Empress of Sark,* preferring sea to air. You're thirty-two, the third-richest man in Australia, you own cattle, sheep and gold, mines, you're single, you get bad-tempered after two or three drinks, but you can hold your liquor well ...'

Anson stared.

'How in hell do you know all that?'

'It's all a matter of practice,' Diana told him. 'He takes one look at your eyes ...'

'Quiet, America!' said Loftus, mock-severe. 'Point is, Anson: we knew Myra was interested in you, and we wondered why. What we haven't learned, is why you're in England?'

'A pleasure trip,' Anson said promptly. 'I'm just ...'

Loftus lifted a hand.

'Don't try it. Even you wouldn't bring three secretaries on a pleasure trip.' Seriously, he added:

'Look Anson—this isn't a joke, and there's no time to waste. For some reason, you're wanted by the League. I've given you a lot of secret information, in the hope that you'll not hold back. There's a business reason for your trip, and I've got to know what it is.'

Anson hesitated, rubbing his chin thoughtfully. Then suddenly he smiled—an unexpected smile: transforming his face, robbing him of that sullen, sulky expression.

'You don't mince words, do you, Loftus? Well, I *am* here on business. I'm here on a conference called by Lord Nebton and—what the devil's wrong, man?'

And his last words were addressed, not to Loftus but to Carruthers, whose single expletive had made the girls as well as Anson jump.

CHAPTER 11
THE ERROLS AGREE

After that first admission, Anson showed an unexpected reluctance to disclose any further details of his affairs. For the first time, Loftus had a glimpse of the hard-headed businessman behind that youthful, almost boyish, exterior. The man he was seeing now was clearly capable of controlling his large fortune …

'It's just this, Loftus. You may be all you say—and I'll be surprised if you're not. On the other hand, I want more positive proof before I discuss my business with you or anyone else. I've given you Nebton's name deliberately.'

'Why?'

'I haven't much use for him,' said Anson, bluntly.

'Again, why?' Loftus was lighting his pipe, and the questions came casually enough: the tension had eased.

'Well …' Anson shrugged. 'He came to see me when he was in Melbourne, last year—as you may know,' he added, drily. 'And for one thing I don't like men who travel around with a harem.'

Loftus said, easily: 'I don't think Neb is all he seems, in that respect. It would be interesting to know, though, where else he went on that trip.'

Carruthers spoke up: 'It was a round-the-world voyage in that floating palace of his: the *Callay*. It touched on the Riviera, then Cape Town, Bombay, round Australia, New Zealand, up to San Francisco, and then home *via* the Panama Canal.'

Loftus grinned at Anson.

'How do you like our walking encylopaedia? Thanks, Carrie—that's quite an interesting list. Look, Anson: I'm taking you at your word and I won't press for more—yet. But I want you to stay here for an hour of two. My immediate chief is tied up with the Cabinet, right now ...'

He grinned again, as the Australian tried to disguise his scepticism.

'Don't worry—it's a fact. As soon as he's free, we'll go to see him. Until then, I'm not taking the chance of letting you out of my sight.'

Anson's cheeks flushed.

'Look here, Loftus, if you're trying to suggest ...!'

'Don't keep flying off the handle!' said Loftus, sharply. 'Just consider the situation. The League wants you, for some reason or other. We've got you—and men have died for a lot less reason than that. Wally, lead the man to the window—but go easy.'

Anson stared from one to the other, and saw Diana smile her sympathy at his obvious bafflement. Fay had the radio tuned in, very softly, to an orchestral concert and appeared to be listening to it with rapt attention. Yet these were the girls he had seen, earlier that evening, dealing with armed thugs ...

He let Davidson take him by the arm, and lead him to the window. Very slowly, Wally drew the curtain aside. Outside the building, there were two cars. Directly opposite, two men lounged with their hands in their pockets.

Anson stared.

'Who *are* they?'

'Friends of our friends of tonight,' said Davidson. 'We like to feel it's us they're watching—but if you went out, old fruit, your chances of living more than three minutes would be small. Indeed, I'd say ...'

The telephone rang just as Anson was expressing, loudly, his disbelief.

He fell silent as the others stared at Loftus, who had taken the call. They saw his jaw tighten as he listened, heard him say:

'You're sure? Korrel's dead?'

A moment later, he replaced the receiver slowly, and turned, grim-faced, to Anson.

'Korrel—our prisoner of tonight—and two policemen were machine-gunned in Victoria Street, on the way to the police-station. All dead. Well—do you stay around?'

'Too blooming right I do!' said Richard C. Anson.

'So far,' said Mike Errol, 'I don't think much of it.'

Mark held his peace.

'Dumb?' inquired Michael, irritably.

Mark shifted his feet.

'For the love of Pete! Why don't you say something?'

Mark, in the shadows of a small house on the sea front, took a cigarette from his lips and murmured:

'It won't do, Mike. We're agreeing too much. I don't think anything at all of it.'

They were both silent a moment. Then Mike said:

'Who is this fellow Rogerson, anyway?'

'Craigie said he's suspected of being one of the League.'

Mike frowned towards a spot, a mile or so away, where the lights of the pier were reflected on the incoming tide. 'I'm beginning to feel a bit of a mutt. I mean—we took it for granted we'd be doing great work, down here. It looks to me as if we've just been pushed out of the way, while the fireworks take place in town. I can just imagine Loftus telling us, with that lopsided grin of his—hallo! Things begin to happen.'

'Excitement,' murmured Mark, sardonically.

Silent, now, they cupped their cigarettes in their hands to hide the glow.

Bylands—the house they were watching—belonged, Gordon Craigie had told them, to a Mr Cornelius Rogerson. It was a small but expensive villa set in not much less than an acre of ground, which stretched to the sea on the outskirts of Bournemouth, in an obviously good residential neighbourhood.

Their instructions had been simply to watch, and report on callers. They had squeezed their way easily enough through a gap in a hedge, and were near the garage. They could see the front door and also the open gates of the small drive, yet could dodge out of sight at a moment's notice—a positioning which Loftus would have approved.

A car was coming along the private road at speed. Tyres and brakes squealed suddenly and headlights slewed round towards the Rogerson house.

The Errols darted back.

The car, a high-powered Hispano, swung in through the gates and along the drive. As the two occupants, a man and a woman, hurried out, the porch-light went on—and the Errols had a brief glimpse of the woman.

'Wow!' muttered Mike.

'Shut up!' Mark whispered, fiercely.

Richard C. Anson would have recognised the face and figure, the feline walk of Myra Clayton. Her companion was dark-haired and youthful, but they did not see him well enough for future identification.

A servant opened the door.

The callers went in, and the door closed.

'Now that,' murmured Mark, 'was interesting. They were in a hurry, and if that lovely wasn't all het up over something pretty grim ...'

'Decidedly so,' agreed Mike. 'So what happens now?'

'Craigie said: "In any emergency, use your own initiative",' said Mark. 'Hallo! A light in the front room. We'll go see, shall we?'

Quietly, they made their way towards the house. As they neared it, they saw that the lighted windows were open and that mosquito netting covered them, as well as casement blinds. The breeze rustled the blinds ever so slightly, drowning all sound of their approach.

They heard the woman's voice, low-pitched and tense.

'I tell you it was touch and go! We only scraped through by the skin of our teeth ...'

'By the skin of a flatfoot's cheek, my sweet.' It was a man's voice: mocking, casual. 'But, joking aside, Corny, it was a tight squeeze. I didn't know Myra could run so fast! I phoned the Naveling, of course—and inside half an hour, Korrel was *non est.*'

'You're sure?' The voice, presumably, of Cornelius Rogerson was cracked: that of an old man.

'No doubt about it. They used the tommy-gun.'

There was a sigh, suggestive of relief.

'So ... Well, he was the only one who could talk. What of the papers?'

'Loftus won't find them in a month of Sundays.'

'Don't be so sure!' snapped Myra. 'I'm beginning to think Loftus is a damned sight too clever for us.'

'It will not pay you to keep thinking like that,' said the older man, coldly.

They heard Myra swear, and it was not nice from a lady.

'If Korrel had taken my word for it, Anson wouldn't have gone with Loftus! I never was Anson's type— he needs the fluffy kind. Dora or Letty would have held him, but he soon tired of me—so when he saw a fight, the damned fool had to go into it. Look here, Corny, are you deaf as well as blind? Korrel had orders to get hold of Anson. Now, Anson's with Loftus—and he might know enough to talk and do a hell of a lot of harm. Aren't you going to do anything?'

'Not a damned thing,' the younger man cut in. 'We're too hot, my love. It's time *you* left the country, for one; Loftus isn't going to forget your sweet face in a hurry.'

'It is as well Korrel's gone' said Rogerson, testily. 'He had failed far too often. Now, let me see.' His voice quavered, rose and fell uncertainly. 'There's no doubt you must get abroad, Myra, and quickly. As for you, my friend ...'

Mike grimaced at Mark.

The names already mentioned were firmly registered on his mind and would be brought out for Craigie's benefit as soon as possible. The casual talk of a tommy-gun—of an obvious murder—the inference that the three people in the room knew something of the day's outrages, would ordinarily have incensed them into risky action. But a caution had come upon them—they were both very conscious of Craigie's order that they must never act precipitously, but wait till they knew there was no chance of learning more. They were so intent on listening that they did not hear the soft-footed approach from behind them—until the man kicked against a stone.

Mike left Mark to handle trouble from that direction and watched the window.

Mark saw a shadowy, thickset figure with his hand upraised, and something in it—not a gun: probably a cosh … As it swished down towards him, he closed with his man, missing by a fraction the full impact of the blow. He drove a short-arm jab to the attacker's stomach, but he was too late to prevent the man yelling:

'Boss—look out …!'

A shadow loomed at the window.

Mike, crouching tensely to one side of it, saw the blinds pulled aside—and the girl and the young man standing there. The man had a gun in his hand—and the light revealed the struggling figures.

Mark's back was towards the window: a perfect target.

Mike struck at the unknown's hand.

As the gun fell from the man's grasp, Mark twisted his man's wrist and sent him thudding to the floor, while Mike grabbed the man at the window and vaulted into the room. He heard Cornelius Rogerson's cracked voice call urgently:

'Myra—come away, come …!'

The girl disappeared.

In a free-for-all, Mike was as happy as a sand-boy. His opponent gasped in mingled pain and fury as he followed a blow to his *solar plexus* with an uppercut which made his teeth rattle.

Mark appeared at the window, breathless.

'My man's out—Mike! *Jump for it, for God's sake!'*

Mike, intent only on finishing his man, had seen nothing. But Mark saw the spluttering fuse in the hand of Cornelius Rogerson—and the urgency of his voice made Mike swing round for the window.

Mark's heart contracted with fear as he watched, help-less. Could Mike get out—or would the explosion come first?

Chapter 12
Up She Goes

Mr Cornelius Rogerson was a man of resource, and indeed often claimed that he had never been taken by surprise. There was always the possibility of a raid on Bylands, and he did not propose to allow the records he kept there to fall into the hands of the police—or of anyone else, for that matter.

In a drawer of his desk he kept a home-made bomb—dynamite with a fuse, in fact—and at the warning from his guard outside, he dragged it out, struck a match, and called for Myra.

Obviously, her companion could not get away from the intruder.

As Myra reached Cornelius at the doorway, he flung the bomb, and together they turned and ran. Mark's warning cry still echoed as they dashed through the house and they were out of the door and into the car before Mike reached the window. Mark was far too concerned for his cousin's safety to even notice the car start up and roar off down the drive …

Mike leapt for the lawn—and Mark flung himself to the ground. There was a moment's pause; a second, perhaps more, of utter silence save for the scrabbling of the young gunman as he tried frantically to follow Mike's lead.

But he was still only half over the sill when the explosion came.

It shattered the windows of a hundred houses, sent the unknown man fifty feet through the air, and showered bricks, dust and debris over the Errols. A piece of mortar struck Mike on the back of the head, sending him right out.

The whole estate was lit for a moment in a vivid glare, and then a thunderous *boom!* shook all Bournemouth. The earth seemed to tremble, and one wall of Bylands sagged ominously.

Hundreds of people, holidaying nearby, headed for the scene. Reporters raced from the town—and policemen in dozens. So did the fire-engines—but they would have no chance of stopping that holocaust.

When Mark staggered up, half-conscious, the room where the three had been talking was a blazing inferno. Shaken, he wiped the dirt and dust from his eyes. Then he saw Mike, lying there unmoving, still. Alarmed, he knelt down, and turned him over gently—and swore in his relief as Mike's eyelids fluttered.

'You bloody goat—you had me thinking ...'

He forgot his thoughts as he took a whisky-flask from his pocket, unscrewed the cap and held it to Mike's lips.

One swallow was enough. Mike sat up, bemusedly—then saw the flames, and his mind cleared in a flash.

'Thanks, Marko,' he murmured, solemnly.

'Forget it,' growled his cousin. 'Just get on your feet as fast as you can: we've got to get away without a lot of questions—if we can manage it. I wonder if grandpa and the beauteous Myra got clear?'

He peered towards the road: subconsciously, at least, his mind had registered that precipitant flight …

Myra had driven like mad from the house, and they had reached the road as the explosion came. The car had slithered from side to side as the blast of air hit them. The debris, though falling close, had done no damage.

Cornelius Rogerson and Myra, at that moment, were already two miles away.

Mark left Mike shakily finding his feet, and walked slowly over the lawn. People were already approaching: the light from the burning house revealed their vague, shadowy figures. Mark searched along the hedge—and found what he had suspected he must find.

The unknown was there; or what was left of him. Mark gave up any thought of establishing his identity.

He went back to Mike, and said bleakly:

'I could have given him a hand. I …'

'Don't be a damned fool!' snapped Mike. 'It would merely have meant three corpses instead of one—and he was fated for a violent end, anyhow. Let's move!'

To avoid the police, they slipped through the hedge at a point where there were few people about, and merged with the crowd. The Talbot was covered with dust, but fortunately not damaged.

As they drove towards Bournemouth, thousands of holiday-makers were on the way to the fire, which was burning so fiercely that it spread a lurid light about the west side of the town. They parked the car near the pier and went to telephone Craigie. There was no answer from the Whitehall number: Craigie, rarely for him, had left his office and gone to Loftus' flat.

They tried the latter, and Loftus' deep voice answered.

Mark began to spell his name backwards.

'All right,' said Loftus, 'anything up?'

'Everything's up, including Bylands,' Mark told him. 'How much can I say over the wire?'

'Cautiously, anything.'

Mark obeyed—and Loftus' only rejoinder was:

'Good work. Get up here as soon as you can, will you? Eh? … Yes, we'll look after the identification. You needn't worry about a thing.'

Mark replaced the receiver and eyed his cousin.

'Feel fit to drive? Good. Let's go!'

Craigie had been to an unofficial Cabinet meeting, and as usual had found several Ministers openly disbelieving in a League of a Hundred-and-One, or its connection with the outrages. The shortsightedness of Cabinet Ministers was one of Craigie's most regular problems, and the changing faces at the big table at Number 10 increased the difficulties.

The Rt. Hon. David Wishart, the then Prime Minister, was on his side. So was Bryce-Scott, the recently-appointed Foreign Minister. Kingham, of course, would not commit himself one way or another. At the end of a difficult meeting, Craigie was exactly where he had been at the start—he was asked to continue his investigations.

He would have returned to his own office had not a remarkable-looking man accosted him.

The man was short, particularly of leg. His back was slightly hunched, his shoulders broad and full. His face was red, with a Punch-like chin and a beak of a nose, and his eyes were very blue. He was in evening dress, but his black Homburg was on the back of his head, revealing a broad, smooth forehead, and a stretch of baldness.

Thus was Sidney Peter Athelstan Thornton—Spats to his friends, and for many years Craigie's resident agent in Paris. Spats, more recently, had a roving commission.

He fell into step with Craigie.

'As usual?'

'Worse,' said Craigie, shortly.

'Too bad.' Spats had a remarkably deep voice. 'Never mind, we keep living. Bill 'phoned me—Anson's at the flat. There's been a shindy of some sort at Moorton Road—does that mean anything?'

'A great deal,' said Craigie.

They were passing under a light, and Thornton, glancing at his Chief, thought that Craigie looked greyer and older.

'Loftus suggested that you went there, using the second entrance.'

Craigie considered a moment. 'All right, Spats ... Are you coming?'

'Think I should? What's it about?'

'Today's business.'

'Is it, begad! Yes, count me in.'

In Brook Street, there were a surprising number of cars parked, and a surprising number of young men in sight. Loftus, in fact, had called for eight agents, to watch the two men who were watching the flat. It was significant, however, that the two men of the League keeping Loftus under their eyes spared hardly a glimpse for Thornton and Craigie as they entered the house next door. They would have been shocked had they seen them, five minutes later, enter Loftus' big drawing-room.

Carruthers and Davidson were playing bridge with Diana and Fay. Anson was looking on, and stared in disbelief as the newcomers appeared from a bedroom.

As Loftus introduced them, giving a brief but vivid résumé of the Moorton Road affair, Craigie's manner changed. Something of the strain and disappointment dropped away.

'Well, Mr Anson, it seems we have a lot to thank you for!' From a small, leather pocket-case, Craigie had assembled and was now smoking one of his favourite meerschaums. 'And of course you are fully justified in wanting further evidence of our authority.'

'I don't,' Anson assured him. 'I'm satisfied. It's all fitting too well to be a trick. Well, now, this conference ...'

'Before we go quite so far,' Craigie interrupted, 'do I understand you are here on the direct invitation of Lord Nebton?'

'Well—he's the chairman.'

'I see. Do you know the other members?'

'I know some.' Anson reeled off seven names. 'The fact is, Mr Craigie, we're all more or less interested in armaments, one way or the other.'

Loftus stirred and the four at the bridge table looked towards Anson.

Craigie's eyes smiled.

'You are, of course, the managing-director of Ventors Australasia Limited, Mr Anson.'

Anson stared.

'Secrecy has its limits,' Craigie said, drily. 'Yes, I was particularly interested when your name was first mentioned, because of your interest in armaments. Exactly what was the purpose of the conference?'

'You mean you don't know?'

'I knew that several Empire manufacturers were visiting the country. But not why. Can you tell me?'

Anson rubbed his nose.

'Yes, I can. There's talk of nationalisation, you'll know. We're opposed to it, for good reasons. I don't mean the profit aspect,' he added firmly, as though expecting to be challenged. 'I don't care if I don't make a pound out of armaments or aeroplanes ...'

'It is not a general feeling,' murmured Craigie.

'Too right it's not—but it's my feeling,' said Anson, sharply. 'But we are all opposed to nationalisation. I haven't seen a thing this country or mine does well on those lines. Nationalisation means muddle, with a capital M—and we can't afford any more of it.'

Craigie nodded, and Loftus felt his own opinion of Richard C. Anson rise considerably.

'I don't give a tuppenny damn about profits,' Anson reiterated. 'I can't answer for all the others, but there are more than one who think the same way. Anyhow, we decided to get together, talk it over, and put up a proposition to the different governments. We,' added Anson impressively although without undue emphasis, 'control the armaments of the British Empire. Every damned bullet, every gun, every ship and every 'plane. That's a fact, Mr Craigie.'

Craigie was staring.

The bridge party put down their cards.

Loftus seemed carved out of stone.

Carruthers and Davidson, for once, looked wide-awake and very serious. Spats Thornton was rubbing his chin thoughtfully.

After a long pause, Craigie said:

'I see. You seriously imply that every armaments concern is to be represented at the conference?'

'It's a fact.'

'When is this conference to take place?'

Anson hesitated.

'Well, it's officially secret, Mr Craigie. Still, I've told you plenty: I may as well finish. On the first of September.'

'Where?'

'I don't know, yet. All I know is that it might be a day's journey from London.'

'I see.'

Craigie did see; more than Anson realised. Loftus, too, saw the possibilities of the situation far more clearly than most could have done. Here was a conference of the big arms manufacturers, the men who controlled the complete output of British armaments. There could be only one reason for the League's interest in members of the conference.

To influence them.

But how?

In what direction?

Anson found the silence worrying, and cleared his throat. Craigie hesitated, wondering just how much to say to the Australian, just how far he could be trusted. And then, cutting across the tension, the telephone rang.

Loftus lifted the receiver, spoke shortly, waited, and then said:

'Good work. Get up here as soon as you can, will you? Eh? … Yes, we'll look after the identification. You needn't worry about a thing.'

He replaced the receiver, and turned slowly. Anson felt the intensity of the big man's gaze, but his voice was quiet enough.

'That was the Errols,' he said. 'Does the name Rogerson—Cornelius Rogerson—mean anything to you, Anson?'

Anson stared.

'Too right it does. He convened the conference for Nebton. Why?'

Loftus shrugged, casually, but he knew just how important that statement was.

'He's quite definitely mixed up with the League. Myra went to see him, but she got away again. Gordon. I'm afraid we'll have to have a chat on our own. What's the wise thing to do about Anson?'

'I'm going to my hotel,' the Australian cut in, quickly.

'Do you carry a gun?' asked Craigie.

'No … Look here—are you trying to throw a scare into me? There are limits …'

'There isn't a limit known,' said Craigie in his precise convincing way, 'to people who will organise terrorism as we are beginning to know it. I'm warning you seriously, Mr Anson, that your life is in danger—and will be, for some time.'

Anson forced a smile.

'I'll risk it, thanks.'

'Spirited, but unwise,' said Craigie.

'You're not trying to tell me that I can't move away from here! I can look after myself, thanks, and …'

'I don't want you to go away from here without a guard,' Craigie told him. 'And I want you to take on two new secretaries. They'll call on you ten minutes after you get to the Regal, and you will be able to rely on them.'

'What the devil do you expect to happen? Am I liable to be bumped off?'

'You're much more likely to be approached by the League, with a view to doing what the League wants. And unless I've misjudged you, you'll refuse. That's when the danger comes in. I hope you'll be sensible.'

'Sensible? The whole thing sounds such absolute bunk—'Anson grinned, suddenly, disarmingly. 'All right, I'll bite. Only I'll bar Loftus, as a secretary.'

Loftus gave a lopsided smile.

'I've more important things to do. Wally, will you go along with Anson, and collect one of the lads from downstairs? Take it easy.'

Anson, although he would never have admitted it, felt jumpy as they reached the street. But nothing happened, except that a colourless young man nodded as Davidson lifted a hand, and walked on the other side of the street, to be followed in turn by one of Craigie's men.

While Craigie turned to Loftus:

'What was the call from Errol, Bill?'

Loftus explained. Carruthers started talking, about Nebton. Craigie jotted down the names of the seven men Anson had mentioned as being concerned in the conference, and altogether they saw more than enough to keep them busy for a long time to come.

They had to check up on:

1. Lord Nebton.
2. The other seven armament kings.
3. Myra Clayton.
4. Cornelius Rogerson.
5. The unknown victim of the explosion at Bournemouth.
6. Mr Richard C. Anson, who might not be all that he seemed on the suface.

'And other things.' Loftus had, throughout the spell at the flat, been preternaturally serious: 'The papers I collected from Moorton Road, Gordon. I'm more worried about them than anything ...'

'What were they?' Craigie's voice was sharp.

Loftus said heavily:

'A full list of the particulars of today's explosions, plus dates for another series, without the particulars. At midnight tomorrow they start, according to Korrel's card index. They called it Operation B. Today's business was Operation A. And one thing seems certain—it will be a lot worse than we've seen already.'

Craigie and the others saw now why he had been so solemn. Like him, they saw not only the explosions to come. They saw panic.

Panic, unavoidable and uncontrollable ...

Unless Operation B could be stopped in time.

Chapter 13
Seven Gentlemen

In the past, during times of crisis, Craigie had been able to judge the temper of the public as few other people could. He had a natural respect for the coolness of the average Englishman, and in his lighter moments would admit that, as a Scot, he had learned to expect the Englishman to pull out just that little extra in a crisis.

He had seen London calm enough when an air invasion had seemed only a matter of hours. He had listened and watched with cold disapproval a system of news distribution which had the unhappy effect of looking like deliberately-created panic—and had seen it fail.

But he knew there were limits even to the phlegmatic calmness of the English. In common with most peoples, they would be more worried by something they could not understand than by anything, no matter how menacing, which was competently explained.

The explosions presented such a problem.

One of the wilder national dailies went so far as to suggest that the outrages had been deliberately engineered by a foreign power, aiming to paralyse the country before it struck—and although the paper in question was severely reprimanded in the best Home Office tradition, the rumour gained ground.

London and all the other big centres were on the alert, and in the man in the street there was nervousness and even fear. Craigie had received a hundred reports to that effect, and they had worried him far more than anything else the League might have done.

He knew—and the Cabinet knew—that there *was* no proof that the outrages had not been deliberately organised by a foreign power.

And with the papers which Loftus had secured from the unfortunate Abraham Korrel, it seemed there was every reason to believe it possible. For those papers, which mentioned no names and used only numbers for identification, included one headed:

GENERAL PLAN

1. The object of the League is to instil a lack of confidence in the public, leading to (a) anxiety, (b) panic.
2. Operation A will be instrumental in creating general anxiety. Operation B should cause the first stages of panic. Operation C should put the finishing touches to the preparations for the final and effective Operation D.
3. Operation A will take place at midday on August the 12th. It will be followed by operation B at midnight on August the 14th.
4. Times for the further activities will be advised after the effect of A & B can be adequately judged.

There were other statements, but none more comprehensive than these four. Loftus had seen from the first—and Craigie needed no more telling of it—that to fully understand the General Plan, a good knowledge of the League's proposed activities was essential.

They had no such knowledge.

But there in black and white was the statement that the first objective of the League was to create panic. And all about them, that night, there was evidence of the fertile ground on which the further seeds of terrorism could be spread. Even an open declaration of war from one of the aggressor-powers would not have had the same unnerving effect.

No one *knew* what might happen.

But Craigie and Loftus knew *when* the next stage was to come.

'One of the first things,' said Craigie, 'is to get something from Nebton. That's not going to be easy. He's still popular with the powers that be, in spite of rumours about his reputation. You can get busy, Bill.'

'Thanks,' murmured Loftus, drily. 'Just how?'

'If we believe Anson, and for the time being we've got to assume that he wasn't lying, Nebton is the principal representative of the conference. He may or may not know anything about the League. There's nothing to stop him—or any other armament manufacturer—convening a meeting. There's no proof that he knew his convenor was connected with the League. In short ...'

'The police can't work.'

'So we must,' nodded Craigie. 'And quickly.'

'We'd better have the Errols' report, first. And we ought to get on to Bournemouth and see what we can do about identifying the man who was killed down there. If Miller …'

'I'll talk to Fellowes. But it can wait for five minutes.' Craigie frowned. 'Let's try and get things in the right perspective. Nebton has called this conference, and the members have kept their movements so close that there was no reason for suspecting it before.'

'Far, far too secretive,' Thornton agreed. The fat cigar sticking from his Punch-like face made him look more of a caricature than ever. 'I was going to report tonight, Craigie, that Amondier is coming to England at the end of the month.'

Craigie's eyes widened.

'So the French might be in it, too? I wonder if it's bigger than Anson knew?'

Loftus looked thoughtful.

'I wonder if Anson told us all he knew? But assuming he's on the up-and-up, all the important English and Empire arms manufacturers will meet at some place unknown on the first of September—and probably pass resolutions and go into methods against nationalisation of armaments. That's innocent enough. The problem is—how many, if any, are working with the League? Was Anson the first to be approached—through Myra—or is he the last?'

Carruthers was scribbling on a piece of paper, and he pushed it in front of Loftus. It read:

Mr Benjamin Morely—Canada.
Mr Eustace Jaffrey—New Zealand.
Sir Jabez Gorton—England.
Mr Andrew McKenzie—Scotland.

Lord Hubert Lore—England.
Sir Ronald Frazer-Campbell—S. Africa.
Mr Matthew Tiarney—England.

'Thanks,' Loftus nodded. 'The seven men Anson mentioned. And to them we can add Anson himself, Nebton, and Amondier of France. But it's not a quarter of the big men in armaments.'

'It may be all whom Anson knows are concerned,' said Carruthers.

'Or all he wants to talk about,' suggested Loftus.

Craigie frowned, tugging at his pipe.

'Are you thinking Anson was deliberately holding back, Bill?'

'Hardly that,' said Loftus, 'but at least it's possible. He was reluctant to talk at first—in fact he was a constant contradiction of himself. When I first started talking to him at Moorton Road, he was all up in the air. Then he quietened down, and grew reasonable. After that he demanded proof of our good faith, and'—Loftus grinned—'without disrespect; Gordon, there doesn't seem any reason why he should take you at your face value. We could have offered him Fellowes, or even one or two from Downing Street. Instead, he suddenly decided to let us know all he could—and it just didn't seem in keeping.'

'He seemed temperamental,' Carruthers offered.

'Yes … And money does work like that, I know. All the same he needs watching. The new secretaries was a good move, Gordon—who are you sending?'

'Wally, I think—and Graham.'

'Good enough. If Anson deliberately dodges them, we'll have considerable reason for doubting the gentleman. Well now—Neb certainly had that world-trip last year, and it might have been connected with this. Someone must find the connection between him and Rogerson.'

'It's a pity Oundle's laid up,' murmured Craigie.

'I'm not.' growled Thornton, in his deep voice.

'Better let him do it,' said Loftus. 'It'll keep him out of mischief for a while, anyhow.'

'My hide,' Spats assured him, 'is impervious to sarcasm, little man. But didn't I gather that an unofficial investigation of Neb himself was on the bill?'

'Yes, but we need to approach him from both angles,' said Craigie. 'You get busy at once, Thornton—you can take any one of the men downstairs you want. Wait there a minute—I'll get you to come as far as Downing Street with me.'

Thornton went off, and Craigie pushed a hand through his sparse hair.

'You and Carrie will look after the Nebton end, Bill,' he said, slowly. 'And do it carefully, for the Lord's sake!' Craigie's untypical outburst showed the others just how deeply he was feeling. 'You'll use the Errols, I suppose?'

'Yes—they're new, and not likely to be known. And for Neb, I think we'd better use Diana.'

Craigie hesitated.

'Yes … All right, Bill, I'll leave it to you. But be careful. Let me have the Errols' report as soon as you get it in order.'

When Craigie had gone, Diana and Fay approached the second flat, to find Carruthers saying:

'There's one thing worrying me, Bill, Neil Clarke—you don't know him, but he's an old acquaintance of mine. He was on the *Luxa*, and I caught a glimpse of him at Moorton Road—he was one of the few who got away.'

'What is he?'

'On the 'Change.'

'H'mm. We'll get Miller busy, for a start,' said Loftus. 'For the rest—hallo, America, you look as though you need some beauty sleep!'

Let it be said that between Diana Woodward and William Loftus there was an affection as strong as most—in fact, Carruthers was apt to say, stronger. They were engaged, but they were postponing their marriage until such time as the work of the Department was slack enough for Craigie to train a new leading agent. Diana, late of the American Intelligence and co-opted by Craigie, found relief from strain in Bill's genial, almost off-hand manner, knew how deliberately it was calculated to ease the perpetual suspense and uncertainty.

That she could and did enter the spirit of *camaraderie* so successfully was a tribute to Diana's courage, and her complete acceptance by Loftus' friends was a compliment of the highest order.

'Thank you, darling,' she said, now. 'Actually, I've been thinking that it's past time I was busy. Nebton …'

Loftus grinned.

'We're doing well—I'd just fixed it with Craigie. With Spats working on the Neb-Rogerson angle, myself, Carrie and the Errols working on Neb under-cover, and you trying to win a place in his affections, the poor devil will probably end up in an asylum. All of which serve to illustrate,' he went on, putting his arm about her shoulders, 'the need for that beauty sleep. Only the best will do, for Neb.'

Diana laughed.

'Just where,' asked Fay, 'do I come in?'

'Sad though it is to relate,' said Loftus, 'you stay here and nurse Ned. He'll like it, even if you don't.'

Fay looked mutinous.

'Look here, Bill …'

'Look here, lass, Ned's gone to a nursing home today—but he'll be back tomorrow, and if there's no friendly face to greet him, he'll droop. We can't have agents drooping. What's the matter with Ned, anyhow?'

'Oh, he's all right,' said Fay, too casually.

Loftus widened his eyes, but said nothing, and the discussion was cut short when there was a ring at the front door. In a few seconds the Errols, reasonably presentable now, if grazed in places, came in. They did not look light-hearted.

'We'll get to bed,' Diana said, and retired, with Fay.

Loftus, as always blessing the tact of Diana, found beer and offered it to the new agents, who accepted with alacrity. Carrie's offer to get sandwiches was refused with thanks.

In five minutes Loftus understood what had made the Errols more sober than of yore. The experience at Bylands and the blasting to pieces of the unknown man with the mocking voice was a grim initiation into the work of the Department.

'Myra and Korrel we know about,' said Loftus, after the full recital was over. 'Dora and Letty are strangers, and as for the Naveling—it doesn't sound unfamiliar. How was it used?'

'The cove said: "Of course, I 'phoned the Naveling".' said Mike. 'A pub, possibly?'

'It isn't impossible, anyhow. You two get a bath, while I do some telephoning—we're going to be busy.'

As the cousins disappeared, Loftus murmured:

'They'll do. I wish I could be as sure of Anson. Push that 'phone over, Carrie—and get on the other line and tell Craigie just what the Errols reported.'

Carruthers obliged.

Loftus sent messages to the Yard and replaced the receiver, then located a directory and checked Nebton's address in St John's Wood. He telephoned the Yard again, and learnt that the peer had a cottage in Hampshire, near the Test—for he was a fishing fanatic—and a house in Scotland, near Loch Awe.

'The conference might be a day's journey from London,' Loftus reminded himself.

Mike Errol, clad in a bath-towel, poked his head round the door.

'The Rogerson bird looked all of eighty,' he offered. 'What put you on to him?'

'Fay heard Korrel and Myra mentioned, so we watched them both—and Myra visited Rogerson a week ago. Quite simple. Did you see him?'

'For a split second, yes. Old, wrinkled ...'

'Long or short?'

'Short, definitely. Myra—if it was Myra—was inches taller. I suppose he blew the place up to destroy all papers and what-not?'

'Glimmerings of intelligence do show through,' Loftus said earnestly.

'Thank *you*. Did you hear the story of the ...'

Brrr-brrrr.

'Later,' said Loftus. He pulled the telephone towards him and heard Superintendent Miller's gruff voice.

'That you, Loftus? ... Yes, I've word about the man Clarke—he's handled a lot of buying and selling, lately, for Lord Nebton.'

'Has he, by George!'

'Don't shout,' Miller reproved. 'I've been through to Bournemouth, and there's little chance of identifying the dead man, but they found another fellow nearby, named Grossman—you might call him Rogerson's bodyguard. He says he knows nothing, but that he saw two people looking through the window just before the explosion. Would that be your men?'

'It would, Miller: thanks.'

'Good. And then Rogerson himself, and the Clayton woman, caught the night boat from Clarence Pier to the Isle of Wight—they were in a hurry, that's why a man took note of them. They left an open Sunbeam ...'

'Have the Island advised at once,' Loftus urged. 'If we can get that brace it'll be a big thing, Miller. You'll do all you can?'

'Yes—will you be sending there?'

'I will. Two men by the name of Errol—they'll fly from Heston in an hour's time. Have them given all facilities, there's a good fellow.'

'It's as good as done,' promised Miller.

'Thanks.' Loftus rang off and turned to find Mike half-dressed by the door, and Mark towelling just behind him. 'You heard? Well, can either of you pilot a 'plane?'

'Yes,' said Mike.

'You'll find one at Heston—here's a note that will release it.' Loftus scribbled quickly. 'Things are moving, so try to get this into your thick heads: if you find Rogerson, force out of him what's going to happen at midnight tomorrow. Never mind his age or infirmity—go to any lengths but get that information. Clear?'

'Oke,' said Mark.

'Then get going—Oundle's clothes will fit you more or less if you want a change of anything.' Loftus had not wasted a word, and the Errols turned with a united purpose. Carruthers, recognising the signs of coming action in full blast, was not surprised to hear:

'Carrie, get on that 'phone and locate Nebton. Never mind what you say to him or his, just find where he is, we'll go and see him. I—*damn* the thing!'

For the telephone under his hand rang sharply. He lifted the receiver and heard Wally's voice. But for once it was not weary. In fact it was sharp:

'Bill—Anson's been shot—one of his secretaries. I got the little runt, but he turned the gun on himself ... No, Anson's not dead but it's touch and go, and an ambulance is coming ...'

'Keep the ambulance waiting till I get there,' said Loftus. 'Don't argue, keep it there! Anson's not to be taken away until I've seen him!'

And in Loftus' eyes as he replaced the receiver was hope, mingled with fear.

Chapter 14
Fast Work Fails

'What do I do?' demanded Carruthers.

'Just get on to Neb, and as soon as you've found him, 'phone me at Anson's hotel,' said Loftus. He grabbed his hat from a chair and hurried out. Carruthers heard the front door bang as Mike Errol emerged, fully-dressed and looking puzzled.

'Any change in orders?'

'No—get going as soon as you can.' Carruthers dialled a number. 'Hallo—Lord Nebton, please … he's not? Can you tell me where to find him? Yes, it's important—a message from Mr Anson … all right, thank you.'

'Damn!' He replaced the receiver, then lifted it again, dialled, and: 'Can you tell me if Lord Nebton is there …? Yes, I'll hold on …'

But Nebton was not at his club; nor at his houseboat. Carruthers was still trying to get him, as the Errols left for Heston and the Isle of Wight.

Loftus reached the Regal to find Leroni, the manager, waiting in the foyer in some perturbation and outside, an ambulance from the London Hospital. Leroni came towards him with hands outstretched.

'M'sieu, I beg, I implore you …!'

'Get Mr Farquharson on the telephone,' said Loftus, shortly. 'Give him my name, tell him that he is wanted for an emergency operation here …'

'Here! *Santa Maria!* M'sieu Loftus. I beg …'

'Get him!' snapped Loftus, then realising that the tension that gripped him could not be understood by Leroni, he added more easily: 'It's essential, Leroni. I'd avoid it if I possibly could …'

'But *here,*' moaned Leroni. 'I …'

He found he was talking to Loftus' back, and swung round on a staring reception clerk. 'Why do you stare like ze fool? Did you not hear M'sieu Loftus say 'phone ze doctair—hurry, hurry!'

In the royal suite, Loftus found two frightened secretaries, an inspector from the Yard, Wally and a small, immaculate man named Graham—one of the lesser lights of the Department. In an inner room was a doctor, a nurse, and Anson, who was unconscious.

He was lying on the bed, his shirt-front soaked with blood. His mouth was shut tightly, as though he had clenched his teeth, and there was blood on his hair. The rest of his face was deathly white.

The doctor swung round as Loftus entered.

He was a dapper man, grey-haired, and with a considerable reputation—and he knew Loftus by sight. His eyes hardened.

'Mr Loftus, every moment you keep Mr Anson here you are lessening his chance of life …'

'Yes, I know,' said Loftus. 'And every moment he's outside this room there's a chance of another attack. Listen,

Forbes, I wouldn't do this if it weren't essential. I've sent for Farquharson, and he'll operate here. Get the necessary things ready, will you?'

'*Here?*' Dr Forbes looked startled. 'It's impossible! He won't have the facilities—confound it, man, the London is only ten minutes' journey!'

'It's ten minutes too far.'

'I cannot accept the responsibility,' said Forbes, stiffly.

'I can and do—and if you want to save his life, get those things ready!' snapped Loftus, and as Forbes gave in, added more calmly: 'Sorry, Forbes, there's more to this man than you know. What are the chances of him talking in the next hour or two?'

'None,' said Forbes. 'Unless—' sardonically—'you care to hear what he says under the anaesthetic.'

'Even that might be useful,' Loftus told him.

He went into the outer room as Leroni arrived to say that Mr Farquharson was on the way, and Forbes—hearing, through the open door—decided that if Farquharson would come in such a hurry at his behest, Loftus must wield considerable influence.

Preparations were hurriedly made.

Farquharson arrived in fifteen minutes. By that time, a table had been procured, instruments were being sterilised—and Davidson was completing an explanation to Loftus.

He had arrived with Anson, waited till Craigie had 'phoned his orders to stay, with Graham, as the Australian's new secretary—and told Anson, who had laughingly agreed that he probably needed a bodyguard.

'There was a little runt here, named Wiseman,' he was saying now. 'Bowing and scraping—you know the type. He had a telephone call—we traced it to a call-box in Piccadilly—said "yes" three times, turned round and shot

Anson before we knew he'd finished talking. I went for him, but he put the end of the gun in his mouth and kept his finger on the trigger.'

'How many bullets did Anson take?'

'Three—Bill, why stop the ambulance?'

'If the League can get Korrel in a police car, they can make sure of Anson in an ambulance,' said Loftus. 'I'm going downstairs to a 'phone booth, and I'm getting half-a-dozen men here. Watch everyone closely—they'll probably try to get through, knowing that the operation's being done here.'

'Anson's as important as that, is he?'

'Be yourself, Wally—be yourself! Anson knows a whale of a lot he forgot to tell us, and they tried to make sure he didn't have a chance of changing his mind. If he jabbers under the gas, Farquharson will tell us if there's anything interesting. Keep awake, old man!'

Davidson said something unprintable and Loftus grinned and hurried downstairs. He gave instructions for men to come to the Regal and, as he stepped from the booth, was told by a clerk that there was a call waiting, from a Mr Carruthers.

'Put it through here,' Loftus told him.

Carruthers said:

'Nebton left by air for an unknown destination two hours ago, Bill.'

'Did he, by George! So he's had an alarm, too. Have the Errols gone?'

'Yes.'

' 'Phone the landing field at Ryde, and tell them to look out for Neb as well as the others. Then call the Yard again, and have a call put out for Neb as well as the rest of the bunch. Got it?'

'What then?'

'You and I will probably make some calls,' said Loftus.
'Get Di and Fay out of bed, tell them to go—separately—to
Morely and Jaffrey, the first two men Anson mentioned, to
represent themselves as newspaper special correspondents,
and ...'

'Damn it, it's after midnight!'

'Yes—and just twenty-four hours before Operation B,'
snapped Loftus. 'I want both men's reactions to a statement
that the Daily So-and-So understands they're attending an
important armaments conference on the twenty-first of
August—give them the wrong date, it'll look more natural. When you've finished all that, get to Gorton and then
McKenzie. I'll tackle the other three.'

Upstairs again, he learned from Davidson that the operation was expected to take an hour, and promptly left the
Regal for Craigie's office.

Craigie had just returned from Number 10.

The proof he had been able to offer had been all the
confirmation Wishart wanted—and four members of the
Cabinet who had been talking with the Prime Minister were
at last convinced that the League of the Hundred-and-One
was not a figment of Craigie's imagination. Extraordinary
measures were already being put into operation. Special
constables would take over the normal duties of the police
from eight o'clock the following night, and the regulars
would be concentrated at all points likely to be affected by
the mysterious Operation B.

The press had not yet been informed.

'You can't stop them getting the precautions story,' said
Loftus, 'but they can be asked to repress it. Did you put that
up to Wishart?'

'Yes—he'll do it, provided nothing is yet in print—he won't risk a sensation by half-suppressing it. Well, Bill …'

'Listen,' said Loftus.

He plunged into an account of what had happened and what he had done—and Craigie nodded approval. But:

'I don't think there's much chance of getting anything stopped, Bill. It's nearly one o'clock, now.'

'A lot can happen in twenty-three hours.'

Craigie's tired eyes narrowed.

'What's in your mind?'

'Rogerson almost certainly knows more, or he wouldn't have gone to those lengths to get the house destroyed. Anson might know. Any one of the seven might yield something. And here's an idea. Generally speaking, daylight's the time for terrorism as we know it. More crowds, more to suffer and to see what happens. Why have they chosen midnight?'

'I'd thought of that, but—well, main services might be affected …'

'Not so much as by day.'

'But more easily.'

'Yes …' Loftus took out his cigarettes slowly—for the first time since the shooting of Anson, he was at half-speed. 'All the same, I've a strong feeling they're choosing midnight because it's something which will be more effective when the country's asleep—the majority of people, anyhow.'

Craigie drummed his fingers on the arm of his chair.

'Yes … But I'm fogged.'

'Aren't we all!' Loftus drew a deep breath. 'Let's be fantastic, Gordon. The League wants panic. Destroy a building, say with two or three hundred people in it—sleeping people. Do the same thing in twenty places. Let the country wake up next morning to learn that some thousands of people have been wiped out—*in their beds.*'

The tension in the room increased.

Craigie stared—his eyes filled with horror.

Loftus said:

'It's been on my mind, Gordon. It makes everything else unimportant—even finding who is behind the League. If anything like that should happen tomorrow, the country will be in a ferment. Oh, I know it's wild—but it would be so easy! No precautions could stop it, now ...'

'Bill'—Craigie's voice was strained—'have you the slightest reason for believing this could be? ...'

'*Operation B should cause the first stages of panic.*' Loftus intoned the words, then went on more normally: 'General Plan, paragraph 2, Gordon. I tried the old trick. If *I* were controlling the League, what would I do to create panic—at midnight?'

Craigie's face looked grey.

'All right, Bill,' he said, bleakly. 'Get busy.' The telephone rang and he answered it, then turned to Loftus.

'Carruthers wants a word with you.'

Loftus took the receiver and for once, Carruthers sounded excited.

'Bill, I've seen McKenzie, and he didn't like it. He said definitely that there was no such conference, but he was lying—and badly, at that.'

'Yes, he would keep it close—they all will. What's the trouble?'

'Simply this: I recognised McKenzie for the first time as a man who was on the *Luxa.* I've an idea that all seven men Anson mentioned were on the houseboat, and I know *five* of them were. How does it sound?'

'More and more like Nebton,' said Loftus, grimly.

He left the Whitehall Office and, not without difficulty, interviewed Lord Hubert Lore, a big, gruff-voiced man who also denied the suggestion of a conference, but too categorically and bluffly to deceive Loftus.

Next, he interviewed Sir Ronald Frazer-Campbell, the South African armaments manufacturer. There, he received the same denial in a cold, detached voice which appeared at the same time to want to know what the devil Loftus meant by forcing the interview. Sir Ronald was a short, well-proportioned man: grey-haired, aristocratic, authoritative.

The last of the seven, Mr Matthew Tiarney, was out of town, and his whereabouts unknown …

Loftus returned to the flat, to find Diana and Fay already back. Fay seemed amused. Mr Eustace Jaffrey had scoffed at the idea of a conference, and assured Fay that she was far too pretty for newspaper work.

'Did he get as far as a dinner suggestion?' asked Loftus.

'Yes—for the day after tomorrow,' said Fay, demurely. 'I told him I was sorry …'

Loftus gulped.

'Fay my sweet, it was exactly what we wanted. I …'

'That I was engaged for the rest of the week,' Fay went on, her eyes gleaming, 'but that I was free tomorrow. Jaffrey has cancelled another appointment—it *is* better before midnight tomorrow, isn't it?'

The smile had gone from her eyes, something of the horror which Craigie had shown replacing it. Loftus said, gently:

'It is, Fay—thanks a lot. But be careful, tomorrow night! Any luck, Di?'

Diana nodded.

'A lot, I think. Mr Benjamin Morely also denied the idea of a conference. He had a lady friend with him, and

he addressed her as Dora. Hasn't a Dora been mentioned
before?'

Loftus snapped.

'By God she has! By Myra, at Bournemouth—bless the
Errols—and not forgetting you. What was the relationship?'

'Friendly. She was just leaving.'

'H'mm—did you follow her?'

'No, but I had young Bimbo with me, and he did.'

'The Fates be praised!' murmured Loftus. 'It …'

But Carruthers returned, a Carruthers who was thoughtful, for his second string—Sir Jabez Gorton—while denying
the idea of a conference, had seemed a very frightened man.

'He was clinging to a fluffy little creature called Letty,'
Carruthers reported. 'And Mike Errol said Myra mentioned
a Letty.'

'Did she stay with Gorton?'

'No—she left just after I did. But she was too smart for
me—I lost her in Piccadilly.'

Loftus picked up his hat.

'Gorton was scared, you say?'

'Yes, but …'

'Let's see if we can frighten him some more,' said the big
man, gently. 'He might do in place of Neb, for the night.'

But Sir Jabez Gorton, one of the biggest armament
manufacturers in England, virtual controller of the big
Gorton-Mayer combine, with branches in ship-building,
aircraft-building and explosives, would never be frightened
again in this world. For when Loftus and Carruthers reached
his Kensington house the lights were blazing, two Flying
Squad cars were standing outside, and a Chief Inspector
who knew Loftus, was trying to get a coherent story from a
hysterical housekeeper.

He failed, for some time: and when the truth was out, it transpired that Gorton had sent her to bed, and answered a knock at the front door himself. The woman had heard the knock—and the three shots which had followed it.

And in the armament king's head were three bullets.

The question that obsessed Loftus was: which others would die?

Chapter 15

Operation B

'**P**reposterous,' said the Home Secretary.
'Absurd!' said the Minister of Defence.
'Fantastic,' said the Minister of Labour.
'Quite beyond reason,' opined the First Lord.
'What kind of evidence is there?' asked the Rt. Hon. Jonathan Bryce-Scott, the Foreign Secretary.

'Very little,' admitted Wishart. The Premier's face looked drawn, his eyes lack-lustre. He was not yet sixty but he seemed to bear a burden far greater than his years could carry. 'But the very suggestion is frightening, gentlemen.'

'My dear Prime Minister,' boomed Sir Oscar Willingham, Minister of Transport, 'Craigie has raised a mare's nest this time,' Big, bluff and genial, Willingham shook a large forefinger. 'Man can't always be right, after all. Er—is there anything we can do?'

'We can have all thickly-populated areas watched,' said Wishart, 'and of course that is being done.'

'If the public gets this idea'—Bryce-Scott's downright manner made him the least popular man in the Cabinet, but did not affect his efficiency—'it will cause a lot of trouble. I …'

'I have made the necessary approach to the press,' Wishart assured him. 'Well, gentlemen, we can only hope that this is a grotesque blunder, but I shall be happier after midnight. For the moment, however, there is another thing. Just as important, in its way.' Wishart was right below par, thought Bryce-Scott who liked and pitied the Premier. 'Despite German denials, official confirmation comes from Lagrade of troop concentrations on the Lagra frontiers. The latest figures are ...'

As Wishart went on, the minds of twenty-two Ministers of State left home affairs for foreign ones—and things happened up and down the country.

The Errols found no trace of Myra, Rogerson or Nebton on the Isle of Wight, and the police could not assist them.

The remaining six men mentioned by Anson steadfastly refused to admit that they knew anything about the coming conference, even when the question was put to them officially.

Anson hovered between life and death.

Neil Clarke did not appear at his flat during the night, nor at his office next morning.

Mr Eustace Jaffrey had broken a dinner engagement with some difficulty, and wondered whether it was worth it, until Fay arrived at his Anne's Gate house in a wine-coloured evening gown which threw her loveliness into a vivid relief that sent his doubts to the four winds.

Mr Benjamin Morely, managing director of the biggest firm of armament manufacturers in Canada, who was staying at the Lenster Hotel in Piccadilly, received a visit during the afternoon from a pert, raven-haired, frivolous-looking woman named Dora—a fact which interested Wally Davidson, who was watching the hotel very much.

Dora had been followed by a young agent named Bramley—otherwise Bimbo—to a two-roomed flat at the top of a Chelsea mansion block, and had not stirred until she had started out again for Morley's hotel. Wally went into the hotel in her wake and, without arousing her attentions, saw her enter Morley's rooms without knocking, which indicated a certain degree of familiarity. It was a three-roomed suite, and in the room next that into which Dora had disappeared, Wally found a communicating door. It was locked, and he cursed his luck: he could hear nothing.

Nevertheless, he waited hopefully.

Loftus and Carruthers spent one of the grimmest days they had ever experienced, trying to make the wounded Dodge and convalescent Kalloni talk—but they failed, although they knew most things about third degree methods on both sides of the Atlantic.

The only progress that was made was through the police, who were able to advise Craigie, late that evening, that Cornelius Rogerson had accompanied Lord Nebton-Hart on his round-the-world tour of the previous year, that he was an antiquarian of some distinction, that he was seventy-one years old, and that his past life, as far as the police could find had been blameless.

'Which is a mistake,' said Loftus to Craigie, just after eight o'clock that night. Loftus looked gaunt, and he felt dismayed, for the idea which had come to him persisted ...

He had spent some time in the streets, and the panic—called 'anxiety' in the General Plan— was obvious enough. Trains still travelled with light loads, buses were filled to overflowing, private cars were thicker than ever in London, and taxi-drivers did a roaring trade.

But the anxiety was there.

It only needed a touch to bring the panic ...

'Short of visiting the half-dozen and threatening them with violence,' said Loftus, 'we can't do a thing. Wally reports that the woman Dora left Morely at half-past four, after she'd been with him three hours, and went back to her flat.'

'Is he questioning her?'

'I told him not to—I can't imagine she'll know much. It's reasonably obvious that she's another Myra, just there for catching the fools.' Loftus spoke bitterly. 'God damn it, Gordon, we've *got* to find what's coming! In less than four hours ...'

'Easy,' Craigie protested. 'You're only guessing, remember.'

'I know, but—oh, well, Di and Carruthers are dining near Fay and Jaffrey. I think I'd better drift along and see what's happening—they're at the Éclat. Fay,' he added, with something like a smile, 'stood out for the high lights rather than the private apartment. I'll 'phone you when I come away.'

'Right,' said Craigie, and Loftus went out.

He knew that he was followed by a swarthy-faced man who in turn was followed by the enthusiastic and somewhat tubby Bimbo Bramley. Both followers stayed outside the Éclat, where Diana and Carruthers appeared to be enjoying themselves immensely, So, it seemed, were Fay and Jaffrey.

Jaffrey, virtual owner of the Jay-Grantham Company, manufacturers of heavy armaments, and managing director of one of the biggest firms of shipbuilders on the Clyde (which had recently started work on two battleships) was a handsome man of middle height, inclined to greyness. In a more subtle way than Richard C. Anson, he created the impression that the world was his own special sphere. He carried his clothes with an air: he wore a gardenia in his buttonhole, and from his lapel there dangled a monocle he rarely used. His features were just a little too regular, but his pleasant, cultured voice was often used with great effect on the political platform as well as in the few remaining saloons of Mayfair. He was interested in the theatre—as Fay was learning.

'My dear,' he assured her with a quick, charming smile, 'your talents, as I suggested last night, are wasted—entirely wasted. The stage …'

He smiled, and Fay jumped to the bait—as he expected. Her eyes widened. She said:

'The stage? *Me?* Oh, but that's nonsense!'

'I'm not flattering you, my dear Fay.' Jaffrey had taken for granted permission to use her Christian name, and Fay was wondering just when to try a gentle 'Eustace'. 'Looks, a figure, if you'll forgive me saying so, that could hardly be bettered—personality …'

It was nearly nine o'clock before Fay felt she could safely try a minor question. By then, Jaffrey had primed himself well with champagne, but he was only a little brighter about the eyes, a little more careless with his 'dears' and 'darlings'.

'It's a wonderful idea,' she admitted demurely, 'but I don't understand, I thought you were only interested in ship-building and …'

Jaffrey laughed lightly.

'That's the serious side, my pet—we needn't worry about that, tonight. The theatre …'

'I warned you,' said Fay, 'that I wanted a story from you
tonight. If I tell my editor you talked all the time about theatres, I'll be out of a job.'

'Not for long Fay, don't be foolish—and don't worry
about your editor ...'

'I must live.'

'*I'll* look after that ...'

A waiter came up and Fay shook her head slightly, for
Carruthers' benefit, to indicate that she was not progressing.
There was time, for the evening was young—but she knew
how desperately results were wanted—in time to let Loftus
and company get to work before midnight. The devil of it
was that there was no certainty that Jaffrey knew anything ...

The waiter said:

'He is waiting, sir ...'

'Oh, all right.' Jaffrey looked annoyed, but smiled at Fay.
'My secretary is on the 'phone, my dear: I'll be back in a few
minutes.'

'Don't hurry.' Fay radiated forgiveness.

Loftus, drinking alone at a bar which commanded
a good view of the dining-room, hid his face as Jaffrey
appeared and hurried to the telephone. Loftus shifted to
another convenient bar, where he could watch the man
clearly, through the glass.

He saw the man's lips widen, saw the expression of alarm
on his face—even heard the barked:

'*What?*'

Never before had Loftus been more anxious to get at
close quarters, but for the moment he could do nothing.
Jaffrey lowered his voice. He spoke for nearly a minute without pausing, and when he stepped out of the booth his face
was pale, his eyes glittering.

'Get my hat and coat, please.'

A passing attendant hurried off, and Loftus disappeared towards the cloak-room. He came out after the attendant, and saw Jaffrey put his coat on and hurry from the hotel—without a word of explanation to Fay.

He hailed a cab, and Loftus had no trouble getting another to follow.

Wally Davidson, no longer watching Dora, was in his Frazer Nash outside the Éclat, and he followed Loftus.

The first cab drew up at Jaffrey's St John's Wood home, and both men saw him hurry inside. Loftus alighted a hundred yards further down the road, and Wally drew up beside him.

'A man,' he said, 'who can leave Fay flat, is capable of anything. What happened?'

'He had a 'phone call that worried him. I—Lord, that's quick work!'

For a Rolls-Royce had suddenly pulled up outside Jaffrey's house, and they saw a servant bring three large suitcases to the car. Within three minutes of entering the house, Jaffrey was coming out again.

'Ready for a long journey,' murmured Loftus. 'I'll follow with you, Wally, but no further than the outskirts of London. He *might* make a call on the way.'

'Yes ...' As the big car passed the Frazer Nash, it went under a street lamp, and Jaffrey's face was visible. It looked deathly white, and Loftus was sure, now, that he had received inordinately bad news.

The Rolls sped through Marylebone, into Edgware Road, Park Lane, Grosvenor Place, Victoria, Sloane Square—gathering speed wherever possible. Chelsea, Fulham, Fulham Palace Road and then left, towards Putney Bridge ...

By making judicious use of traffic lights, Davidson had made reasonably certain that they were not observed. But now there was less chance of it, and he said so.

'You'd better keep on the trail,' Loftus told him. 'I'll drop off at the Southern Railway Station—it's about the last place I'll be able to get a cab.' He glanced at the dashboard clock: nearly a quarter to ten.

Just over two hours to go.

Two hours—and what?

Would his nightmare theory become reality?

Behind the Frazer Nash as it was stopped by a red light on the far side of the bridge, came a Daimler car. The curtains were drawn, a fact which Loftus noticed as it passed them. He frowned.

'Watch that Daimler, Wally …'

They were in the middle of Putney High Street. The Daimler reached the Rolls, and drew alongside it: a criminal piece of driving, in that narrow thoroughfare, if nothing worse.

Then Loftus yelled:

'*Brakes!*'

Wally jammed on foot and hand brakes together. The Frazer Nash jolted, smacking them both painfully against the windscreen. But not so painfully that they missed anything of what happened.

From the back window of the Daimler as it passed the other car, a stream of fire came, yellowish-red. The *tap-tap-tap* of machine-gun bullets followed. There was a shriek from the driver of the Rolls, loud explosions as two tyres were punctured, and then the Rolls left the roadway and crashed into a window. As it went, the Daimler, shot ahead, narrowly missing those who were rushing to the scene of the accident.

Loftus jumped from the Frazer Nash.

'After them Wally!'

Davidson let in the clutch and sped off, while Loftus ran towards the smashed Rolls. He reached it before anyone else, and wrenched open the nearside door. Jaffrey was sprawled on the seat, blood on his shoulder, face and chest.

But his eyes were open.

Loftus knew there was no hope for the man, knew that it was a matter of minutes before he went. Quietly, urgently, he demanded:

'Jaffrey—what made you rush off like this? *What do you know of the League?*'

Jaffrey licked his lips. He did not look afraid of the death that was coming, and he tried to speak.

'Mayden ... Man-sions ... Twelve—o'clock.'

'I'll be there,' Loftus assured him. 'They're going up, aren't they?'

'Yes ... Other—places. See ... see ...'

An outraged voice came from behind Loftus.

'Now then ...!'

'Shut up, you fool!' snapped Loftus, and the policeman was so startled that he obeyed. Jaffrey choked, but tried again to speak, despite his lacerated lungs.

'See ...'

He stopped. There was a rattle in his throat, and then a dreadful coughing. Loftus tried desperately to ease him, but failed. And in his anguished awareness of how close he had come to real discovery, he turned on the innocent policeman.

'You—damned—fool!' he blazed. *'You—damned—fool!'*

✤　✤　✤

'It's taken me twenty minutes to convince the Putney police,' said Loftus, in a voice Craigie hardly recognised. 'Jaffrey told me that Mayden Mansions were going up—he tried to warn me of other places, and failed. Anyhow, I'm having the Mansions searched—the basements, of course. No, not another word. Gordon—I'm afraid it looks as though I was right.'

'I'll get at the others at once,' Craigie said quietly.

'I don't see that I'll do much good here,' Loftus added. 'I'd better—just a moment ...'

He was in the police-station at Putney, and a man had just rushed in, carrying an attache case.

'Explosives! Enough *to* ... ' he was almost shouting.

'Right!' snapped Loftus, and told Craigie: 'Yes, they've found it here. I'll try McKenzie. If you could try ...'

'I'll look after the other three,' Craigie assured him.

Loftus reached the street to see one of the senior officers who had refused to believe that danger threatened the select residential block of mansion flats on Putney Hill.

'You were right, sir. I ...'

'I want a car!' snapped Loftus. 'And two men—in a hurry.'

'I'll come with you, sir—this is mine. If you'd prefer to drive—? Wright!'

A plainclothes man left a small party who were carrying cases loaded with explosives, and hurried over.

Loftus took the wheel—and fifteen minutes later, screeched to a halt outside the Kensington home of Mr Andrew McKenzie, Scotland's biggest shipbuilder and an armaments manufacturer of renown. Leaving the engine running, he jumped out and took the front steps in two strides. He waited only twenty seconds after his first ring, then thundered on the door.

The footman who opened it looked outraged.

'Did you …?'

'Is Mr McKenzie in?' Loftus demanded.

'Mr McKenzie is not at home,' said the man, superciliously.

'Which room?'

'Really, sir …!'

'Which room?' roared Loftus, and took a gun from his pocket. The man gaped, swallowed hard and pointed a trembling finger towards the stairs.

'The—the first …'

'Lead the way—*and hurry!'*

The footman needed no second bidding. On the spacious landing he gestured towards a door—and backed away as Loftus threw it open and strode in.

In that moment Loftus was enough to frighten most men, and McKenzie's slate-grey eyes showed real alarm. A plump, dowdy-looking woman seated with him looked equally startled.

'What's the meaning of this?' the Scotsman began, sharply. 'Who …?'

'Jaffrey's just been shot to pieces,' Loftus told him, brutally. 'He told me that Mayden Mansions was to be blown up, and tried to say more. He died too soon. What do you know, McKenzie? Of that—and of the League …'

McKenzie was staring at him blankly.

Loftus could not be sure whether the bafflement was genuine, but he was grimly determined to find out—and McKenzie clearly knew he was in earnest. But before the Scot could speak, there came a roar …

It shattered the windows of the room and sent pictures thudding to the floor; it made McKenzie stagger and his wife shriek—and then another explosion came. And another …

And Loftus knew that they had started before midnight, and his soul was sick.

CHAPTER 16
PANIC!

O peration B was in action.

If Loftus had any lingering doubts, a second series of explosions—coming from further away and before the rumbles of the first had properly ceased—confirmed it.

McKenzie and his wife stared at the big man: the woman in fright, McKenzie with an expression impossible to read.

Most of the glass had fallen outwards and some was still falling. When some fell into the room, just behind her, Mrs McKenzie screamed—and then, with complete suddenness, she crumpled up. As her husband went down on his knees at her side, the Putney policeman came through the door. The Inspector strode to the broken windows and looked towards Chelsea.

Across the roof-tops, a lurid red glow was widening, getting brighter …

Fire!

Loftus said:

'Mr McKenzie, there is a state of emergency in London, and because of it I must ask you not to move from here until I give you permission. I've asked for information about the League—the League of the Hundred-and-One, and anything you know might well be indicated to Inspector … '

'Morgan,' the policeman supplied.

'Morgan, of the Putney C.I.D.'

McKenzie, raising his wife with the plainclothes man's help, nodded but did not speak.

Loftus reached the door as yet another explosion shook the walls with convulsive fury. He could see flames reflected on broken glass in the windows opposite, leaping skywards from somewhere in Chelsea.

The second explosion had been in the Marylebone direction.

The third, as far as he could judge, from the west: probably the far side of Lambeth.

Men, women, and children, at least half in night-attire, were now crowding the streets. A red glow illuminated their upturned faces, and he caught the word 'bombs'. He saw fear—and the beginning of panic ...

His own heart seemed frozen with the horror of it all: the nightmare come true.

He brushed broken glass from the car seat, and climbed in. Grimly, he noted that the crowd—those of its members who were fully clad—was moving, now, in the Chelsea direction. At every door, people were talking: some in dressing-gowns, some simply in pyjamas or nightgowns. He could hear the hum of voices—*frightened* voices—on every side. And over all, came the strident jingling of bells, as London fire-engines rushed to the scenes of disaster.

In four directions, now, the red glow spread over the star-spangled skies.

And all he could do was to see Craigie ...

He let in the clutch savagely—then stopped as the plain-clothes man came running out of the house.

'Sir—a Mr Craigie—rang through—' he panted.

'Yes?' Loftus snapped.

'You're to go to—Effley Mansions Fulham ...'

The engine roared.

'Anything more?'

'He's not sure—of the timing.'

'Right!' Loftus, surveying the ever-growing crowds, hesitated a moment; then turned the car and made for Fulham by a roundabout route which avoided Chelsea. He had to go along the Fulham Road for half a mile, and there the crowds were thicker than ever.

Special constables, A.R.P. units and volunteers were keeping them back, leaving just enough room for two-way traffic. Fire-engines still clanged their way from every side, towards the Chelsea outbreak—and now blackened fragments were falling thick and fast. Even here, the heat was intolerable.

Every street was the same.

Every house had its anxious group standing outside—talking, gesticulating, looking towards the fire. Here and there, women who had fainted were being attended at the roadside. Children cried and whimpered, instinctively sensing the fear all around them.

Panic.

Across Stamford Bridge, by the Chelsea Football Ground, a dense crowd was moving towards him. The explosions must have taken place somewhere in the Lots Road direction.

He was forced to slow down, and heard a man say:

'Beasley Flats, that's where it is ...'

'Where're they?'

'Y'know, where old Tom lives ...'

A working-class district, this time, Loftus noted. And noted, also, an angry undercurrent growing in the general hum.

The sound of people realising their fear.

Effley Mansions ...

Effley Road was near the Fulham Football ground and before he reached it, he saw the towering blocks of recently-built, low rent flats. Turning the corner, he saw people streaming from the various exits and as he drew up, he was glad to see Superintendent Miller hurrying from his own car.

'*Miller!*' he shouted, and jumped out. 'What is it?' he asked, joining him.

'We found a note at Gorton's place—there's one due here between eleven and twelve.'

'Got many men?'

'As many as we could find. I'm just going in.'

Loftus glanced at his watch. Eleven o'clock, exactly.

'Just emptying the place, or searching?'

'Both—will you tackle the top floor with me?'

'Yes. I'll take the left wing—you take the right.'

Neither man spoke of it, as they pushed their way through, yet both recognised the risk—knew what it would mean to be on the top floor of that building if it went up. But to get every family out was essential, and Loftus was appalled by the handful of police.

'There're a hundred alarms,' Miller explained grimly. 'Took us right by surprise—we were watching the power stations and services—God, there's a man somewhere whose neck I'd like to wring!'

'We will, before it's over. Here, you—and you ...' Loftus shouted to a group of men standing nearby. 'Get inside will you and lend a hand!'

'Not bloomin' likely!' one retorted. 'What d'you take me for?'

'I wouldn't like to say,' Loftus rasped.

But three men came from the group, and after a short: 'It's damned risky,' Miller gave them orders. They nodded understanding, and went at once to join the party searching the cellars and low flats for explosives.

There were no lifts.

Loftus raced up the left staircase—and on the tenth floor, saw an elderly woman in a bath-chair being wheeled down a passage by a boy no more than thirteen. He drew a deep breath.

'I'll carry you, Mother—' he offered, and his smile eased some of the fear in her eyes. Half-way down the stairs others took her from his grasp and he hurried up again. He went through the flats at speed—finding, incredibly, some couples still lying fast asleep, others awake but scared and inactive. He hustled them down, and when he had emptied the top floor, went to the one below.

He was wringing with perspiration.

He stripped his coat off—his waistcoat—his shirt …

From time to time, he shot a swift glance at his watch. At any moment, the explosion might come …

No, it was twenty to twelve.

Within twenty minutes, at most then …

Fifteen …

On the next floor down, he stumbled across Miller, who was carrying a paralysed child.

'Another five minutes,' Miller said, 'and they'll be all out. Don't stay a minute longer.'

'Right. Thirsty?'

Miller found a smile.

'Damn you, doesn't anything worry …'

But Loftus was already back with the work of rescue. At ten minutes to twelve, he was on the ground floor again and knew the place was empty. He saw the cordon of police well back along the road, saw furniture and personal effects strewn about the pavements—belongings the tenants had taken with them, but been forced to relinquish.

Ten short minutes …

Were the people far enough away?

His head was aching and his limbs seemed like lead, as he ran, stumbling, to where the crowds were still being pushed back by police and volunteers. A few stragglers were just ahead of him, including Miller.

'Zero hour,' Loftus said, as he caught up.

'Yes. Any second. I've done my damnedest to get the neighbourhood evacuated—but look at the bloody fools!' Miller glared at the crowds, who seemed unable to comprehend the danger.

'I've sent for some loud-speakers, but they'll never get through this lot,' he added. 'Daren't use the radio—it would put the whole country in panic.'

Loftus nodded, too spent for comment. His eyes felt filled with sand, and he could hardly put one foot in front of the other. But the explosion had not come when he reached the police cordon just as loud-speakers somewhere towards the back of the crowd began to raise the alarm.

'Everyone must clear the area at once. There is every danger that Effley Mansions will be blown up. Get back! …!'

There was an audible gasp from the crowd.

The effect of the words, repeated time and again, was instantaneous. Loftus saw the mass of white faces turn away, heard the roar as the crowd surged forward, and saw what amounted to a stampede.

And there was nothing—nothing!—he could do.

Screaming, shouting, crying, fighting, the crowd surged forward along the street towards a main road already jammed with people evacuated from other streets. It would be impossible to confine the effects of the explosion, and the huge Effley Mansions building, ten stories high, housing nearly two thousand people, would crush a thousand surrounding houses ...

It was small consolation to realise that it could have been worse: that on the river side, at least there would be little damage. On ... on ... on ...

The crowd has passed from Effley Road, leaving a dreadful trail. A dozen women, two or three men, and perhaps twenty children had been left behind, trampled and wounded. Small articles of furniture, clothing of all kinds, boots, slippers—the street looked as if it had been swept by a hurricane.

With Miller and a dozen other policemen Loftus set about carrying to safety those of the helpless who were alive: at least five were already dead.

He reached the main road carrying an unconscious woman across one shoulder, two screaming children over the other: both kicking, struggling, panic-stricken.

He turned the corner.

He saw Miller and the other men, similarly burdened—and then *felt* the earth trembling beneath his feet: *knew* it had started. He dropped to his knees, and somehow managed to keep the youngsters with their faces to the ground. His right arm was holding the unconscious woman down, his left was forcing the children close to the pavement. His own head was hunched into his shoulders.

It came.

A flash of light that blinded him and made his head spin. A whine, as of a high wind. A *boom* that seemed to shatter his ear-drums. And a blast that lifted all four of them bodily and dropped them again like rag dolls.

A fourth—a fifth—a sixth ...

And mingling with the roaring of the explosions, was the thunder of falling walls and debris. More wind came, screeching and whining. There were crashes like the constant smashing of guns, glass crashed all about him from the windows of the evacuated houses, as they began to topple, to crumple up.

Fire lit the heavens.

The roaring of flames and the rumbling of falling masonry added to the din. It was like being caught in some monstrous thunderstorm.

Something crashed, close to Loftus. So close that he thought it was *finis*. Dirt and fragments of stone and plaster showered over him, and his cheeks were suddenly damp. The woman went very still. A scream from one of the children was cut short, but the other still whimpered.

His head cleared a little, and he dared to lift it. The wind had ceased, but the continual noise had not, and although every street lamp had been extinguished, the glow from the fire of what had once been Effley Mansions showed everything in a lurid yellow glare—a nightmare of devastation laid bare by a light which seemed to come from hell itself.

Houses in ruins all around—with a few standing freakishly intact.

Roofs ripped off.

Gaping holes in walls that sagged.

Deep craters in the roadway.

Lamp-standards crashing, or swaying perilously.

A constant rumble as more walls collapsed and more roofs fell after them.

And now there were people running wildly to and fro; others simply standing, staring helplessly towards the fire. Loftus looked at the woman—and swallowed hard.

A piece of masonry had crushed her head and shoulders. The 'damp' on his cheeks was her blood. He did not stop to marvel, then, that he had escaped almost unscathed. Dully, instinctively, he made sure that the unconscious child was not badly hurt and the other unharmed. Then he staggered to his feet, and with both in his arms, walked on.

Past falling houses and tumbling walls.

Past water-spouts from broken mains shooting hundreds of feet into the air. Through a pungent smell of escaping gas. Past a hundred smaller fires already started.

And yet there was no unreality about it for Loftus; no feeling that it could not be. He had lived with the fear of this for days ...

Not until he was half a mile away did people meet him, take the children from his arms, lead him into a house which was windowless but otherwise unaffected by the explosions. He felt water at his lips, coolness at his forehead, his cheeks. He did not know that he was talking wildly, on the borders of unconsciousness; did not know how long he rested there, nor how often Diana's name was on his lips.

The first thing he really understood was Diana's voice, cool and detached yet with a fierce undercurrent of passion which he recognised before either of the other factors.

'Come along, Bill—it's all over. All over ...'

He opened his eyes, which ached abominably, saw her face blurred and yet unmistakable, and put a hand on her hair—for she was on her knees and very close to him.

'I wish—it was,' he said with an effort. 'Just—started ... I'm afraid. Chin up —America.'

And then, even to his dulled ears, came the ominous roar of another explosion, distant but unmistabable—telling a tale that Loftus could picture with dreadful vividness.

It was not over—it was *starting*.

CHAPTER 17
GRIM MORNING

A doctor—bandages—and sleep.
Deep and intense, although short-lived.

Loftus seemed to be coming from a deep well, seemed to hear waters swirling in his ears. His eyes were leaden, and when he opened them, his vision wavered erratically. It cleared at last and he struggled to a sitting position. Vague figures materialised.

He saw Craigie, sitting dozing in one chair; Diana leaning back in another, fast asleep. Wally and Carruthers. Two faces which looked like one.

The Errols.

That did not make sense: they were in the Isle of Wight.

Mark Errol was sitting at a table, pouring out coffee. That humdrum sight did more to revive Loftus than anything else—and the coffee itself helped even more. Yet it was ten minutes before he could talk, and even then his tongue was like a rasp and his head thumping, his eyes still blurring.

'Hallo, folk—who called the party?'

'He's obviously no crazier than usual,' said Mark Errol. 'More coffee, William?'

'Thanks. Don't wake Di, drat you.'

'Nothing would, at the moment,' grinned Mike. As his cousin poured coffee, he explained that the house was virtually a field-dressing-station for those not sufficiently hurt to need hospital care.

The ease with which the Errols had fallen into the spirit of Department Z pleased Loftus, and for the first twenty minutes the gravity of the situation was less apparent to him than it might have been. For one thing, he was fighting against letting it get too deep a hold on him. He knew from past experience that if he let himself go—as, for instance, when he had rushed to McKenzie's house—he would be less effective in the long run. A quip, an apparently carefree smile—those things were far, far better than emotion;

'Is there a bathroom?' he asked.

The Errols said there was a bathroom; it was being used by nurses. But there was a W.C. and a bucket of water waiting for him ...

Loftus doused his head and wished he could shave. But with a cigarette between his lips and his eyes feeling more normal, he re-entered the room in better shape. Craigie was awake, now, and already assembling his inevitable pipe.

Through the broken windows Loftus saw a queue, mostly women and children, waiting for attention. Some had minor injuries so far not attended: others had rough, dirty bandages. The women had one thing in common—an expression of despairing resignation.

Inside the small house, four nurses were hard at work: it was nearly half-past eight and they had been there over eight hours. Loftus learned that a hundred nearby houses had been turned into similar emergency dressing-stations; that the hospitals were full to overflowing. He did not ask what else was happening.

He knew ...

He could envisage all too easily the collection from shattered streets of the bodies of the dead, the weary firemen battling the endless flames, the vast stretches of London cordoned off, too dangerous for occupation. He needed no telling of the fear that so many would feel—the fear of illness, through broken sewers and the breakdown of sanitary arrangements.

Craigie was stolidly stuffing his pipe.

Diana still slept: She had been playing nurses, Wally told him, until she had dropped asleep on her feet some two hours before. Fay was somewhere in Kensington, doing similar work.

'How many?' Loftus made himself ask, at last.

'Seventeen,' said Craigie. 'We stopped three—the Mayden place, one at Hampstead, and another at Lambeth. The last two more by luck—after the Mayden business we started searches in all big modern blocks and tenement buildings. But of course there wasn't time to get round them all. We learned of the Effley Mansions job from some papers at Gorton's house, but no particulars of where the explosive was hidden …'

'Miller's lot searched pretty thoroughly, he tells me.' Wally Davidson for once had an excuse for looking tired, but in fact seemed wide awake.

Loftus nodded, grim-faced. 'Well, it can't be undone. Casualties?'

'At least ten thousand,' Craigie told him. 'And at least a thousand dead.'

'*God!*'

'Emergency measures are in operation,' Craigie added, bleakly. 'The more thickly-populated areas are being evacuated, as in time of war. It's the only thing we dare do—panic would get the upper hand, otherwise. At least the A.R.P. training has helped a little.'

Loftus nodded again, then glanced towards the Errols. 'Why have they come back?'

'All right, go on!' Craigie smiled, drily, and Mike shrugged.

'We had a spot of bother on the island, William—we located sweet Myra, but she managed to put one across Mark ...'

'You damned liar,' said Mark bitterly. 'It was you ...'

'Not just now,' Loftus stopped him. 'Myra could put one over most people. Was Nebton there?'

'I'm not sure. Rogerson was, and another man—we didn't recognise him. The three got away in a 'plane near Ryde. We came after them, but lost them over Hampshire somewhere—they had the edge on us for speed. Se we came back ...'

'Find anything on the island?'

'We told the police to go through the house we located,' said Mike. 'But we haven't had word yet—telephone communication is pretty difficult. Thank God the radio's working, and Broadcasting House didn't get any presents.'

'H'mm. What about you and the Daimler, Wally?'

'It lost me,' said Davidson, shortly.

'Pity. Any idea who it is, Gordon?'

Craigie shook his head slowly.

'No, Bill; nothing definite. Nebton might be in it, and the other armament men, but it's impossible to believe that it's not being engineered from abroad. The public mood ranges from inertia to anger. So does the Government's, for that matter. Half the Cabinet wants an immediate air attack on Germany and Italy. They're busy getting reassurances from Rome and Berlin,' he added, bitterly. 'But it's up to the House—it's meeting now, and there'll be an announcement about midday. Whoever's behind it, comes later—our problem is: what's next?'

They were all silent for some minutes; thinking hard, trying to get order out of chaos.

The facts were unanswerable.

The series of explosions, all aimed at places where the population was thickest, had created a state of national emergency. With justification. But there was no one to fight, no one definitely to guard against. If, as seemed possible, it was being controlled by enemy powers still talking glibly of friendship and 'misunderstanding', there was proof to be found. But could they get it in time to take steps to counteract the devastating blows already delivered against the most vital item of defence—the *morale* of the general public?

'All we've got,' Loftus murmured at last, 'is Nebton, Rogerson and Myra—definite. Anson, possible. Ditto, Morely, McKenzie, Lore, Frazer-Campbell and Tiarney. Gorton's murder as well as Jaffrey's reasonably proves they were implicated some way or the other, and the inference must be that the others are in the same boat. Do you know where they are?'

'All we know,' said Craigie, 'is that each man is being watched. We ought to have reports in as soon as we can get the telephone service in working order again. You've missed two things, Bill: Dora and Letty, for what they're worth.'

Loftus grimaced. 'Cyphers. We've also got ninety-odd members of the League so far unaccounted for.'

'They're not identified,' Craigie pointed out. 'Meantime, every known residence of the possibles is being searched, right now—our fellows and Miller's are busy. That's all we *can* do!' Craigie looked very, very old—and Loftus knew that this thing was different from anything else he had ever tried to tackle.

It was no longer solely the work of the Department, for one thing.

But more important, it had reached this stage without any effective counter being made. In most of those tasks which had confronted the Department in the past, Loftus and his men had been able to get the other side on the run before damage of this magnitude could be contrived. The opposition had been well-known—but now?

Korrel, Jaffrey and Gorton, all possibles, had been ruthlessly murdered—obviously to prevent them from talking. For all Loftus knew, the others might have escaped their followers. Even if they had not, there was no evidence to *prove* that they were members of the League.

'How's Anson?' he asked, suddenly.

'He was "as well as could be expected", the last time I heard,' said Craigie, 'and he seems our most likely contact. I'm going to get you to talk to him, Bill. Dangerous to him or not, he's got to talk.'

'Yes … And I can try Dodge and Kalloni again.'

Craigie shook his head.

'Kalloni was taken from Cannon Street last night—the only two men left on duty there were murdered. Dodge has committed suicide.'

Loftus said sharply:

'How well is Anson being guarded?'

'With a detachment of the 9th London Regiment,' said Craigie, drily. 'We're taking no chances, Bill. Well, can you move?'

'I can try. Where's Fay, by the way?'

'Working at Kensington.'

'We'll need her,' said Loftus. 'And we need Diana, too, but she'd better have her sleep out. Wally, will you stay around and bring her to the office as soon as she's fit?'

'Y'know,' said Wally, ingenuously, 'the Errols need more sleep than I do.'

'That's why you're here—to keep awake.' Loftus gave a tired grin. 'The Errols can have two or three hours' sleep, if they're lucky. Same to you, Carrie, after you've escorted us to Whitehall.' He tried to introduce a note of levity, but it was not a conspicuous success, and he stopped trying entirely when he went outside, for the chaos was appalling.

Hardly a ten-yard stretch of road was free from bricks or damage of some kind, and houses without broken windows, from Fulham to Whitehall, were few and far between. The explosions, Craigie explained, had been concentrated on three areas—south-west London, including Chelsea, Fulham, Kensington, Battersea and Wandsworth. A south-eastern area, starting at Lambeth, and one in the north-west—stretching as far apart as Hampstead and Wembley. Central London had hardly been touched, and the extreme suburbs in the south and south-west had also escaped.

For the time being …

Their car stopped after its slow, grim journey. Police and troops were as thick as bees about Parliament Street, the House, Westminster Bridge, Whitehall and Scotland Yard. Arrangements were already being made for the removal of vital papers to previously prepared underground offices, and the Government was to move a motion of adjournment until the next day, when it would meet again in Oxford.

But before then, the big decision had to be made.

Should this be treated as an hostile act by one—or more—admittedly antagonistic Powers?

Or was it internal?

Loftus leaned to the opinion that it was war—without a declaration and begun with a cunning which could never be surpassed. It had the ring of dictatorship about it—the policy of invading small, helpless countries under the threat of force, aiming at those who were defenceless, in this case the people.

It was damnably clever …

It …

Loftus, climbing out of the car, stopped as a piece of paper fluttered past his face. Craigie felt one touch his hand. The Errols grabbed simultaneously at one falling between them, and Carruthers was the first to see that they were falling like leaves from a clear, blue sky.

High up, aeroplanes glinted in the sun.

'What the devil …!' said Loftus.

'*My God!*' Mike Errol was reading his copy.

As the others followed his example, every mouth set tightly and every eye was steely hard.

For the leaflets said:

THIS IS THE BEGINNING

WE have constantly tried to persuade the Government to change its policy.

Hitherto we have failed.

Force is the only pressure it will understand. WE are applying that force. WE are determined that the democratic form of government in this country is at an end. WE have the interest of the country at heart.

WE SHALL DELIVER AN ULTIMATUM TODAY.

The Government's rejection of it will be followed by stronger measures than those yet used. WE can paralyse every city of consequence within forty-eight hours.

TEN MILLION OF THESE LEAFLETS WILL BE
DISTRIBUTED
TODAY—AT SEVEN O'CLOCK
TONIGHT
OUR ULTIMATUM WILL BE BROADCAST

Craigie dropped the leaflet like a man who had been stung. Carruthers and the Errols stood motionless. Loftus stared towards Parliament Square, where police, troops, territorial reinforcements, and civilians alike were grabbing at the leaflets, reading them wild-eyed.

And at that moment, the same thing was happening throughout London and the big provincial cities.

Mr Cornelius Rogerson, who looked so much older than his seventy-one years, was leaning back in an easy chair and smiling. Opposite him were three men—men who had once met at a houseboat in Maidenhead.

'Well, gentlemen,' Rogerson was saying, almost genially, 'I think we can claim considerable success. Efforts to block our campaign have, of course, failed completely. Most satisfactory!'

As he rubbed his hands together in glee, his lined and wrinkled face was like a dried Egyptian mummy's, his eyes almost buried beneath the criss-cross lined, parchment-like skin.

The short man, who at Maidenhead had been the spokesman, cleared his throat.

'We're doing well, yes. But there have been—tcha!—three efforts prevented, more by luck than judgment. Jaffrey's disaffection was the chief cause. He will do no more damage.' Rogerson cackled, and the sound was obscene. 'Nor will Gorton—I have always wanted to see the end of Gorton—he was so easily frightened.'

The florid-faced man whose nerves were not too steady swallowed a lump in his throat.

'It—it's been successful, but—will the—the people stand for it? The—the Government ...'

'The Government!' Rogerson's contempt was unmistakable. 'It has virtually ceased to exist! Wishart looks likely to die at any moment. The others—pouf! Are *you* frightened, my friend?'

'No, no!' the florid man blustered. 'I'm with you, always have been! But a mistake now ...'

'There need be no mistakes.' Rogerson cackled again. 'You will see—it will prove easy. Understand that I have planned this for years—*years,* not months. The fools of public! Democracy—the Constitution—these outworn shibboleths! Cattle, that's all—cattle! And *they* elect the Government!' His voice became more powerful and resonant, lost its querulous note. 'Understand, the emergency Government has been formed, and will operate immediately after the collapse at Westminster. The League—*our* League ...'

Rogerson licked his colourless lips in evil satisfaction.

'They *thought* they had caught some of us. We gave our workmen numbers, and they thought ...'

The short man said sharply:

'Korrel was a member! Jaffrey—Gorton ...'

'They were all fools. Pah, fools! Are we weakened by their loss? No—a thousand times no! We are strengthened, my

171

friends: strengthened a hundred times! But enough of that. I have news—news of first-class importance. The Italian and German Governments have promised us all the support we may need. The League undertakes immediately on assuming power to cancel the bi-lateral agreements with Poland, Greece, Rumania and the others, and on the assumption of control by the League, we shall give our allegiance to the Rome-Berlin Axis, and the anti-Comintern pact.'

The short man stirred uneasily.

'You will never get the Army, Navy, the Air Force ...'

'Tcha! We don't need them. We can render them useless! We have forces ready to assume control of all armament factories and store-houses. I have forgotten nothing! And remember—remember!' cackled Rogerson: 'before Wishart resigns and the Government breaks up, they will issue orders to the Fighting and Civil forces to accept the government of the League. *Our* government—the League's government—can't you see? Every member of the League will benefit a thousand times! Every one of us stands to lose most of his fortune, his influence, in the event of war. I, alone, have a million pounds in Germany. Will it be handed back to me if Great Britain goes to war, or remains hostile to the Führer? No! Nor will your German and Italian, your Spanish and Hungarian commitments. Remember how much you will lose if these fools continue with their enmity to the totalitarian states. Remember that once we have joined the anti-Comintern pact, that danger disappears! With Great Britain, it cannot fail. Russia—the smaller countries—then America. And then,' Cornelius Rogerson hunched his shoulders and looked craftily from one man to the other—'*then* will be the time for this country to usurp the power of Rome and Berlin. *After* they have served us! It will be easy, so very easy. The League will control *the world!*'

Rogerson stopped abruptly, and glanced at his watch.

'Seven—seven o'clock, wasn't it? You will read the ultimatum, my friend.' He indicated the short man, who saw that it wanted ten minutes to the hour.

A voice from Rome said:

'*Are you sure? Would it not be wiser to strike now?*'

A voice from Berlin said:

'*Wait! Wait until they have control in England—then we can move.*'

'*You are sure they will get control?*'

'*I am sure.*'

'*Your arrangements are made?*'

'*I can land a quarter of a million men in twelve hours.*'

'*I will wait,*' said the voice from Rome.

Simultaneously, two receivers were replaced and the speakers sat back, brooding yet satisfied.

'Obviously,' Bill Loftus was saying, 'the ultimatum will be broadcast, so we'll find where it comes from by tracing the transmitting station—that's all been arranged.'

'*Every* available man is waiting for seven o'clock.' Craigie shrugged dispiritedly. 'But what can we do? I have never felt defeatist before, but this time …!'

Loftus pursed his lips.

'We can keep trying, Gordon. God knows there isn't much chance of getting through in time, but odd things happen. At least we've breathing space.'

'Yes …'

The Government had been persuaded—correctly—that there was no direct intervention from Foreign Powers. It had decided that the disturbance was internal, and had expressed—through Jonathan Bryce-Scott, speaking for the Prime Minister—the Government's view that the revolt, if it could be given so high-sounding a term, would be over within twenty-four hours. The Government, Bryce-Scott had said so convincingly that at least half his listeners believed it, knew exactly when and where to find the perpetrators of the outrages.

And the House had adjourned.

Lord Dryton had made a similar statement to the House of Lords, with similar effect. The Lords, too, had adjourned ...

The newspapers brought out special editions with two-inch headlines, reiterating the Government's complete control, and the radio blazed forth statements that there need be no alarm ...

And the country waited for seven o'clock.

Craigie, Loftus and the others remained in Craigie's office. No word had come from the agents who had followed the men named by Anson—and it was beginning to look as though they had been prevented from sending information. The Cabinet, meeting in secret and not at Number 10, waited for the ultimatum with almost equal despondency.

Both the Cabinet and Craigie's men *knew* that their bluff would be called, and they could take no decisive steps—unless the transmitting station was located in time.

Tension, awful and unbearable, increased as the seconds ticked by.

CHAPTER 18
ULTIMATUM

The effort to follow the 'planes which had dropped the leaflets over England failed, for the 'planes used had been faster than any of the squadrons sent up belatedly in pursuit. The state of mind of the public would be better estimated after seven o'clock, but Loftus and Craigie had faith in the steadiness of the people. If this was an attempt at invasion, the people were likely to rally strongly behind the Government.

But it was an interval of fear and apprehension.

Of dread …

At one minute to seven, Craigie began to twirl the wave-length control of the set in his office. The British stations, except one in Scotland, had closed down at six-fifty-five, 'to enable listeners to hear an announcement of general interest.' Nothing, it seemed, could perturb the equaunimity of the B.B.C. announcers.

Seven o'clock …

Ten seconds past …

Craigie got the station at last, picking up a slow, measured voice using perfect English. Loftus wondered for a moment whether he should be with one of the vans trying to locate the 'pirate' station. But now he listened, fascinated by that steady voice with its outrageous demands—a pistol being held to the head of the British Government with a matter-of-factness quite as disconcerting as the B.B.C. announcer's aplomb.

'I will repeat that. The League which has been instituted to replace the present Government of this country has only the good of the nation at heart. The British Government has for years possessed the powers of a dictator: the so-called democratic constitution has for a long time been a thing of the past.'

There was a pause. Then, emotionlessly, the voice went on:

'The League will continue to operate all civil and military services, but will completely eradicate the wastage, the muddle and the hypocrisy which has been typical of the present Government.

'The Government will signify its acceptance of the authority of the League by a unanimous vote in the House of Commons—and must sit at Westminster and *not* at Oxford, as arranged. Representatives of the League will take over, and for the present, will govern the country from unspecified headquarters.

'Let there be no misunderstanding.

'Owing to the stubbornness of the present Government, it was necessary to reveal the strength of the League. But the incidents of last night were mild in comparison with others which can occur—and *will* occur—unless the national Government and the people of Great Britain accept without conditions the change of constitution, and the control of the country by the League.

'This statement will be broadcast again at nine o'clock and eleven o'clock.

'The House will meet by noon tomorrow. Or else ...'

The voice stopped. There was a hush in Craigie's office, until Loftus drew a deep breath, easing the tension.

In millions of private homes, in thousands of cafés and cinemas throughout the land, the quiet, unemotional voice of the man who had made that audacious statement had been heard. In millions of hearts, there was a contraction of fear—a dread of what might come. The tension which had broken in Craigie's office lasted longer almost everywhere else.

Political meetings had been called to listen to that message.

Officials of all parties had heard it—and their reaction was in all cases the same. For the first time for fifty years there was not a voice raised against the ruling Government of Great Britain. From the extreme right to the extreme left, leaders and party members were united.

The man in the street, afraid though he might be, on the verge of a panic which had threatened to engulf the country, felt the same surge of indignation, the same spirit of outrage and defiance.

They were being *told* what to do …

Dictatorship—*here!*

There was a change over the face of the country, a change Loftus had hoped for, even prayed for—yet had hardly expected to see in so sweeping a fashion. Within an hour, it was obvious which way the tide was going. The Militia, of course, was already at full strength. The Territorial Army, far short of the million men appealed for, months before, had a rush of volunteers unrivalled even by the rush during the early days of the First World War.

Thousands besieged recruiting offices, A.R.P. and National Defence headquarters ...

The news trickled through to Craigie and Loftus: to the Cabinet; to other officials. The ultimatum had hardened the spirit of the British people as nothing else could have done. The threat of force had to be resisted, would be resisted, was being resisted. The Territorial and the Regular Armies would, at that rate of increase, pass the million total before the day was out. Other services, more than fully-manned, would have no need to appeal for personnel.

But ...

There was nothing for the Army to fight. Nor the Navy. Nor the Air Force.

There was no knowing whether the next attack would come from the air, or from the ground.

The only information that did come through was from Post Office radio officials, concerning the location of the 'pirate' transmission station.

The ultimatum had been broadcast from an aeroplane flying over the Channel.

'Anti-climax,' murmured Loftus, with a wry grimace. 'Our friends of the League have their wits about them. It'll be interesting to see who are with them.'

'Interesting!' snorted Mike Errol.

'The new recruits getting out of hand again,' Loftus said lightly. 'Everything considered, we can call ourselves lucky, my friend. By the time you've finished, you'll probably wish you'd never heard of Department Z.'

'Here—' Mark frowned in puzzlement: 'You had an idea of what would happen last night, didn't you? How come?'

'I used my thinking-cap,' Loftus grinned.

Craigie was at the telephone, waiting for a call from Berlin. One from Paris and another from Rome had already been through, but the Z men abroad had, so far, no worthwhile information.

Mark Errol was still puzzling.

'Odd, just the same. He *did* know ...'

'Forget it,' said Davidson wearily.

'Let them alone,' Loftus reproved him, genially. 'They'll wake up, one long-distant day.' His lips were smiling, but his eyes were alert. 'Here's another prophecy. The next step from our League friends is gas—and if you think that's imagination ...' He shrugged. 'Did Myra or Rogerson see you yesterday?'

'No,' said Mark, firmly.

'They might have had a glimpse of me as I jumped into the room at Bournemouth,' Mike offered. 'But it's not likely. Why?'

'I was wondering,' Loftus was frowning, now: 'whether Dora and Letty might be useful ...'

Craigie spoke quietly into the telephone, then replaced the receiver and said flatly:

'The Führer and the Duce had a personal talk at seven o'clock, or just afterwards. That might be interesting. It ...'

Another telephone rang.

Another and another.

Craigie had seven on his desk, and within three minutes Loftus, Craigie, Davidson and Carruthers were talking into one apiece. Which at least meant that certain cables damaged during the night had been repaired, and junction lines were in order again.

Agents came through one after the other, with long-awaited news.

Lord Hubert Lore had disappeared.

Frazer-Campbell and Tiarney were missing.

Dora and Benjamin Morely were in conference at Dora's flat.

Letty had been traced to the Naveling Hotel, Bloomsbury which was already being watched by Craigie's men.

'On the whole, pretty useful,' Loftus summed up, when the influx of messages was over. 'McKenzie is the only one of Anson's friends who remains at large—or more accurately, under surveillance. Are you going to have a show-down with him, Gordon?'

'He's due here at eight o'clock,' said Craigie.

'Right. Well, the next item is the Naveling: we've decided it's time it was raided. Not that we'll get anything more than the small fry, but even they'll be useful. Mike, I'm going to be unkind, and separate you from your cousin and friend ...'

'Just separate me—there's no need to apologise,' Mike assured him.

'I'll pay you for the service,' Mark offered.

'Be quiet,' said Loftus, but his own brighter spirits seemed to have infected everyone present. It was—although they could not have defined it—the fact that there had been a reprieve. 'Mike will come with the rest of us to the Naveling. We'll let Letty get out, and you'll do the Sir Galahad act, Michael. The strong silent man and these wicked police-men. She'll ask you to take her to somewhere unknown, and you'll let Craigie know, as soon as you can. Failing him, any policeman—but be sure you tell him the message must go to Miller, at Scotland Yard, at once. All clear?'

'Absolutely,' beamed Mike.

'Damn it!' protested Mark. 'What do I ...?'

'You have a far more delicate task,' said Loftus, cheerfully. 'You fall on to Dora's neck when Morely is arrested— and arrested he's going to be. All right?'

Mark smoothed his hair.

'This is getting places. Why didn't you think of it before?'

'We had to play it canny, then—but it's time for the battering-ram, now,' Loftus told him. 'We've a dozen men at Naveling—Gordon, you said we'd better have some policemen, to make it look more official?'

Craigie nodded.

'Yes, I'll 'phone Miller.' He and Loftus had worked out this new plan of attack earlier in the afternoon. But everything had been held back until after the ultimatum.

'Then,' added Loftus, 'Morely, after questioning, is released. You think Diana …?'

'She'd better try,' Craigie agreed.

'Right—I'll leave you to arrange it with her. Give her my love! Does Fay come in?'

'McKenzie?' suggested Carruthers.

Loftus grimaced doubtfully.

'Too hard-headed and hearted, I'm afraid. And a man with a wife like that probably wouldn't believe in Fay if he saw her. Still …'

'I'll arrange for Fay to meet him after he leaves here,' said Craigie. 'I can't see anything else that we can do, yet.'

'No … Right, then—Wally, you come to the Naveling with me. And you, Carrie. All fit?' He glanced at Craigie, and the chief of Department Z—who, a short while before, had looked all in—nodded. The tiredness, the near hopelessness, seemed to have dropped from him like a cloak.

The Errols secretly marvelled at the change in him. They did not know how long and how bitterly Craigie had fought to get at the League, did not realise the heart-breaking effect of months of work without results, followed by the disasters and devastation which had come.

'On with the dance, then,' Loftus announced. 'Out, knaves!'

Craigie pressed a button beneath his desk, and the sliding door opened. Loftus and the others saw the men standing outside. A dozen men in all; three of them carrying tommy-guns—and slightly ahead of them, his shoulders hunched, was Mr Andrew McKenzie.

Loftus recovered first from the shock.

'Well, well,' he said. 'You're a bit early, Mac!'

'Early for what?' snapped McKenzie.

'My dear man—you did have an appointment.'

McKenzie grinned, not pleasantly: 'I'm always early, Loftus. Get back by Craigie's desk! All of you …'

'More massacre?' murmured Loftus, 'I should be very careful, McKenzie. We …'

'Stop your blether, damn you, or … '

'Supposing I speak for him,' said Craigie, in his softest voice. 'I expected you, of course, McKenzie—but hardly like this. What can I do for you?'

'You can keep your mouth shut, for one thing!' snarled McKenzie. 'I told you all—get back! If one of you goes for his pocket, he'll be shot out of hand. I want,' he added. 'to talk to you. Craigie—first. Never mind what comes next. Now …'

He took a wary pace forward, obviously afraid of a trick. The odds seemed heavily on his side, but the activities of Department Z had a cautionary effect—too many attempts on Craigie's men had failed.

Loftus was smiling, apparently unconcerned, and Craigie seemed in complete control of himself. The Errols were more affected than Davidson or Carruthers and Wally actually contrived a convincing yawn.

'If you try—' McKenzie was advancing cautiously into the room, while the men on the far side of the sliding door moved slowly in his wake. 'If you—' he began again, warningly.

Then heard the single, united gasp from behind him, and swung round—to see the machine-guns and automatics clattering to the floor, and the rigid horror on the faces of his men.

'Simple electricity,' murmured Craigie. 'Won't you come further in?'

CHAPTER 19
MIKE AND LETTY

As the steel guns met the steel-lined floor, there were a series of sharp cracks—and one man collapsed. A moment later, the lot went down, crumpling up as though they had been shot, and Wally said easily:

'I'll leave our Scottish chum to you, Gordon—come on, Errols.'

'But—!' Mike was staring at those prostrate figures.

'The current's off,' said Craigie, drily. Loftus, too, was smiling with real humour for the first time that day.

He gripped McKenzie's arm, and found it rigid. Offhandedly, he told the Errols:

'We hoped for this, but whether friend Mac, here, is a little fish or a big one, we don't yet know. Those fellows have had enough juice to keep them quiet while you get them to a police-station.'

'Have them sent to Wandsworth,' Craigie added.

'Right …'

Dazedly, the cousins followed Carruthers and Davidson out, and as they began to move the men from the landing, the door slid to behind them.

Wally chuckled.

'Don't look so daft, you two! We knew there was a crowd outside—each man that trod on the top stair lit a red light on the mantelpiece, You don't know the half of Craigie, yet!'

'It seems not,' murmured Mark Errol. 'Oh, well …'

'I'll collect some flatfoots,' said Carruthers. 'Be seeing you.'

It had not been pleasant.

McKenzie, his collar and tie off, his shirt damp with sweat, his eyes red-rimmed and fearful, his teeth chattering, stared almost blindly at a grim-faced Loftus and a Craigie who had not turned a hair.

'Th-that's all—I swear th-that's all! …'

'Let me repeat it,' said Craigie, but at that moment Loftus put his hand in his pocket for his cigarette case. McKenzie screamed and cowered back, and Loftus told him coldly:

'Keep telling the truth and you'll have no more.'

Craigie continued:

'As far as you know, twenty-one members of the Empire Armaments Manufacturers Association are members of the League. That includes the two dead men, Jaffrey and Gorton and yourself. You're not sure about Anson?'

'No, I swear …!'

'Just say no,' said Loftus. 'Or yes, as the case may be.'

'Nor are you sure of Lord Lore, or Benjamin Morely?'

'N-no … I don't—don't think Morely is … The—the girl Dora—has been trying …'

'To get him with you,' Craigie supplied. 'Wasn't Myra Clayton trying to get Anson?'

'I—I don't know!'

Loftus was sure McKenzie was telling the truth, now; so was Craigie. It had taken half an hour to break down his resistance, and only the memory of what had happened at Effley Mansions had stiffened Loftus enough to use the refinements of persuasion it had needed.

'Nebton is also an unknown quantity?'

'Yes—yes!'

'Rogerson, as far as you know, is leading the attempt?'

'He—he's Number 101 ...'

'And you are 94?'

'Y-yes.'

'The conference of Armament Manufacturers Association has been called for the first of September—where?'

'I've told you—I don't know! It's not decided yet. But it doesn't matter—I told you! Rogerson didn't intend to let it meet, *ever.*'

'Just why was Rogerson anxious to get you—and others—working with him?'

'We—we were rich.'

' "Were" is good,' said Loftus, gently. 'But there's another reason. What is it?'

'We—some of us ...' Sweat was trickling down McKenzie's face, and for the first time he hesitated. Calmly, Loftus took his cigarette from his lips, and McKenzie shivered. 'We c-could, if necessary, d-destroy the stores of ammunitions, if the G-Government decided to f-fight ...'

'So that's it!' snapped Loftus, and Craigie's eyes gleamed.

'Yes ... You were prepared, McKenzie, to prevent the Government getting reserves of ammunition in the event of the League trying to reduce the country to a state of civil war. That's right?'

McKenzie was sweating.

'I—I had to, I ...'

'You had to make more money, somehow!' Craigie's contempt was monumental. 'Who introduced you to the movement?'

'A—a man named Korrel.'

'Hallo,' murmured Loftus. 'We're beginning to get at the bottom of it, Gordon. Korrel was a recruiting sergeant, was he? Myra, Dora and Letty are others. It makes sense.'

'Where are the headquarters?' demanded Craigie.

'I—I don't know! We met at the houseboat, once—four of us …'

'The others being?'

'I don't know their names! They would never talk! They always met at different places. I was asked to make a report on—on the condition of two cruisers I'm—I'm building for the Government. That was all! I don't know them …'

'They weren't in the Association?'

'I don't know—I'd never seen them before!'

'Where else have you met?'

'At—at the Éclat. The Regal. A little place in Bloomsbury. On Nebton's yacht, the *Callay*. At the Coventry Street Corner House, other restaurants!' The words were pouring from McKenzie now, and he was difficult to understand. 'I always had a letter to be at such a place, I always saw the same three men, reported, and then …'

'There's just one thing that doesn't fit in,' said Craigie. 'You're Number 94 of the League. You tell us that in the event of the League usurping the Government's position, you would have been in the High Council, equivalent to the present Cabinet. But—when it comes to a push, you lead a gang of cut-throats here.'

McKenzie drooped forward to Craigie's desk, his eyes almost starting from his head.

'I—I had orders! We've lost men—someone—someone had to interrogate you properly, learn what you knew …'

'Thanks,' said Craigie, drily. 'Where were you going to report?'

'I don't know. I would have been telephoned at—at my house. I …'

McKenzie saw Loftus move again—and slid from his chair, quite unconscious. Loftus lifted him, not ungently, back into the chair, and turned to Craigie.

'That's as much as we'll get, I think. Thank God we're beginning to see the light! It's a stinking business—but at least you can give orders for getting another eighteen of the swine, now.'

Craigie nodded, glancing at the notes he had made of the men McKenzie had implicated. There was a lot to do before they could strike at Rogerson and the mysterious trio McKenzie had talked about. But for the Department to get at eighteen members of the League—important members, unless McKenzie had lied—would shatter Rogerson.

The risk was, thought Loftus, that it might move him to further acts of chaos; they had to be careful. But Craigie would watch that, he knew.

'All right, Bill,' Craigie said. 'You get to the Naveling. You'll have the Errols followed, of course?'

'I will—but more with the idea of reinforcing them in emergency. They're sound enough.'

Craigie's hooded eyes twinkled.

'We *can* make mistakes.'

'You've got my resignation if the Errols turn out on the wrong side!' said Loftus, cheerfully. He looked down at the unconscious McKenzie. 'Odd how they will fall for the easiest trick, isn't it? The one place our League friends should have kept away from is this office.' He shrugged, and turned to go then added, soberly: 'Tell Di to be careful with Morely ...'

Craigie pressed the control panel and he went out. As the door closed behind him, he smiled grimly. There were exactly seven doors from the Department office, and there had—as the Errols had learned—been ample evidence of the gathering of men outside.

To see McKenzie had been a shock, and to realise there were quite so many men outside had also jolted him. If they had simply opened fire ...

He stopped smiling.

For half an hour, things had gone well. The skeleton of the thing was in their hands, and—thanks in a large measure to the ultimatum—they knew which way events were driving.

Rogerson probably imagined himself another Hitler: older, even craftier, but driven on by the same megalomania. That much seemed obvious.

But there were others behind Rogerson. Just as Hitler was 'advised' by his party leaders, so was Rogerson.

Who were the mysterious trio?

Anson? Tiarney? Frazer-Campbell? Morely? Lord Lore?

Five possibilities, in short. But the list might well be longer ...

He reached Whitehall to see the unfamiliar men in khaki patrolling it, with a smattering of policemen. Davidson and Carruthers, with the Errols, were taking the air just outside Scotland Yard, and talking with Superintendent Miller, who had made arrangements to handle the prisoners—already on their way to Wandsworth.

Four pairs of eyes regarded Loftus keenly.

'Anything?' asked Carruthers.

'Pointers, but nothing definite. McKenzie cracked, but he's not one of the Mighty Men Who Matter. His house had better be looked through, Horace,'—Miller found a smile at that—'and you can also ask how Inspector Morgan let him slip through his fingers. Will you look after it?'

'I'll deal with Morgan,' Miller assured him, and left them.

'Poor Morgan!' grinned Loftus.

His own car and the Errols' were parked nearby. They piled into both and drove quickly towards Bloomsbury, where they found that the evacuation order now being carried out in London was leaving a preponderance of men and youths in the streets, although women were reasonably plentiful, still. Little groups were gathered everywhere, and paperboys were yelling. Newstand placards mostly showed just one word:

ULTIMATUM!

The Naveling Hotel, Bloomsbury, proved to be—rarely, for that part of London—fully detached. It was not large, and it looked dowdy. In the crowded streets, it had been easy for the Department men, all youthful, to pass unnoticed. A dozen policemen had also been detailed to take part in the raid.

The Errols separated—Mark somewhat reluctantly, for he wanted to see the fun; but he had to find Morely and the little-known Dora. Young Bimbo Bramley accompanied him, and another two agents followed at a discreet distance.

Mike was curious.

'Are the police starting it, William, or ...?'

'Or,' said Loftus. 'The police stay outside to catch any strays, and I'll bring Letty. I'll let her get away, and you'll be parked fifty yards or so to the left. Act fast—but the details are up to you.'

'I will not fail us,' grinned Mike. 'Right-ho!'

They were round the corner from the front entrance of the Naveling, and he walked to his car, buying an evening newspaper as he went.

Loftus, Carruthers and Davidson led the way to the front door.

There was more than a chance of a fight, but Loftus wanted to get it over quickly. The house was surrounded at such speed that few passers-by noticed there was anything happening. Loftus rat-tatted on the door, and it was opened after a brief pause by a miserable-looking man in black.

'Who ...?'

Loftus gripped his arm, and the narrow hall was suddenly filled with muscular young men. The man in black opened his mouth—and shut it again as Loftus snapped:

'Keep quiet, or you'll get what's coming to you. How many men here?'

'There ain't—there ain't many. And they're what...'

'Women?'

The man in black looked mutinous for a moment—and Loftus clipped his ear.

'There's only Miss Letty! Mister, I din't mean no 'arm ...'

There was a sense of anti-climax about the raid, not to mention disappointment. The miserable one needed little persuasion to lead the way to the first floor room where, he said, the woman named Letty lived.

He tapped—and a pleasant voice said: 'Come in.'

Loftus opened the door.

A fluffy-haired, indubitably pretty girl was sitting in an easy chair, her legs crossed and showing plenty of silk stocking, her hands holding lightly to a picture-magazine. Her grip tightened as she jumped up, alarm in her eyes.

'What …?'

'Letty, my sweet,' said Loftus. 'I would have words with you. About many things. Put a coat on, if you want one.'

She had gone deathly pale.

'Who are …'

'Call it the police,' Loftus told her. 'I want to know all that you know about the League, my pet—and don't try throwing fits: I'm hard-hearted.'

She looked ready to faint, and it was some seconds before she recovered enough to put on a hat and coat.

Loftus wondered whether she would have the pluck to try to escape. As he led her past the men outside and below, he felt her trembling. She was pretty enough, but not up to Myra's standard. She had a figure, too, and the clothes she was wearing did little to conceal it.

They reached the street.

As Loftus had ordered, four policemen were on the right, but none on the left. He beckoned the men in blue, and at the same time eased his grip on Letty's arm.

She was away in a flash!

Two of Craigie's men essayed to catch her, but let her go—and Loftus, although running, saw Mike Errol look around in surprise, for people were shouting, and saw him open the car door. Letty drew level, hesitated …

'In a hurry?' drawled Mike. 'I'm free, darling …'

'Fast—for heaven's sake, fast!' she gasped, and Mike let in the clutch as she jumped in. Police whistles shrilled, but as he drove at speed, turning one corner—a second, a third—the echo of the whistles died away.

He looked down into Letty's pert but frightened face with a dry smile.

'What have you been up to? Cat burgling?'

'No—oh, hurry! I can't thank you enough ...'

'I wouldn't be too sure,' smiled Mike, and Loftus would have revelled in his acting, then. 'What direction? I know a nice spot for supper ...'

'Never mind that! I—oh, please!' She seemed to remember abruptly that he was a perfect stranger, and that charm was necessary. 'I—I've got to get on the Maidenhead Road quickly. I wonder if—if you would ...'

Maidenhead, thought Mike Errol grimly. The houseboat?

'As I'm free, and if you'll promise to have supper with me ...'

'I'm ...' She changed her mind suddenly, smiled, snuggled closer to him. It was not difficult to understand why Sir Jabez Gorton had found her persuasive. 'Of course, I'd love to ...'

Mike admitted aloud and to himself that he was satisfied. A fast car, with Carruthers and Davidson up, was on his heels, and he did not think they would be likely to lose him. As he went out of London, taking the Slough Road for it was likely to be clearer, his Bentley gathered speed.

Letty sat rigidly at his side, remembering him only when he forced her to. Mike Errol noticed two things: she was very frightened—and her nose-tip tilted very attractively ...

He got out of London after three-quarters of an hour, which was not bad going considering the number of pedestrians on the road. The man in the street was wondering whether the ultimatum would be backed by further demonstrations of force that night.

'Where now?' asked Mike.

'I—oh, just straight on,' she said.

He hesitated, then went on. He might have stopped for a while, for conversation, he might have demanded to know just where she wanted him to take her. But he could not reach a decision. He felt that Letty would be an ample handful, and hoped Carruthers and Davidson were close behind him.

They were not, for a careless pedestrian and a clumsy motorist combined to make them crash, and they were stranded.

As was Mike, although he did not know it.

Chapter 20
Mark Meets Dora

A colourless little man, a useful agent for work abroad because he was so easily disguised, but pressed into service in England because of the emergency, informed Mark Errol that Dora was still at her flat. Benjamin Morely had also arrived, five minutes before.

'The problem,' said the colourless little man, 'is whether it's just a case of Benjamin heading for the divorce courts, or whether the present interview is important. I've a feeling that our Benjamin was rattled when he came in.'

Mark considered.

'If he has any idea of what's happened to gentlemen of the League, and he's a member of it, he has cause to be scared. On the other hand, his wife might be proving obstreperous.'

'Yes … Going to barge in?'

'Barge?' Mark looked pained. 'Finesse, little man, is the essential in this game—or so Loftus says.'

The little man grinned.

'Oh, of course—finesse with fists. However …'

He broke off, and Mark, at the wheel of a Lagonda supplied by Loftus, saw without appearing to look at the entrance of the flats, that a short, florid man was hurrying out. He did not look happy, and he bounded into the road, lifting a hand for a passing taxi. The colourless one gestured.

'My job,' he murmured. 'Luck with the lady!'

He appeared to melt into thin air.

Actually he reached a battered-looking Austin 7 which was parked some fifty yards away and drove off ahead of the taxi which Benjamin Morely had managed to secure. That the florid man was Morely, Mark had no doubt.

'Luck with the lady,' he repeated ruminatively. 'I wonder why in Hades they thought I could handle Dora? And I wonder,' he added as he made for the entrance, 'how Mike's getting on? Letty's probably persuading him to stand her a supper. I—I beg your pardon!'

She was short, pert-faced, and raven-haired.

Like Morely, she looked harassed and unhappy.

She was dressed in a tailor-made linen costume which could have had a bewitching effect on many young men, and she had come out of the flats at a speed which put the blame of the collision clearly on her shoulders.

She looked up at Mark, as she recovered herself.

'I'm sorry! I …'

'Don't be,' said Mark promptly, taking what might prove a godsent chance with alacrity. 'There are a dozen ways of being introduced, and this …'

He thought she was going to hurry past him, but her dark eyes narrowed, and she pulled herself up short.

'That's very nice of you. I—er …'

'I was thinking of dinner.' Mark looked humorously hopeful. 'For a start, anyhow.'

'You mustn't be too optimistic.' Dora had the same quick, easy manner as Letty, although that night at least—perhaps because she had less immediate cause for worry—she exploited it more capably. 'I'm really awfully fed up—a friend of mine was going to give me a run into the country, and he can't manage it.'

'I now believe in Fate,' Mark announced, taking her arm masterfully. 'I had an appointment, but it can wait. What part of the country?'

'*Any* part.' She spoke with a quiet vehemence, almost as if she were afraid of being overheard. She looked past him.

Expecting—fearing—whom?

'Please yourself,' he said. 'I've a fast bus, and …'

'I know a glorious little place near Winchester.'

He had half-expected her to say Maidenhead, and was certainly surprised that she should have picked on somewhere so far from London. Mark Errol had always been possessed of an ability to think quickly, and a few days in the service of Department Z had given a fine point to that talent.

Why Winchester?

It was on the Bournemouth Road, and not far from Southampton. Dora probably did not know of the mishap to Rogerson's house—on the other hand, she might want to get something to the docks …

She was scared, he was sure.

As they moved towards the Lagonda, she looked over her shoulder, and up and down the street. Although her voice was steady, her smile vivid, and her laugh convincing, her hand was trembling on his arm.

Why?

'I'd give a lot to know,' thought Mark Wyndham Errol. 'It's beginning to look as if Morely brought news that wasn't good …'

He heard nothing.

He saw a car, a Frazer Nash, disappearing along the street, and felt Dora's fingers clutch his arm. He put a supporting arm about her, quickly, but the left side of her white-linen suit was already stained with blood ...

She died without a word being spoken.

'I didn't get a chance of trying to stop it,' said Mark, into the telephone. 'Sorry, Craigie ... No, not a word. All I know is that Morely called at her flat ...'

'Morely was killed outside his house, five minutes ago,' Craigie told him. 'Don't let this worry you, Errol—we're fighting desperate odds, and there's no quarter either side. We've heard nothing from your cousin, which suggests he's getting somewhere.'

'Mike will, if anyone can. But what can I do?'

'Not a great deal. You'd better stay outside the flats, and if anyone connected with the job calls, follow them. You're speaking from a nearby kiosk?'

'Yes. But the police ...'

'Stay outside,' ordered Craigie. 'I'll see to the police.'

In fifteen minutes a sergeant of police, who had been more than suspicious of Mark's story, apologised so convincingly that it was obvious he had had orders from Scotland Yard. That relieved Mark of an annoyance, but did not make him feel any happier.

He should have saved the girl.

He had known she was worried, had even told himself that she was afraid of an attack, and he had let it happen in front of his eyes—had been too shocked and startled even to shoot at the car which had flashed by.

He had let the girl down.

And the Department ...

He felt flattened, useless. The task of waiting on the off-chance of someone coming along did not make it any easier. But he could hardly blame Craigie for giving him a job just to waste his time. He was as much use as a school-girl ...

A Rolls drew up outside the block of flats.

From the driver's seat stepped a big red-faced, hearty-looking man, whose name was familiar to many people, for he had recently given a quarter-of-a-million pounds to charity.

Lord Lore, in short.

Mark's eyes narrowed.

Lore went inside. He spoke for two minutes to the por-ter, and when he came out he looked deathly pale.

He drove off at reckless speed.

That day, those few police not engaged on special duties were being harassed by small bands of hooligans—many of them organised, Craigie believed—who took the opportu-nity of having what they called a good time. So that at over fifty miles an hour, Lord Lore drove through the main streets of London, to pull up eventually outside the Magnolia Restaurant.

The Magnolia, in a small turning off Piccadilly, was high class in every respect, and a place where Lore might be expected to go. Mark, after a decent interval, followed him in.

And then had a shock.

For in the restaurant, which was no more than half-full, Lore was sitting at a table—deep in conversation with Fay Loring!

'There isn't,' Mark told himself 'a shadow of doubt. There might be others as pretty, but—this is absurd!'

He had parked himself in a corner table, where he could see Fay clearly, and Lore with some difficulty. Fay was doing more listening than talking. Twice she glanced up, looked straight at him, and appeared not to notice him.

Why Fay?

Did Craigie know that she was working on Lore?

A waiter approached the table where Lore was sitting, and Mark heard:

'If you'll order, Hubert, I'll be back in a moment.'

She left her table, walked past Mark without looking at him, and disappeared. Mark scowled. Was she leaving Lore to him or …

He had not made up his mind when a waiter approached.

'M'sieu—I 'ave been ask to give you this.'

'This, was a folded note, and Mark nodded, smiling a little in admiration for the way Fay handled things. He ordered a coffee and, while the waiter was away, opened the note.

Fay's writing was small but easily readable:

Get out, you mut. Don't let him see you!

'Oh, my Lord!' muttered Mark Errol. 'I've put another foot in it! This is not my lucky day.'

It was not.

Fay returned, and Lore stood up to move her chair back. Doing so, he glanced across the restaurant—and saw Mark. To the best of Mark's knowledge, they had not exchanged a word in their lives; he knew Lore only by hearsay, and from photographs.

But the red, hearty face paled.

Lore sat down quickly, leaned across the table and spoke in a whispered undertone to Fay. Within three minutes they had left the Magnolia, and Fay's sidelong glance at Mark Wyndham Errol had not been one of congratulation.

Miserable, Mark reported to Craigie.

'No,' said Craigie. 'I didn't know. But Fay's been working on her own, and she's probably picked up a useful trail. Again, don't let it worry you, Errol. You've done no damage—although one thing's interesting.'

Mark growled:

'Yes—Lore recognised me.'

'Got it in one,' Craigie approved. 'He recognised you as an agent, and that means that he's not only learned that you are one …'

'But has reason to be scared!'

'Again, in one.' Craigie sounded satisfied.

Bill Loftus was there, and listening, as Craigie added:

'Go back to your flat, then, and I'll send any further orders for you there. Better get some sleep while you can.'

'If I can,' said Mark gloomily, and rang off.

Loftus looked lazily across at his Chief.

'Mark, I fancy, doesn't feel too pleased with himself. Actually, he's doing damned well, if only by accident. And Fay, the pet, is on to Lore.'

'Yes … She's done good work.'

Loftus stuffed a pipe.

'I wish we didn't need the girls. Diana's after Frazer-Campbell, and he'll be a different proposition to Lore, I'm afraid. Cold beggar, Campbell. You'll have Lore watched?'

'Of course.'

'And then?'

Craigie hesitated, and it was some minutes before he spoke.

'I don't know any more than you do, Bill. The situation's virtually unchanged. We've got to wait until we know what the League will do after this set-back. We've just got to wait, with what patience we can. Word ought to come in from Mike Errol before long …'

'M'mm. Gordon, the thing I like least about this show is that *everyone* we get a line on is warned. Usually scared to death, or murdered. Gorton, Jaffrey, Morely, Dora—they've all died pretty soon after we got at them.'

Craigie pulled at his lower lip.

'I know. I don't like to think it, but …'

'There's a leakage of information.' Loftus looked bleak. 'In this damned business, we can't call our souls our own. In a normal job, we'd know it was one of our own people, and it would be reasonably easy to find him. As it is …'

'Forty people outside the Department are getting the reports,' said Craigie. 'I know. Permanent officials, the police …'

He broke off, and again there was silence. While in Bill Loftus' mind an unpleasant thought was growing.

Were the Errols reliable?

Were they what they seemed?

Fifteen miles along the Maidenhead Road, Mike Errol took a chance. Letty had not given him the attention that he might have expected, in view of the manner of their meeting. She was more than preoccupied: she was frightened …

And, of course, with good reason.

Michael Errol did not know what it was like to fear that the police were following him, but just that fear was in Letty's mind. She had twice urged him to go faster, and he had done so. But his own mind was seething with questions, and the most important was whether she wanted to go aboard the *Luxa.*

On that, he took his chance.

'Know Maidenhead well, sweet?'

'Eh? I—oh, yes, of course.'

Mike squeezed her arm.

'Pretty hot, everything considered, in places. I've heard some astonishing stories about a houseboat old Neb owns. Don't believe a word of it, myself ...'

He felt her stiffen as he went burbling on, and when he stopped she was looking at him fixedly:

'Do you know Lord Nebton?'

'Well, not exactly "know." We've met. Stunts and what-not. I mean ...'

'I've been on the *Luxa.*' Letty made an obvious attempt to sound casual. 'It's perfectly orderly—and I'll prove it to you.'

'Eh?'

'I'll take you there,' she said, firmly. And although Mike had been hoping to hear just that, although it seemed to prove the active participation of Nebton in the affairs of the League, he did not feel as pleased about it as he would have liked.

There was something intense about Letty that made her far more attractive than he had expected.

'Steady,' he warned himself. 'Falling for fair ones is not in the agenda. Poor little devil ...'

He took two wrong turnings on the way to the *Luxa,* and she corrected him immediately, confirming her knowledge of the place, and the fact that she had travelled to it by road. Mike remembered that the owner himself was missing, and found it hard to believe that they would find him on the river.

But as they passed the spot where Carruthers had been 'stranded' they could hear light strains of music coming from the houseboat. Letty's pretty mouth tightened, and her small, lithe body was rigid. Mike found it difficult to appear casual while he felt so strung up.

Surely Craigie had men in the vicinity?

By design, he believed, a bush near the river-bank moved: beyond it he saw the head and shoulders of a man. Not one whom he recognised, yet one who seemed more likely to be a Department man than one of the cut-throats working for the League.

Would the *Luxa* be raided, now?

At the river bank car park used by Lord Nebton's guests, a uniformed, middle-aged attendant stared hard at Mike and was about to speak, when Letty said quickly:

'A friend of Mr Clarke's, sergeant.'

'Oh-oh.' The attendant nodded: whatever question he had been about to raise was silenced.

But the name of Clarke had stabbed through Mike like an electric shock.

Carruthers' friend, the stockbroker!

A man, although Errol did not know it himself, who had lately handled most of Lord Nebton's accounts.

A key man, if of minor position—and Letty was either familiar with him, or knew that his name would be an open sesame to the *Luxa*.

They went on board across a pontoon bridge, and were shown to separate cloak-rooms. Mike washed hurriedly and was ready to rejoin Letty within three minutes of entering. He did not want her to make any contact without being observed.

But she, too, was in a hurry.

As he left his cloak-room he saw her hurrying from hers, to meet a sharp-faced yet good-looking young man. Mike knew Neil Clarke by sight, and knew also that this encounter would be of overwhelming interest to Gordon Craigie.

He felt on tenterhooks.

He saw Letty and Clarke start dancing, the girl apparently oblivious to the man who had brought her here. Clarke spoke at some length, and smiled frequently, but the smile seemed forced. The band stopped, at long last. Mike looked put out as he approached Letty.

'I say …!'

'I'm so sorry, darling,' Her smile was ravishing, as she took his arm, pressed close against him. 'Neil, this is a friend of mine …'

'Delighted,' said Neil Clarke, and thus smoothed over what might have been an awkward social moment.

Mike was out of his depth.

Letty seemed to have lost her fears, although he did not see that Clarke could have passed on her message to anyone.

The night was warm, and despite the open windows—curtained with mosquito netting against the river insects—the atmosphere was sultry and oppressive.

Oppressive …

Mike could not rid himself of a feeling that some kind of trouble was coming.

As far as he could tell, there was no one even remotely connected with the League of the Hundred-and-One present. Certainly no one named in his talks with Craigie and Loftus.

He had been there an hour, forcing laughter and simulating gaiety with increasing difficulty, when it struck him that the whole frame-up was absurd.

The hilarity was at its height.

There were thirty people present, mostly young, all wealthy, all—as far as he could judge—English.

Their country was under threat of God knows what domination.

Twenty odd miles from where they were dancing and laughing and drinking there were stricken homes, thousands of dead and injured, emergency laws in operation—panic's ugly face already leering, in London and the big towns. There was death and destruction, the threat of disaster, of the collapse of the oldest and soundest democratic Government in the world.

Politicians were in a frenzy.

The Army, the Navy and the Air Force were standing by.

Even at that moment, more dreadful attacks on innocent people might be in progress— 'Operation C' might have started …

Yet these people laughed and joked and danced …

Why?

'You—damned—fool!' Mike Errol swore at himself. 'They *know* what's coming. They *want* it! They're celebrating it!'

He felt suddenly very hot.

Letty had caught the eye of a young man in evening-dress, and he claimed her for a dance. Sick at heart, Errol forced a smile as he let her go and, getting a drink from the luxuriously-appointed bar, went to a window.

The mosquito-net blew upwards a little, and he looked out.

And kept looking, hardly knowing what to think, what to do. It seemed incredible, for he had had not the slightest warning.

The *Luxa* was in mid-stream, and moving rapidly!

Chapter 21
Down River

Mike stood by the open window as the houseboat glided down river, his face expressionless, his heart hammering.

He had not been aware of any motion, but now he realised that the band had been playing hot music for some time past, that the 'Lambeth Walk' and the 'Green Apple' had figured prominently and noisily in the programme.

To hide the movement?

It that were so, it suggested that the majority of the gathering present were also unaware of the movement. He doubted that, and in doubting it, wondered whether the noisy pieces had been deliberately arranged for his benefit.

If so, it meant that he was at least suspected as an agent of the Department.

He did not realise that his body was rigid, his chin set, and his eyes very narrow. But he jumped when a suave voice came from behind him.

'Mr Errol ...'

He swung round.

Neil Clarke was there, smiling without humour. In that moment, Mike knew two things: he had not succeeded in passing himself off as a casual acquaintance of Letty's, and Clarke *was* involved in the League.

He steeled himself to keep his temper.

'Right in one, but ...'

'My name is Clarke,' the stockbroker informed him. 'You will hardly need telling that, however—Loftus and Carruthers must have warned you.'

Mike frowned.

'Loftus and who?'

'We need not be quite so elementary,' said Clarke. 'I know just who you are, and just why you picked Letty up. She has told me the whole story, and I'll admit it was extremely ingenious. Tell me, have you managed to get a message to Craigie? That you were heading for Maidenhead, for instance?'

Mike drew a deep breath, then threw subterfuge aside.

'I wish I had!'

'So.' Clarke smiled thinly. 'It is as well for you! Now, let me be frank: all of us aboard know that we are moving to a place of safety. Believe me, such a place will be necessary. You, also, can be with us, if you give me your parole not to try to escape.'

Mike's eyes held cool contempt.

'Parole,' he said, 'is a question of honour—between gentlemen.'

Clarke coloured.

'Let me be even more frank, Errol. If you give me your word not to try to escape, you may stay here, mix with the crowd, enjoy yourself. Later, you will even have an opportunity for serving the new régime. If you refuse ...' he emphasised, 'you will be held in a small room, tied hand and foot, until we decide to kill you.'

Mike Errol grinned.

'Clarke,' he said, calmly: 'I don't believe you. If you took my word, I wouldn't take yours. Why don't you want to kill me right now?'

'Because,' Clarke said coldly, 'you may be more useful to us alive than dead. However, let us say the issue is between your immediate comfort, and discomfort. Have I your word?'

'No,' said Mike gently.

So gently that Clarke was quite disarmed—the bigger man's arm moved with surprising speed and force. His fist connected with Clarke's chin and sent him rocketing backwards.

He sprawled against two dancers, and a woman screamed as he slithered across the highly-polished dance-floor. Mike snatched an automatic from his pocket, and stood with his back to the window. His eyes glittered, and there was murder in his manner.

'Stay where you are, the lot of you! The first to move will get more than he bargains for!' As he spoke, his left arm moved behind him, searching for the window, trying to make sure that it was open to its widest. There was just the faint chance that he might manage to get away through it.

Clarke scrambled to his feet, his chin swelling.

'You damned fool, I'll ...'

He moved forward, and Errol fired.

There was hardly a sound, for the gun was silenced. But a stab of flame shot out and Clarke gasped as the bullet tore through his shoulder. Again a woman screamed, and the band stopped. Everyone stood transfixed, staring towards Mike Errol.

The window was wide open, thanks be ...

'You've been more than warned,' he snapped. 'If ...'

He did not see the arm stretching past the curtains.

He did see a dozen pair of eyes turn towards the window in unspoken, unwitting warning. He half-turned, but he was a fraction of a second too late. Something hard and heavy crashed on the back of his head. As he staggered, it came again—and he pitched forward, the automatic clattering to the floor from his nerveless fingers.

From outside the window, a steward pulled back the curtains as Clarke crossed to the unconscious man's side and kicked him viciously in the ribs.

'Come and get him!' he snarled to the steward.

And then the band began to play. Hot rhythm swept through the room as the women turned to their partners, and the dancing started again.

That was at half-past nine.

At eleven o'clock, Loftus entered Craigie's office and he did not look pleased with life. He threw himself into a chair and, since Craigie was on the telephone, filled his pipe in silence as he waited.

'Well, Bill …?' Craigie asked, hanging up at last.

'Who was that?'

'Fellowes. There's no news of any kind. The Army's in readiness for martial law, if it should be necessary, but there isn't an inkling of what will happen next. The Government's attitude is defiant, of course …'

'It's got to be,' Loftus stirred uneasily. 'Anything from Mike Errol?'

'Not a word. Nor from the two men I had near the house-boat. It suggests that Errol and this Letty woman didn't go to the *Luxa*—although they were seen on the Maidenhead Road. We'd have had a report by now, I think.'

'Yes ... Better send someone to check up, though—I'll give Carrie a ring.' He went to the telephone, gave Carruthers instructions to get to Maidenhead at all speed and report, then returned to his chair. 'Well, the position's as you were, Gordon. Apart from the men we've got, there's Neb himself, Lore, Frazer-Campbell and Tiarney—not to mention Amondier—all missing.'

'Lore dropped Fay cold, did he?'

A tired grin crossed Bill's face.

'I'm afraid so. What with Jaffrey and Lore, she'll begin to think her charms aren't working as they should. Of course Lore recognised Mark Errol, and that seemed to make him suspicious. If he knew what happened to Jaffrey, it would be enough—and probably Fay isn't as convincing a newspaper-hound as we'd like. However, she tried. Clarke was on the houseboat, and I expect he's still there. Rogerson and Myra haven't turned up, and everything considered, it's safe to assume they've gone to a joint rendezvous.'

'Yes ...' Craigie pulled at his under-lip. 'But I don't like the way these people seem to disappear into thin air. Or ...'

'Into the hereafter,' Loftus supplied, soberly. 'Oh, the organisation is good, all right—more like a thousand-and-one, than a hundred! However, we've done everything we can. Oh, hell—this blasted silence is getting on my nerves!' He pushed his chair back and stood up, glowering down at Craigie as if the Chief of Department Z were to blame. 'Good God—here we are, nearly midnight, the whole country awake and waiting—waiting for some ungodly tragedy that might kill tens of thousands! It's unbearable. It's ...!'

'Steady,' said Craigie.

Loftus stopped. After a moment, he shrugged, shamefaced:

'Sorry, old man. But …'

'It gets you, as it gets us all. But as you said, we've done everything possible, and all we can do is to wait. It can't succeed, of course.'

Loftus looked ten years older.

'No?'

Craigie's lips drooped as he insisted:

'Not over here …'

'It can!' Loftus retorted, sharply. 'They *can* do it, Gordon. They've been preparing for this for years. And we depended on a chance word from Fay to know anything at all about it! Secret Intelligence!'

Craigie lifted a hand.

'It's not as bad as that, and you know it. We were after the men who were after Fay, before she told us what she knew. She only confirmed it. We were late starting, but with an organisation among people like Nebton, Jaffrey and the others—well, what could we do? Men you would imagine to be as loyal as anyone living! And don't say we've never liked Nebton.'

'I won't,' Loftus grunted, and glanced at his watch. In the past ten minutes, he had checked it half-a-dozen times, watching the minute-hand move nearer to midnight.

It was eleven thirty-five …

Zero hour was twenty-five minutes off. Something, God knew what, was to happen. They knew that from the General Plan they had discovered—knew that it was to put the finishing touches to the panic already started by Operation B.

That had been dreadful enough.

Operation C would be worse—much worse …

Brrr-brrr!

The telephone jangled sharply in the silence, making them jump. Craigie answered it, and Carruthers announced himself. He sounded as if he had been running.

'The *Luxa's* missing. Our men were laid out, around nine o'clock, just after Mike and the girl arrived. Locals say it went down-river—it's probably through the last lock by now.'

'Nothing else?'

'Clarke was on board: no one else we know.'

'Clarke again,' said Craigie. 'All right, get there as soon as you can.' He replaced the receiver slowly, and passed the news to Loftus. 'Carrie will be back here, soon,' he added.

And neither of them knew that Carruthers proposed, in fact, to disobey Craigie for the first time in his life.

'So Carrie's little Neil is in it, is he?' Loftus mused. 'You'll have his office and home searched?'

'Yes—and we'll do it ourselves. Miller and Fellowes are too busy on special work. Who've we got handy?'

'Di and Fay, Wally, Dodo, Spats ... That ought to serve.'

'Get the girls on that line,' Craigie nodded. 'There's Mark Errol, too, of course.'

Loftus said, bleakly:

'Seeing there's a faint chance they're not all they should be, let's leave the Errols.'

'Right,' said Craigie.

In five minutes, from their various flats within half a mile of one another, Diana, Fay, Wally Davidson, Spats Thornton—and one Dodo Trale, recently back from Paris—were converging on the St. James' Street flat of Neil Clarke.

In half an hour they were agreed there was nothing of use there and left, in two cars, for his Mincing Lane office, A caretaker, at first obstreperous, was soon overwhelmed by Loftus' manner and Craigie's obvious authority.

It was Fay who made the discovery ...

In Clarke's sumptuously-furnished private office, there was a trap in the wainscoting—as there had been at Moorton

Road. From it, Fay took files of papers, exclaiming as she did so; and Diana working near her called the others from the outer offices. A three-minute inspection proved that they had found enough to incriminate Neil Clarke beyond any doubt, but little else to help them.

For the papers were exact duplicates of those found in Korrel's office at Moorton Road.

'Which,' commented Loftus, 'is useful, up to a point.'

'Useful!' cried Fay, almost in tears. 'It's turned twelve, we're no further forward, and ...'

'Easy, lass,' Loftus soothed her. 'It's a blow, but it can't be helped. There's another thing we might get hold of, Gordon—Clarke's recent transactions. We know he's done a lot for Neb, and others on the schedule might be on his books.'

'Dodo's going through the safe right now,' said Craigie.

Dodo Trale, a man of medium build and considerable good looks, whistled as he sorted through the papers he had extracted from the safe. Dodo was an expert in picking locks—a sign, Loftus was wont to say, of a misspent youth.

They went into the larger office.

'Find anything?' Fay demanded. She was on tenterhooks now; more nervous than they had ever seen her. Loftus sympathised. He felt a heaviness within him; a fear that somewhere not far away, disaster was coming. Zero hour was past: if the General Plan was adhered to, the third operation was about to be demonstrated.

All of them were worked up, brittle, sharp-tempered.

Of them all, Diana seemed to be the least tense. But Dodo's whistling got on Spats Thornton's nerves.

'For God's sake shut up. Dodo!'

'Sorry, sergeant!' said Trale, and the little man with the Punch-like face shrugged wryly. They had taken a number of files apiece, and were going through each of them at speed.

This time, Loftus made the find.

'Here's Neb's papers! I—*hallo!* Jaffrey—Lore—Morely—McKenzie—Fraser-Campbell—*Anson! The* whole damned bunch—he's been working for them all!'

'Anson!' exclaimed Thornton.

'The same ...' Loftus had taken the files and was spreading them on a desk in front of him. The others crowded round. They all read the records of the transactions, all saw—with Loftus and Craigie a little ahead of the others—that Neil Clarke had handled the buying and selling of millions of pounds' worth of armament companies' shares.

The minutes passed unnoticed ...

The extent of the negotiations Clarke had handled was beyond anything they would have dreamed. The stockbroker had been working for years for all the bigger armament firms, and there in front of them was a full record of his activities. They saw, for instance, how many shares of the Anson group Nebton had bought, and how many of Nebton's group had been bought by Anson. The system was intricate: the negotiations must have been delicate in the extreme—but one supreme fact emerged.

Anson and Nebton, between them, held more of all the other companies' shares than the companies themselves.

Anson and Nebton virtually controlled the combined output of the Empire Armaments Manufacturers Association.

'Which makes it look,' Loftus remarked, deceptively mild, 'as if Anson is very deep in this after all. A visit to the Regal is indicated, whether he's still convalescent or not.'

'I can't believe Anson ...' began Fay, oddly.

'We won't prejudge him,' said Loftus, but he looked as if he had already done so. 'We ...'

Brrr-brrr!

The telephone, in the office which was supposed to be empty, startled them all. Loftus was nearest to it and at Craigie's nod answered it crisply:

'Yes—who is that?'

'Oundle. Is Loftus ...?'

'Speaking! Ned, how the devil ..?'

'Fay told me you were after Clarke—I knew you'd be there. Bill ...' Oundle's voice was urgent, charged with alarm—perhaps with horror. 'The Regal's on fire—blazing like a hayrick, *and they can't get to Anson's room!*'

CHAPTER 22
OPERATION C

No human being could have got through.

The Regal, when Loftus and the others reached the nearest point they could approach, some fifty yards away, was blazing at all corners. Flames roared two hundred feet into the air, the smuts falling on the seething onlookers like a blanket of black snow. Debris was crashing all around, and walls tumbling, showering sparks and flame over the cordon which police and military tried desperately to maintain.

The regular and auxiliary fire brigades had given up hope of saving the hotel within ten minutes of arriving on the scene. They were concentrating, now, on the adjoining buildings, some of which were burning fiercely and several of which would be razed.

The hissing water from a hundred powerful hoses, the smell of burning, cries of alarm and of pain, added to the bedlam. Loftus and Diana watched, sick at heart. Craigie, with Dodo and Spats, had gone to see Miller, who was at the scene. Wally had a hand on Fay's shoulder. She was looking white and hollow-eyed, her lips dry and colourless. The strain was clearly beginning to tell on her.

Diana, on the other hand, looked as cool and fresh as it was possible to look under such extremes of heat and smoke.

'Wally had better get Fay to the flat,' she murmured. 'Ned will look after her. She'll crack, if she doesn't get some rest.'

'Idea,' admitted Loftus and spoke, *sotto voce*, to Davidson.

The lethargic gentleman agreed that Fay should be taken to the flat, dosed with veronal, and sent to bed. He helped her through the crowd with some difficulty, a hand on her waist all the time. She walked like a woman in a trance, and as they disappeared, Diana protested:

'It's been too much for her, Bill. Isn't there a thing we can do?'

'Not a damned thing,' said Loftus, savagely. 'The League wanted to stop Anson talking, or it looks that way. They meant to get him, and they've managed it ...'

But suddenly, shockingly, came the start of Operation C—although at first they did not realise it.

'The damned fools!' Loftus roared. 'They've turned the water off!'

From a dozen nozzles near them, the water had receded to the merest trickle and firemen were looking at each other, puzzled and worried. The flames seemed to redouble as they watched, and the adjoining buildings, which had been partly under control, suddenly burst into a roaring, uncontrollable blaze.

Loftus and Diana fought their way to where Craigie and Miller stood with a Brigade Superintendent. A lieutenant reached the little group at the same time.

'It's off at the main, sir—nothing wrong here.'

'Get it on!' snapped the superintendent.

But they did not get it on.

There was no water ...

The mains had been destroyed, by sabotage on a grand scale. From every part of London reports came to Craigie and Loftus, who had gone to Miller's office at Scotland Yard. Fires were starting in a hundred places ...

And there was no water to fight them!

North, south, east and west, the reports were the same. Pumping and control stations had been attacked, in most cases by a dozen or so armed men. The engines had been wrecked and pipe lines blown up: reservoirs had been attacked and thousands of gallons of water were devastating whole areas and driving hundreds of people from their homes.

In other areas, fires had been started at cinemas and hotels, public houses and club rooms, theatres and meeting halls: there could be no doubt that they were the work of incendiaries. And the brigades could only stand by, watching hopelessly. There was no water, nothing to fight the encroaching flames.

London was burning.

Operation A had started the disquiet, with the blowing up of key-points.

Operation B had begun the panic, with the slaughter of thousands and the demolition of their homes.

Operation C seemed planned to raze London to the ground.

But the emergency regulations which had been put into force showed that the authorities were not as unprepared as might have been expected. With speedy efficiency, sand was rushed in lorries to every danger spot. Around the Regal, a dozen buildings were blown up to prevent the spread of the fire, and the same plan was put into operation elsewhere. And although millions of pounds' worth of damage was done, slowly the regular and auxiliary services, with the Army's help, fought back with not a little success.

But the panic was there.

Thousands of people homeless ... Lurid glows in the sky from all directions ... Fear and horror and pain played their part in the mass evacuation of London which started soon after the fires—and quickly threatened chaos.

All roads and highways were crammed with people; in small cars and large, in lorries and vans, on cycles and on foot. They began as a straggling stream, and developed into a surging mass, intent on one thing only: to get away from London, the City that seemed fated.

Main lines were besieged, hundreds of extra trains were put on; but confusion reigned. There was no order in that great exodus. In three places at once—Euston, Victoria and Charing Cross—rioting started. At Victoria, a gang of men seized over-loaded trains and drove them from the station with no real knowledge of what they were about.

Incoming trains had no warning ...

Two miles outside Victoria, there was a crash which involved four trains, each one crammed full with sweating, frightened humanity. Men, women and children were smashed to pieces in the collision, and all the lines from Victoria were put out of action for days ...

Yet thousands besieged the terminus.

A series of crashes added to the chaos, and slowed the traffic to a crawl. And with the roads so crammed with people, many preferred to abandon their cars and join them in that blind exodus to somewhere—anywhere—*away*.

And a hundred parts of London burned.

Panic—chaos—madness.

And on the morrow?

A few—a very few—knew that if plague were averted, it would be by a miracle.

⚜ ⚜ ⚜

The Rt. Honourable David Wishart, grey-faced with anxiety and fatigue, addressed the emergency meeting of the Cabinet summoned when London's water supplies had been cut off.

'There is no way,' he was saying, wearily, 'of communicating with the country, outside of London, except by aeroplane and carrier-pigeon and, in certain places still, by radio. All main routes are jammed, and the exodus increases hour by hour. All telephone services have been cut off, and most of the exchanges deserted. We are doing everything possible, but ...'

He paused.

Bryce-Scott, the fiery little Scotsman, spoke with less vehemence than usual:

'Is the best use being made of the river, Prime Minister?'

'It is crowded with craft of all kind—there, too, there have been tragedies ...'

A stunned Cabinet listened, in growing horror.

On a scale far worse than they had dreamed of, Operation C was having the effect the League had planned for and expected. There was no defence against it: panic had come to London, and would spread.

How could the Government retain control?

It was a matter of hours, they knew, before the people would be demanding submission to the League. The outrageous ultimatum must be accepted—or disease and fire, famine and slaughter, would be rife throughout the land.

Already, they were helpless against possible attack from a hostile power.

The Navy remained, and the Air Force: but both were needed in the emergency.

Submission, Wishart knew, was in all their minds ...

One man voiced it.

Another agreed.

A third, a fourth …

Bryce-Scott, his face red, suddenly shoved his chair back in fury.

'What the devil are you talking about?' His voice was a snarl: his fists clenched as though he would physically assault the next man to speak of submission. 'Are we going to submit to a gang of bloody pirates?' Thumping the table resoundingly, he cried: 'We *can't* give in! If we do …'

'If we do, there'll be a chance for London,' snapped one man. 'We've got to do it!'

Bryce-Scott paused a moment.

He looked around the circle of faces, and he saw despair. These men who formed the Cabinet—ineffective, he believed, for the most part—had been faced with an ultimatum backed up with a power and a force they had never dreamed of experiencing in all their Foreign Affairs debates. Faced, as now, with a need for quick action, for big decisions—they took the easiest path.

The majority was for surrender.

Bluntly, coldly, Bryce-Scott said:

'If you submit, you will be betraying the people. If any of you dare not fight, he can resign—there are others who will do so in your place. Martial Law had been proclaimed in some areas, and can be spread over the whole country. The Army, at least, will resist!'

'And make more tragedy!' snapped Greffly, on his right. Bryce-Scott ignored him.

He said bitterly: 'You're frightened for yourselves. You're all scared—for your own poor skins. There's hardly a man among you who isn't a coward! I'm sick that any one of you would even contemplate submission. Prime Minister—the time for discussion has gone!'

Quietly, sombrely, Wishart said:

'I am against submission, gentlemen—but it is in your hands.'

There were, Bryce-Scott thought, five besides himself and Wishart who would vote for fighting. He knew that the decision was made, and he felt sick. He saw hands moving upwards, and felt a mad desire to throw himself at Greffly, bodily ...

Wishart started to count, aloud:

'For submission. One ... two ... three ... four ...'

There was a tap on the door.

Wishart paused, and Bryce-Scott—jumping at any chance to postpone that dreadful moment—hurried to open the door. An attendant stood back, mutely indicating the visitor: Gordon Craigie.

Bryce-Scott snapped:

'What is it, Craigie?'

Craigie, warned a short while before of what was likely to happen, entered the room, and twenty-two pairs of eyes turned as one to the man whose counsel in the past had, when followed, averted more than one disaster.

'Gentlemen,' he said, quietly: 'I want twenty-four hours. No more. I can bring you results, then.'

There were gasps; a disbelieving cry or two.

'How can you be sure?'

'Are you serious?'

'Quite serious,' Craigie assured them. 'Just twenty-four hours.'

He knew, as he spoke, that he had come just in time. Questions were hurled at him from all sides, and he answered them ambiguously. But he seemed to give satisfaction ... Half-an-hour after he had arrived, the meeting broke up and he was left with Wishart and Bryce-Scott.

It was then that he admitted that he could offer no definite hope, that he had used what influence he had, simply to gain that extension of time. In doing this he accepted the fact with full knowledge, that if he failed the responsibility would be on his head, and his alone.

'This,' said Dodo Trale, who seemed perkier than any of the others in the sadly-decimated group of Craigie's men, 'is the worst show yet, Bill—but you never can tell. Damned thing is, we're blocked all along the line. Never seen anything like it before.'

'Nasty situation, all right,' agreed Spats Thornton. 'Can't even get in touch with our own crowd. Amazing business ...'

'For God's sake stop chattering!' roared Loftus, and the others glanced at each other in mutual concern for the big man's misery and anger at his impotence to act.

They were in Piccadilly, now.

There was hardly a woman to be seen; what few there were, were trying to ply their trade. The men and youths who were about walked listlessly, aimlessly. The attraction of the Regal fire—which had burned itself out—was gone. Hopelessness had replaced it. And apprehension ...

Public houses and cafes were open, but little that was drinkable remained.

Like wildfire, the knowledge had spread that the water was gone.

There were no private cars about.

Fire-engines, army lorries, even a few tanks were standing at the kerbs. Loftus and the others had lost their cars—stolen, like so many others, when the exodus began. There was not a bus in sight, nor a taxi.

They turned down Brook Street.

It was deathly quiet, although lights blazed from most windows. There were still no cars to be seen: every mews garage they had passed had been empty, its doors wrenched off.

They neared 11g.

Diana was with them, but had spoken not a word since they had left Scotland Yard after a call from Bryce-Scott to Craigie, telling him what was likely to happen at Number 10. Wally and Fay, of course, had gone on.

Had gone on ...

It was Loftus who saw the huddled figure of a man lying near 11g, Loftus who broke into a run and went down on his knees beside it.

Diana, Dodo and Thornton were close behind him as he said sharply:

'Wally—what happened? Wally!'

Davidson's right cheek was streaked with blood, but his eyes flickered open.

'Sorry—old man—Knocked—about—Swine got—Fay.'

And then his eyes closed again, and Loftus knew he would not be able to tell the full story for hours to come.

They carried him, gently, into the flat, using the girls' front door. Ned Oundle, able to hobble about now on his wounded leg, saw them and paled. They put Davidson on a bed, and Diana started to clean the wound. Oundle's saucerlike eyes were wide open and apprehensive.

'Where's Fay?' he asked stiffly.

'I wish I knew,' said Loftus. 'Sorry, Ned.'

Oundle sat down, heavily.

Loftus and the others had had an inkling, before, of how Oundle felt towards Fay Loring. They were left in no doubt, now, and they sympathised with him. But there was nothing more they could do. There was nothing more they could do about anything …

There was no means, even, of communicating with agents who might have followed any of the suspects to a rendezvous.

Kalloni and the other prisoners knew less than McKenzie.

And McKenzie had told all he knew.

One by one, the men who might have given them information had disappeared, or died. The ruthlessness of it, the evidence of a perfected underground organisation of which they had had little or no idea, appalled them.

It was still impossible to grasp, even now, that London was an emptying city, that all roads and railways leading from it were jammed with hundreds of thousands of terrified people, flying for their lives from fire, devastation and pestilence.

Panic had come.

The suburbs had been less affected, at first, but it would not be long before Greater London was gripped by the panic which had paralysed the city's centre.

A kind of paralysis, too, had gripped Loftus and the small band at his flat.

Diana had made Wally as comfortable as she could and now she took a glass of beer with the men, who were sitting or standing about in moody silence. Paralysis …

Suddenly, Loftus roared:

'We've got to do *something*, damn it—we *must!*'

'Just say what,' said Spats Thornton.

Diana was about to speak when there was a sharp ring at the front door bell. They heard Butler's ponderous tread—then a strained but familiar voice, which roused them from the stupor which had threatened.

Mark Errol came through.

Without his voice, they would not have recognised him. His clothes were torn and covered with soot: his face was black, and his hair was plastered about his head. His right trouser leg was missing—torn from the knee.

'Loftus …' he gasped.

'What is it?' snapped Loftus.

'Fay …' Mark was breathing very hard, and they suddenly saw that he was hurt. His shirt gaped open to show the red mark of a wound on his chest, partly covered with dirt. Dodo pushed a chair under him, and he smiled wanly as he subsided into it.

'Thanks … I …' He took a deep breath, and tried again, making a visible effort to speak coherently.

'I was fed up—doing nothing … Came round here. Saw three men jump out of a car … tackle Wally. Grabbed Fay—went off with her. I followed … Putney direction—Barnes. House—on the Common, there … Four-five cars outside. Guards around—but don't worry—drove straight past.' He shook his head as if trying to clear it. 'I think … I think …'

They had to guess what he thought, for he suddenly pitched forward on his face without a sound. For a split-second, no one moved or spoke. Then Loftus snapped:

'Ned, you patch him up. The rest—get moving! Butler—Butler!' The face of his manservant appeared in the doorway. 'Take a message to Scotland Yard, Sir William Fellowes—tell him we're in the Barnes area, needing help, and ask him to give word to Mr Craigie. Got that?'

'Yes, sir …'

They raced downstairs: Loftus in the lead, Diana next, Trale and Thornton behind them. Mark's car was still there, at the door, and they crowded in.

And for the first time, they felt hope …

Fifteen miles away, Carruthers—his conscience uneasy about the order he had disobeyed—also saw a glimmer of light in the darkness, yet was afraid.

CHAPTER 23

ACROSS THE SEAS

A big man sat in a white house at Washington, listening to the words of a pale-faced officer of the American Secret Intelligence. The officer had talked at some length, and when he had finished the seated man said:

'As I understand, then, there is no evidence that either Berlin or Rome incited the troubles in England, but enough to suggest that they are preparing to act now?'

'That is so, sir.'

'H'mm ... Thank you, Russel.'

Russel bowed and went out, and the seated man lifted a telephone.

'I want the Ambassadors in Rome and Berlin,' he said, *'At once!'*

And, very shortly, voices travelled across the seas ...

Mr Rogerson, whose face did not look anything like as with-ered and wizened as when the Errols had seen it, sat in a house near Barnes Common. On his right was Matthew Tiarney, the florid-faced and somewhat nervous member of the trio during the earlier discussion on the *Luxa*. On his left was a less nervous but obviously worried man, arrogant of mien, slow and precise in speech.

He was speaking now.

'I do not, of course, know exactly what has happened, Rogerson, but I have heard disturbing reports from the city. Fires, and ...'

Rogerson snapped:

'What did you expect? You, Tiarney, you, Frazer-Campbell—did you think you could win this fight and do no harm to individuals? Panic we wanted; panic we have! The country is ours—ours, ours,*ours!*' His voice rose as he emphasised the last word by a resonant bang on the table before him. He looked suddenly ageless: there burned in him a fever of passion, unleashing the fierce, repressed ambitions of a lifetime.

Frazer-Campbell stirred in his chair and Tiarney was perspiring freely, although the room was cool.

'I—I quite understand it was necessary,' Tiarney muttered. 'But ... Morely! Morely was a lifelong friend of mine ...'

'Pah! He would have talked!'

'But ...' Tiarney protested, wiping his forehead: 'Are you sure McKenzie did not know where we would meet? If they should learn of this house ...!'

'It is obvious,' Rogerson sneered, 'that you are more concerned with your own safety than the death of your life-long friend. Let us finish with this hypocrisy—we have what we wanted! In a few hours at the most. Wishart *must* capitulate. Everything can be put in order immediately—we shall have no trouble, no trouble at all! The people ...' He shrugged his disdain: 'Sheep! They will do as they are told. If any rebel ...' he shrugged again: 'There is a quick way with such fools.'

Frazer-Campbell licked dry lips.

'That's all right, so far, Rogerson. But what of the *Luxa?* Clarke is most necessary, and ...'

'The *Luxa* is already at Gravesend. Clarke and the others will be transhipped, and there will not be the slightest trouble. The man Errol, who managed to get on board, is under guard and the journey from Maidenhead was accomplished without alarm. All is under control, my friends!'

Tiarney muttered:

'How—how many have died?'

'None who needed to live!' snarled Rogerson. 'Would you repent, now? We are changing the face of England—the face of the world! In a few short hours ...'

'We're talking too much,' Frazer-Campbell said. 'We're worried, in case it fails. Operation D might be necessary. What is Operation D, Rogerson? Only you know about it.'

Rogerson looked cunningly from one to the other.

'Operation D, my friends, is magnificently simple! Our men are placed in positions of vantage all over the country. We shall know, soon, when the Army and Navy are to be called—if Wishart decides for general martial law. And with Operation D—*we shall make sure they have no arms.*'

Frazer-Campbell stared, aghast.

Tiarney gasped.

'You—you would destroy ...!'

'Everything which stands between us and our ambitions! Everything!' Rogerson's eyes glowed fanatically. 'Have you not understood, even now, how cleverly we have worked? Do you not know that vast consignments of armaments supposedly sent abroad are in this country? Waiting—for us, should we need them! The Government's stores, I can have destroyed in minutes—in seconds! What use will the army be without arms, without ammunition? As much use as the people without water! They will panic ...'

Frazer-Campbell muttered:

'It's devilishly clever, Rogerson. But surely ...'

'There are no buts! We have control of everything, *every-thing* that matters! The damage to any important services can be put right in two or three days. Nothing, now, can halt our domination! In a thousand places up and down the country our men are waiting for my word of command, by radio, to act. Every Government store of arms, bombs, aeroplanes, can be destroyed! Our own supplies are safely hidden. We have not the men to use them, *yet*—but they will come! There is Crosby, with his Red shirts—he is only waiting for the call. And with a hundred thousand armed men—the only men in England with arms—the cattle can be easily subdued. Oh, I have studied my subject, gentle-men! And now, when we have ...'

'It's done,' Frazer-Campbell broke in, involuntarily, as though thinking aloud. 'It can't be undone. But there must be no mistake now, Rogerson!'

'Have I made a *single* mistake?' demanded Rogerson, icily.

'There was one,' Tiarney muttered. 'When you let that girl go—Lor ... Loring. As we know, she went straight to Craigie. A girl whose father we had killed because he would not help us! Was that wise?'

Rogerson glowered.

'Has it hurt us? Has it delayed us?'

'No, but—she knew many things. Too many ...'

'You suggest that I would take stupid risks? No, my friend! I have been very careful to have her—looked after, in every way.' His high-pitched cackle sounded almost insane. 'Department Z! Fools like Craigie, Loftus—trying to run a Secret Service! Wait till our Secret Police take over—you will see the difference, then, my friends!' He glanced at a clock. 'I am waiting, now, for word from Downing Street—they are meeting tonight: they cannot hold out longer. If they do …' His eyes gleamed: 'If they do, I shall send armed bands to Downing Street—to the homes of every one of those fools! I shall make the public cry out for surrender! I tell you—*everything* has been planned!'

'Yes …' Frazer-Campbell looked dubious. 'What about Anson? And Nebton?'

Rogerson grimaced.

'Yes, yes—they are to be remembered. Poor Anson! Fool that he was! And my respected employer, Lord Nebton …'

He went off again into that cackling laughter—the man who expected to be in supreme control of the country within twenty-four hours.

He was still laughing when there was a tap on the door.

He stopped abruptly, and called: 'Come in!'

The door opened, and Myra Clayton—svelte and sleek in dark green velvet that suited her tawny beauty to perfection—sauntered arrogantly in.

Rogerson smiled a greeting. Tiarney grunted. Frazer-Campbell stood up and inclined his head stiffly. Both of them, for different reasons, deplored the influence this woman had over Cornelius Rogerson.

A strange, personal influence.

In business, she had none at all, but outside it …

'Well, my dear?' Rogerson indicated a chair. 'You have contacted Clarke?'

'Yes. He's all right—they're leaving the *Luxa* now …'

'Excellent! And the others?'

'Nebton, Lore and Amondier are quite safe.' Myra's amber eyes looked from one man to the other. 'We are all ready, I think, to take over. Craigie went to Downing Street,' she added. 'They've dispersed—but no decision, yet. I think Craigie gained time.'

'That man!' snarled Rogerson. 'He—and Loftus …'

She laughed.

'Loftus and the others, what few there are left, are at his flat. They found Davidson, and he'll have told them about Fay Loring. They will not be pleased.'

'They shall be the first—the very first!' said Rogerson viciously, 'to know what the new order is like! So still the decision is postponed …!'

He broke off and stood up abruptly, his gnarled fists clenched and shaking, his body trembling.

'*We will not delay!*' We shall start Operation D at once—we shall destroy the one thing on which they might depend! We shall send word *now,* to the men who are waiting!'

He pushed his chair away, and swung round.

Behind him, built into the wall of that innocent-looking house at Barnes, was a radio-transmitting station of a wave-length known only to the League of the Hundred-and-One. He had not used it for the ultimatum—for then the chance of an effective police raid had been high.

Now, it was a negligible risk.

He pressed a bell, and within ten seconds a man had responded.

'Get all stations!' snapped Rogerson. 'Get them at once!'

Myra was watching him, tense and expectant.

Tiarney looked as though he wanted to interrupt, but dared not. Campbell sat like a figure carved from stone.

Operation D …

The whole of the Government's stores of armaments, to be destroyed. Lives lost by the thousand in the explosion that would have to come. Sabotage on a scale never before conceived. Bloodshed beyond compare …

And a defenceless country.

Defenceless!

A voice from Berlin reached the ears of a man in Rome.

'Yes, yes, I have heard of the insolence from America! Insolence beyond endurance! But if the Operation D is carried out, in England, we begin at once—and before the fools in Washington can hope to interfere, we shall have conquered. And then—then they *dare* not interfere!'

A voice from Rome said:

'And Russia?'

'There is no need to fear. With the collapse of Great Britain, the whole Peace Bloc will be forgotten. Turkey, Greece, Rumania, Poland—they will make terms: they will not rely on France or Russia. And then, when we have them ...' He stopped, as though he had said too much. 'If Operation D is put into action, then we strike!'

'Let it be so,' said the voice from Rome.

'Caution,' warned Loftus, lightly, 'is the watchword. Myra's inside, bless her little heart, so we'll have something of a bag. The gentry who brought Fay are probably still here, and ...'

'We might get a few big fish,' supplied Thornton.

'We've got to!' snapped Diana.

'Nothing's impossible—if they're here,' said Dodo Trale.

They had arrived near the house in Barnes twenty minutes before. They had driven past and seen three men standing near it, obviously on guard. There might, for all they knew, be others. They had no idea of the number of men who would be inside, either, but they were reasonably sure the odds would be heavy.

Craigie, of course, would get men here as soon as possible.

So would Miller.

A company of Regular Army, or Militia, would be enough to turn the scales. But they dared not wait.

'Well,' said Loftus, as they reached a spot a hundred yards from the house, 'Di will go straight to the front door, pitch a story about being stranded, and ask for assistance. We three will approach from different sides, and see how many guards worry about Di. It's reasonably certain that all the beggars will look her way, and then ...'

The others nodded.

Loftus smiled, and pressed Diana's arm.

He knew, as they all knew, that she might be walking to her death. It was possible that the guards had orders to let no one approach, and it was likely that, if she did get close, she would be recognised. But there was no argument: a woman was the more likely to get through.

As she went quickly along the road, Bill Loftus tightened his lips and moved towards the vantage point he had selected.

Dodo and Thornton silently followed suit and they closed on the house from three directions, each with his hand in his pocket about a gun.

They could see Diana clearly, for it was a brilliant, moonlit night.

They saw one man look towards her, as she opened the gate. Then they saw the other two moving towards her, and they moved very fast.

Loftus got near enough to hear Diana say:

'But I tell you ...'

'Never mind what you tell me—clear out!' a truculent little roughneck told her, and Diana hesitated. She sensed how near Loftus and the others were, knew she had to keep the guards' attention for thirty seconds more, at least.

Loftus, in the shadows of a high hedge, was advancing on tip-toe.

It was the one chance, and the last chance, of doing something to stop Rogerson and the League. It might be a useless effort, the house might not prove to be the headquarters, but at least it had to be tried.

Loftus did not know that the wireless operator had just entered the room.

He did not know that in a matter of minutes, the fatal order for the destruction of all stores of Army and Navy armaments in the country, would be going out.

He did not know of the watching eyes in Berlin and Rome.

He went forward swiftly, as the truculent little man put a hand on Diana's shoulder and swung her round.

CHAPTER 24
SHOCKS

Loftus was twenty yards away.

The gun he was holding had a silencer, but the night was quiet and clear, the sound would reach the other guards, and the flame might be seen. He moved very fast. As Diana staggered backwards under the impetus from the truculent one, Loftus jumped!

He knew the two watching guards must see him as he leapt from the shadows, but he had waited until the absolute last moment. A shot from a silenced gun hummed out, and a bullet passed his head as he crashed into his man and sent him sprawling.

At the same moment, Thornton and Dodo went for their quarries. As the three pairs of struggling, fighting men rolled on the ground, a breathless Diana peered through the darkness for signs of other guards.

None appeared.

The man Loftus had tackled was as slippery as an eel. As he managed to wriggle free, a gun suddenly appeared in his right hand, Loftus kicked upwards …

He caught his man's elbow, and leapt forward again. The other, off-balance, could not evade that mighty left swing. Fist and chin connected, and there was a *crack!*

Sharp, clear, sickening.

The man's head was at an odd angle as he hit the ground, and Loftus knew he had broken the neck. But the knowledge only filled him with a fierce exhilaration. In the spilt-second he allowed himself to look around, he saw the others fighting and knew that any fourth guard would have put in an appearance by now.

'Give 'em a hand,' he snapped to Diana, and made for the front door.

It was shut, of course, and probably bolted, but next to it was a long window, the heavy curtains drawn across. Praying that no one inside the house would hear the scuffling behind him, Loftus took out a small diamond glass-cutter and expertly cut out a circle near the latch. Then taking a piece of adhesive tape from his pocket, he stuck one end across the top of the circle, to keep the glass from falling, and knocked the circular piece out with a quiet tap. Then, slipping his hand through the hole, he found the catch.

The window went up.

Not slowly—for the squeaking would be worse. Just one swift movement, one sharp noise, and it was wide enough for him to get through.

He heard a footfall behind him; a whispered:

'Right, Bill.'

Trale had got past his man ...

Carefully, Loftus pushed the curtain aside: there was no one in the hall. He was through the window in a moment, followed by Trale, and they made no sound on the thick carpet. They hesitated a split-second, then Loftus moved towards one of the three doors opening off the hall.

'Try one of the others, Dodo.'

His whisper sounded loud enough to wake the dead. But no other sound came as they opened each door in turn, to find that the rooms were empty and in darkness. On the left there was a glass-topped door, obviously communicating with the servants' quarters.

He hesitated again, for he had no idea of the call that was going out from the room above.

Then a high-pitched, maniacal laugh came sharply, from somewhere upstairs.

'Come on!' snapped Loftus, already racing up the stairs.

They reached the first landing. Voices were coming from a room ahead of them: one high-pitched, the other gruff.

'Get them—get them at once, I tell you! The call must go out!'

'There's a lot of interference.'

'Get them, I said!'

'Second door on the right, Dodo,' Loftus whispered. 'I'll ...'

He stopped, and Dodo stopped with him.

Despite the urgency of the moment. Despite its implient horror, both men's faces were suddenly alight with relief.

For a door had opened—and Fay Loring came through it.

She started, violently. Her clothes and face still showed traces of the smuts which had fallen from the burning Regal. But she was as free as the air.

'B-Bill! I ...'

'How'd you get clear?' demanded Dodo. 'We thought ...'

'Look out!' snapped Loftus, as sudden realisation hit him.

But Fay had her own gun out before he could get to his. She stood there, covering them both with it as Dodo gaped.

Loftus eyed her calmly, his expression unfathomable.

Fay said, very softly:

'Keep right where you are! I don't want to shoot, but ...'

'So,' Loftus murmured, 'you were *with* them.'

Fay nodded, watching them lynx-eyed. While Dodo realised with sickening certainty what Loftus had already guessed—just how those leakages of information had been managed.

Loftus himself was bitterly recognising that both he and Craigie had been cleverly deceived, by a girl they had both judged to be with them one hundred-percent …

The girl who now held their lives in her hands.

But for Diana, who had used the butt of her gun to good effect, Spats Thornton would have been dead. As it was, he was unconscious and with an ugly wound in the side of his head. She had been tempted to stay with him, but she had seen Loftus disappear inside, and if there was need for action in the house, she had to follow.

Racing to the open window, she slipped through. Then as she hesitated, she heard a whispered:

'Keep right where you are! I don't want to shoot, but …'

Fay's voice!

She heard Bill answer, but did not catch the words. She could hardly believe she had heard aright—that Fay was with the League. But sickened, she knew it was so: knew how much it explained. That night Fay had stopped Mark Errol from working on Lore—probably from fear that he would learn too much. And this was the girl who had shared her flat …

A wave of physical nausea swept over her, but she fought it down. With ice-cold precision she moved to the stairs and mounted them silently.

'Well, we get all kinds of shocks,' she heard Loftus drawl. 'But this really takes the cake. It's probably too late to matter, now, so just as a matter of interest—what is it that someone—Rogerson, I fancy—must get, so urgently?'

Fay shrugged.

'He's sending instructions for Operation D.'

'Being?' Loftus invited.

'Oh, a quick stroke to paralyse the land and air forces. Don't worry, Bill, it's as good as over, and ...'

'You little vixen! I've a ...'

'Stop there!'

And then Diana appeared.

She saw then, as she moved: Bill, about to go forward, his back towards her. Dodo standing like a man in a trance, Fay with her index finger on the trigger.

Diana fired.

The bullet, aimed at the gun, hit Fay's forearm. The only sounds were the soft 'snap' of the silencer, and Fay's gasp as her gun fell noiselessly on the heavy carpet. Loftus leapt, without looking round, towards the door from which the voices were coming. Dodo waited long enough to hit Fay Loring, sharply, scientifically, so that she made no sound. It was not pleasant, but she went right out.

Then he followed Loftus.

In that moment, Loftus merged haste with caution. He had turned the handle carefully, to make sure that the door was not locked. He heard Rogerson's voice saying:

'You have? Good! Give me ...'

Then Loftus flung the door open.

He went through, with Dodo, like a tornado, and he saw everything vividly. Rogerson by the transmitter, taking the headphones from the operator. Frazer-Campbell and Tiarney on their feet swinging round towards the door. Myra, her eyes blazing, moving towards her handbag.

Loftus cleared the table between himself and Rogerson in a single leap. His outstretched hand snatched the earphones from the old man's grasp. Then he jerked the lead from its socket and sent the operator crashing back against the transmitter—and heard the tinkling of breaking valves.

Madness was in him.

He saw Rogerson's feverish eyes a foot from his own and he hit the old man, savagely. As Rogerson gasped, aware only of pain, Loftus grabbed him by the waist and lifted him high.

Myra's voice came, tense with hatred, 'Hurt him and I'll blow the place to pieces!'

She was standing by the wall, and her hand was resting on a small lever which seemed to magnify as Loftus stared at it.

There was silence in the room, now.

The transmitting set was temporarily out of action. Tiarney and Frazer-Campbell were backed against the far wall, both frightened out of their lives. The operator was on the floor, his eyes closed.

At the door, stood Dodo and Diana.

And all eyes were on Myra Clayton.

Her amber eyes glowed, and she was crouching a little, like a panther about to spring.

'I mean it!' she said. 'If I push this down, the house and everything in it goes up. We didn't mean to leave anything here for you, if you did get through, Loftus! *Let-him-down.*'

Loftus hesitated—and then obeyed.

Through his mind was running a refrain:

Operation D's postponed! Operation D's postponed!

But for the moment, the woman by the lever had control. He knew enough about the thoroughness of the League to believe that she was telling the truth. She could blow them sky-high, if she chose. And she would choose, unless he obeyed her.

He had to play for time.

There would be other places, besides this house. Other means of getting the order for Operation D to those concerned. That had to be stopped. For the first time, they had come within an ace of success. Rogerson was here, obviously the leader. Tiarney and Frazer-Campbell, too.

The big fish … Loftus dared not make a mistake, now.

He put Rogerson into a chair, and the man gasped as he lay back, with blood coming from his mouth. Diana and Trale stood unmoving, by the door, equally helpless to act.

Myra had her hand on the lever: no matter what happened, she would have the strength to pull that down.

Loftus said easily:

'Check-mate, it seems!'

There were others, he reminded himself again. Others who might be able to take over, even if he finished Rogerson and Myra. And Craigie would be here soon, with enough men to take over the house.

But if they were heard approaching, Myra would act. The thoughts flashed through his mind, as his eyes met hers.

'Check-mate,' she agreed, and her lips curled. 'You're stuck, Loftus. How the devil you got here, is beyond me …'

'Oh, I know lots of things,' he told her, lightly. 'How Operation D will work, for instance, and stop supplies for the Navy and Air Force.'

Myra started.

'You know …!'

'That, and more,' Loftus assured her. 'How the *Luxa* went downstream, with Letty and Mike Errol on board, and probably Neil Clarke, the amiable stockbroker. How Anson and Nebton have managed to get control of the Association. Yes, I should like to interview those gentlemen …'

Myra sneered:

'You damned fool, they were fighting *against us!* They knew someone was aiming to get control—knew someone was hiding armaments, and guessed there was a big reason. They fought us all they could, but they didn't realise it was something more than an effort to corner the arms market. You *think* you know a lot, Loftus! We got hold of Nebton when we knew he wouldn't come with us—you'll find his body in the river! He didn't know his second-in-command was our leader! We nearly got Anson, but we made sure of him tonight. Your beautiful Fay caught Lore for us, also tonight—he's here: alive, but only just. Those three wouldn't work with us, Loftus, *the only three.*'

Loftus said, very gently:

'Thanks. I always liked Anson. Well, my pet, what next? You can blow yourself and Rogerson sky-high, with us—if you're so minded. You'll hardly expect me to come to terms …'

'You'll come to terms!' snapped Myra. 'London's empty—burning—waterless! There's no electricity—there won't be food, for more than a week! Every road is crammed with refugees, every railway station's besieged. We've a hundred thousand men we can arm! You'll come to terms—for if you don't you'll die here with us! And Clarke will give the orders, Clarke will take over from Rogerson. It's all arranged—it will be messier than Operation D, but that's all. Easy, isn't it?'

Loftus took a deep breath.

'It looks that way. Isn't life worth anything to you?'

'If I let you get away, how long will I live? Long enough to be hanged! I ...'

She stopped as a new voice came, from the door. *Carruthers' voice!*

'That sounds like sweet Myra,' he remarked pleasantly, from somewhere out of sight. Myra stared towards the door, her fingers tight about the lever. 'A bit of a shock, I'm afraid—friend Neil can't do all the damage after all. Bit of a shindy on board the houseboat and thanks to one Mike Errol, Clarke's got a very stiff neck. So ease off the gas, sweetheart ...'

She swore, vilely and obscenely ...

Loftus moved forward, stealthily, amazed but all ready to take this unexpected chance—the fruits of Carruthers disobeying an order.

But as he started, he knew that nothing would stop her. Carruthers spoke again—and her hand moved.

The lever clicked down.

They waited, all of them in that room, on the threshold of eternity. They seemed to hear the thunder about their ears, seemed to feel the cold breath of death.

But Clarke was useless.

Clarke could not take over. Operation D would never be carried into effect. It would take months, perhaps years, to get the country really back to normal—but that last, dread blow would not fall.

Only on them.

The realisation flashed through Loftus' mind in a split second—in the time it took for his eyes to meet Diana's, and to read the message that was in them.

Eternity ...

Time stood still.

Myra's hand was on the lever, and she was motionless now: the words of abuse had stopped.

Seconds ticked by.

And the explosion had not come!

CHAPTER 25
... DID NOT TAKE PLACE

A minute had passed.

No one inside the room had moved, but at last Loftus took a step forward. As he went, Myra snatched her hand from the lever, her face twisted in naked fury. And suddenly there was a small pearl-handled gun in her hand. It seemed that even now, murder must be committed.

Then Loftus leapt ...

He struck her hand as the report came. The flame passed in front of his eyes, but he felt no pain. He gripped her wrists and jerked her towards him, struggling and kicking like a wild-cat. And then Carruthers came through, with Michael Errol at his heels.

'Damn it, it's not a necking-party!' Carrie reproached him. 'In front of Di, too—I'm ashamed of you!'

He dragged Myra off, still talking easily—bringing sanity back into that room of horror.

'Just luck, old boy. We got here, guessing there was likely to be trouble if you'd arrived—Clarke had talked about a little mine in the cellar. We knew you were around when we saw old Spats almost out, in the grounds, so we went to the cellar first, and disconnected the fuse. Easy enough, for a bright lad—and the blow-up will not take place.' He stopped suddenly, as without warning, Myra collapsed in a crumpled heap on the floor.

Then Tiarney started screaming …

Frazer-Campbell, until that moment motionless, put his hand to his pocket and before anyone could stop him, slipped a white pellet to his mouth. There was a moment's pause; then he fell, writhing in his death agony—while Tiarney screamed on, his mind quite gone.

And outside the room, Fay Loring shot herself …

It was thus that Craigie and the Rt. Hon. David Wishart found them, five minutes afterwards. And it was then that Wishart knew that Britain would pull through.

The voice from Berlin was choking with fury.

'It did not start! They have all they need now—the Navy has been warned by America! The Air Force is patrolling the coast line! We cannot do it—we cannot do it!'

The voice from Rome said, coldly:

'It was never my intention to contemplate hostile acts against a friendly nation, such as Great Britain. I shall cable immediately an offer of assistance. It would, perhaps, be as well if the offer from you went separately …'

The flat, Loftus said, was a little overcrowded.

There was Oundle, who knew all there was to know about Fay and had taken it quietly, and without fuss. He was about again, although he had to go steady on his injured leg. There was Mark Errol, stretched out on a bed and amply bandaged, but listening through the open door of the bedroom. Wally Davidson, less badly injured, was sharing the bed for that afternoon's gathering.

Thornton was still recovering in hospital, but at least he shared a private ward with Martin Best. Carruthers was at the flat, of course, with Loftus and Mike Errol. Diana was dispensing drinks, for the afternoon was warm, and they were thirsty.

Cars were moving outside.

A skeleton bus and train service was already running, the water supplies had been reconnected, the electric power stations were already working. Auxiliary fire-fighters—in fact the whole of the A.R.P. organisation, with the Regular Army, the Territorials, and the Militia—were hard at work, restoring some kind of order to London.

Debris was being cleared away.

People were flocking back to the capital, and for those whose homes had been destroyed, accommodation had been found in the safety evacuation areas planned for war-time emergency. The radio was busy sending out reassuring messages. Wishart had twice broadcast to the country, and was due to speak again that night.

Tragedy had come, had swept over England like a tornado leaving its tragic wreckage. But now, fear and uncertainty had given way to cheerfulness and hope.

'Well,' Loftus was saying. 'Let's hear it again, Carrie.'

'Hang it,' said Carruthers, aggrievedly: 'you've had it twice, and ...'

'We haven't,' called Mark and Wally, from the bedroom.

'Oh, well!' Carruthers shrugged resignedly. 'There was really nothing to it. I went to Maidenhead, heard about the *Luxa,* pitched my story and showed credentials to a police patrol boat—and we went after it. The river police were in good form—they collected reinforcements, and we reached the *Luxa* as the whole bunch was transhipping to a sea-going yacht. We waded in, and—well, my children, there was fun.'

'Spare us the details, daddy dear,' murmured Dodo Trale, and grinned as Carrie shot him a withering glance.

'Anyhow,' said Carruthers, 'I located Mike, who wasn't in a good temper, and he located Clarke—and Clarke won't ever be in a good temper again. I simply persuaded him to tell us where the headquarters were, and we came over by 'plane from Gravesend. Couldn't do much else; there were no telephones or whatnot. The disconnecting of the fuse at Barnes was Mike's idea.'

Mike Errol chuckled.

'Call it fifty-fifty, I thought of it, and he did it. Anyhow, it worked, and Clarke's waiting trial or whatever they'll call it. We know all about Myra, Rogerson, and the others in the game, Bill. And we know you've raided a hundred places and collected Crosby's mobsmen—the so-called militia of the League. We know there isn't a member of importance left, but we *don't* know much about Neb and Anson. So speak, Oracle!'

'Don't talk so much,' growled Mark, from the bed. 'If he gets obstreperous, Bill, just sit on him. If I were better ...'

'You'd have the sense not to butt in!' Mike grinned. 'It's all right, Di—just cousinly love.'

Loftus drank deeply from a tankard.

'Well,' he informed them: 'Craigie's now telling Wishart just what we know, so you can have it from me. The essentials are simple. Rogerson started it—primarily with an idea of cornering the armaments market and thus holding a gun at the Government's head. But he had trouble, for Anson and Nebton weren't likely to help him. Then the Government plan for nationalising armaments gave him an opportunity. Neb planned to get the whole Association together, in opposition. Rogerson went with him, as his chief assistant. But instead of concentrating on the anti-nationalisation plan, Rogerson put another idea up to the men who mattered.'

He grimaced his distaste.

'Some, as we know, accepted it. Others were uncertain, but agreed to remain neutral. Those who died were opposed to Rogerson's scheme, which at the start was simply to keep control entirely in the hands of private manufacturers and force the Government prices up.

'Some, such as Tiarney, Frazer-Campbell, Jaffrey, Gorton and Morely, were in the whole fantastic scheme—the League of the Hundred-and-One. Clarke, as the chief stock-controller, played his part well. But Nebton and Anson—at least one of whom we were sure were in the League—separately opposed it tooth and nail. Had they seen the full plan, they would have talked. Neb did learn of it, and was killed—the police found his body yesterday, so it's not surprising we couldn't locate him.

'Anson told us practically all he knew, but Rogerson was afraid Anson's big share in the various companies would be dangerous. He couldn't buy Anson's share, or win his help, so he planned his murder.'

'Meanwhile, Rogerson had hired a couple of hundred cut-throats, and had no trouble in getting what he wanted done—most of them were satisfied simply to be rewarded with the loot. But he was cunning enough, and used anarchist organisations—Crosby and suchlike. Anyhow, he got through up to a point, and we don't need telling just how and why he failed ...'

'Your pardon,' Mike Errol corrected, stoutly: 'Mark, lout though he is, started you off ...'

'Rule 3, sub-section G. Special Orders to Department Agents,' said Diana, gently: 'No personalities!'

'In that case,' Mike conceded, abashed, 'I withdraw.'

'Just shut up, you ass!' Mark bellowed wrathfully.

'When the cousins have finished,' Loftus announced, grandly: 'I'll go on. Our own big mistake was with Fay Loring. Not a subject to dwell on for long … We thought we'd rescued her from the League—we didn't dream she was a member of it. Her father—well, they didn't get on. She wanted him to join, and he refused. His murder, and the chance of planting her with us, enabled Rogerson to keep tabs on most of what we were doing. However, I don't think it made a lot of difference.

'But she did get hold of Lore, at the last minute—when he suspected the real truth. She also advised Rogerson that we were going all out on Jaffrey, Morely and the others—and for that reason they were killed. In each case, they were scared by a 'phone call from Rogerson, saying they *were* being watched.

'Dora and Letty had come-hither parts—catching the big fish for Rogerson and Myra and the others to fry. Amondier, by the way, was in it only because he had shares in English companies: he was never on the active list. He's back in France, and a much happier man. The man killed at Bournemouth—Errols please note—was Neil Clarke's partner who was also in the game. Others we met were simply gunmen and general operatives. And that's …'

'Not quite the end!' protested Mike Errol. 'Weren't Carrie and Wally to follow me to Maidenhead, after Letty? And what *about* Letty?'

'They were held up on the road, and lost you,' said Loftus. 'And somehow Letty got away on the *Luxa*. Just one of those things, friends!' He held up his empty glass. 'More beer, Di? I'm getting a thirst on me.'

'*Getting*,' murmured Mike Errol.

'Peace be on you,' said Dodo. 'All in all, the kidnapping of Fay was about the neatest job, I think—Wally had better be reduced to the ranks, Bill.'

'You go and reduce yourself,' growled Wally, from the bed.

'Y' know,' Ned Oundle offered, with the suddenness of a man visited by inspiration: 'this has been the nastiest job we've tackled, and I've just learned why!'

'Why?' demanded four voices in chorus.

'I was knocked out too early,' murmured Oundle, gently: and Loftus was more than pleased, for it meant that the effect of Fay Loring on his friend was wearing off.

Mike yawned gigantically.

'Well—so it's over … I must say Neb and Anson are my chief personal regrets. The Aussie was a good scout …'

Loftus chuckled.

'*Is*, little man! Anson was taken out of the Regal just before the fire—he recovered well enough to insist on it. He's at the conference in Downing Street, right now, with Craigie. They'll both be along soon.'

They came, and helped to lower the stock of bear—Craigie in smaller quantities than the young Australian—and finally the party broke up, leaving Loftus, Diana, Anson and Craigie at the flat. Anson was able to get about, with care—for this was ten days after the affair at Barnes—and he was subdued: he had lost the arrogance that once had spoiled him.

He had also, it transpired, agreed to take a part in the Government's control of armaments—the Bill for which was being rushed through the reassembled House at the earliest opportunity.

'We only chance on a thing like that once,' he said with a smile. 'I'm right glad to have known you fellows, though—right glad. I don't know which of you did the most.'

Loftus smiled.

'The Errols, I think, when all's said and done. And they'll be arguing from now until the next job which one really came out best. They'll make first-class agents, Gordon.'

Craigie nodded, very slowly.

'We'll need them,' he said. 'You and Di, the Errols and the others—we'll need you all, before Europe's settled down.'

The thing that Anson couldn't understand, was that Diana and Bill seemed actually pleased to hear it ...

DEATH BY NIGHT

JOHN CREASEY

Chapter 1
Two Gentlemen Return

From the Boat Train at Waterloo stepped two large, weary-looking men who created the impression that for some time past they had slept in their clothes. Nor was the impression unjustified, for it was precisely five nights since they had known the luxury of a bed. Even then the bed had been a single one, and they were broad as well as tall, each used to four feet of spring-interior mattress, blankets and luxury eiderdown. To them it seemed that such amenities were never likely to return, for Waterloo Station, with the dim, blue gleams from the lamps hanging from the glass roof, and the bookstalls, was a place of gloom. Vague figures walked past them in either direction.

On the roof pattered heavy rain, while it was piercing cold.

'I am not,' said Mark Errol, 'going another step without a porter. Unless you would like to carry my bag.'

'If you carry me, it's a deal.' Michael Errol stifled a yawn, and tried to pierce the gloom—unsuccessfully. He felt too tired even to exchange witticisms with his cousin. 'Oh, well, we can't stay here all night. What's the time?'

'Just after nine.'

'Half an hour late,' reflected Michael; 'it might have been worse. I—porter. *Porter!*'

'Coming, sir!'

A weedy figure materialised, revealing a wizened face decorated with a wispish moustache. The man jumped into the carriage and pulled down two small suit-cases. The two large men eyed him as they would any phenomenon.

'Two trunks in the van, porter,' Mark said.

'Aye, aye, sir, I'll just get a truck. Got your name on?'

'Errol. Put them all in a taxi, and tell the cabby to wait; we're going to have a drink. And,' went on Mike, passing over a pound note, 'tell him he may have to wait a long time.'

'All okey-doke, sir.' The porter disappeared towards the luggage van, whistling tunelessly. The Errols walked stiffly towards the gates, their eyes lack-lustre and their mouths dry. The sweeping Errol chin which characterised them was not entirely hidden by the gloom; nor were their claims to handsomeness, for they were impressive young men, each topping the six foot mark, each turning the scales at fourteen stone, each possessed of the Errol cleft in the chin but minus the Errol Roman nose. Their noses were straight. Their eyes were grey and fringed with long lashes, their hair dark brown—Mark's straight and well-brushed, Mike's unruly—and that their clothes, although untidy, were from Savile Row.

They were oblivious of those about them as they went towards the buffet—but two people, one a short man with a Punch of a chin and a beaked nose, approached them from one side.

The second man was taller, and very thin.

Again the light prevented strangers from seeing the swarthiness of his skin, and the unpleasant closeness of his eyes. He sidled, and sidling out-walked the short man, and drew alongside the Errols.

'Excuse me, gentlemen...'

His voice was low-pitched, and possessed a note that did not sound English. The Errols stopped with one accord. Mark, who did most of the talking, raised a brow.

'Yes?'

'I've brought a message from Mr. Loftus, gentlemen.'

The close-set eyes were narrow, but that might have been because of trying to see through the black-out. Had the Errols disliked all they could see of the stranger, their immediate uncertainties would have been removed, for the name of Loftus was virtually a password.

They liked to think that they were useful agents of that remarkable organisation called Department Z, but it often appeared that Loftus and others took all the plums, and that if there was a job where it was impossible to triumph, Loftus—Agent Number 1—handed it to them. Certainly he was not popular with them at that moment. All they wanted was drink and food and sleep.

'We do not know a Mr. Loftus,' stated Mark clearly.

'I—I beg pardon, sir?'

'You heard,' said Mark, and then resignedly: 'All right. Where is he?'

'In the booking-hall, sir, in the corner on the left. He doesn't want to be seen contacting with you.'

'Hmm,' said Mark. 'All right, whoever-you-are, lead the way, will you?'

'Yes, sir.'

The thin man of the furtive face led the way, and behind the trio followed he of the Punch-like chin. The station was not crowded, and yet they contrived to bump into several people.

The shadows of the booking-hall engulfed them. Peering across, they saw no figure lurking in the left corner, but the darkness might deliver anyone up at a moment's notice. Approaching the corner, the thin man fell behind.

There was a sharp cry from behind them, and on the instant they came to a standstill.

'Mark—be careful!'

Then the thin man moved.

He snatched something from his pocket which showed a dull glint and then the something went flying from his grasp, for Mike Errol forgot weariness and moved. He leapt at the man, crashing a clenched right fist towards his stomach, and the man doubled up; a gun fell from nerveless fingers. Mike struck again, a left swing this time to the chin. The furtive one's feet lifted inches from the ground and he went backwards like a pole-axed bull.

Mike drew a deep breath.

'Now that,' he said, 'is what I call a warm welcome. Hallo, Spats, nice of you to come to meet us. What's the matter?'

Spats Thornton, one of Craigie's most useful agents since he did not look like one, put one hand in his pocket and contemplated the Errols with his chin jutting out.

'You're the matter,' said he dispassionately. 'I heard every word, and you fell for it.'

'So it seems,' said Mike ruefully. 'But we can go into that later. Here are two men wearily returning from Italy after a damn' fool journey, and the moment we get back to London someone draws a gun on us. I want to know why.' He did not sound over-curious, for he had worked with the Department too long to be surprised at anything.

Mark stooped down and picked up the gun.

It was a Webley automatic, and the safety-catch had not been released. Not that a shot would have caused much disturbance, for the small snout of its improved Maxim silencer poked from the muzzle.

'If he'd fired,' said Mark more dreamily than his wont, 'it would have been death in darkness and no mistake. What and who is he, Spats?'

'I haven't a notion. I noticed him come up to you and heard about the message from Loftus.'

'Good Lord!' exclaimed Mike, and he seemed positively enlivened. 'There wasn't a message, we can have that drink! Look after this little dago, Spats; if I don't lower something...'

'Silence,' said Spats Thornton.

There were occasions when he could make his voice sound sepulchral, and it did then. There were folk who claimed that he always seemed to be putting on an act, and in a measure that was true. It was equally true of most of the Department men, for they worked in a world where little was natural, where death lurked in every corner, where it was impossible to know from one moment to the next what was going to happen. Living like that, they developed an unseen armour of what some called humour. It was a peculiar brand, mingling sarcasm with facetiousness, and it puzzled folk who did not know them well.

'All right,' said Mike, 'we're silent.'

'What really puzzles me,' said Spats, rubbing his chin, 'is how he knew that there was a message. Bill wants to see you at once and I've come to meet you. Someone else knew you were going to be here, and the someone doesn't want you. If you want a drink there's just time for it. I've got a cab.'

'What about that?' demanded Mike, nodding towards the man on the ground.

'I'll watch it,' said Spats. 'Go and get rid of your repressions.'

The Errols walked towards the buffet. There was a certain humour in the fact that they had been sent out on a quest which had carried them through most of Southern Europe where they might have expected excitement, and the first sign of trouble had come at the moment of their return to London.

Drinking, they considered the mystery of the fact that someone knew that they had been due at Waterloo on the 8.37 (arrival) train.

From Southampton they had sent a telegram to Bill Loftus, announcing their impending arrival, and to their knowledge no one else in England knew that they had landed. Therefore, it seemed, the leakage was through Loftus.

'Ye-es,' admitted Mark. 'Well, let's get back.' He yawned, lit a cigarette—Mark refusing—and they strolled back towards the booking-hall. The gloom and the ghostly blue light remained. Thornton lurked in the darkness, and the man remained on the floor.

'Our friend still sleeps,' said Spats, but he smiled, 'which one of you hit him?'

'I,' said Mike with satisfaction. 'We'd better get him round; they'll see us carrying him to a cab even in this. Whisky?'

Spats drew a flask from his hip pocket, adjusted the knee of his trousers, and knelt down. Unscrewing the top of the flask, he held it to the man's lip, and a trickle of whisky forced itself through.

'He can't be as bad as that,' he said almost irritably, while the Errols stood and peered down. 'Wake up, you lump of sin, or—*God!*'

He straightened up, spilling whisky over the dusty platform, where it ran in little globules. Mark replaced him—and Mike also bent down, to see the small hole in the man's temple, the little trickle of blood coming from it.

The man had been shot while Thornton had been on guard.

Want another Perfect Mystery?

Get your next classic Crime story for FREE

Sign up to our Crime Classics newsletter where you can discover new Golden Age crime, receive exclusive content and never-before published short stories, all for FREE.

From the beloved greats of the Golden Age to the forgotten gems, best-kept-secrets, and brand new discoveries, we're devoted to classic crime.

If you sign up today, you'll get:

1. A free novel from our Classic Crime collection.
2. Exclusive insights into classic novels and their authors and the chance to get copies in advance of publication, and
3. The chance to win exclusive prizes in regular competitions.

Interested? It takes less than a minute to sign up. You can get your novel and your first newsletter by signing up on our website www.crimeclassics.co.uk

CPSIA information can be obtained
at www.ICGtesting.com
Printed in the USA
LVOW12s2205041217
558590LV00005B/1330/P